WHAT I TELL YOU IN THE DARK

WHAT I TELL YOU IN THE DARK

JOHN SAMUEL

The Overlook Press
New York, NY

This edition first published in hardcover in the United States in 2016 by
The Overlook Press, Peter Mayer Publishers, Inc.

141 Wooster Street
New York, NY 10012
www.overlookpress.com
For bulk and special sales please contact sales@overlookny.com,
or write us at the above address.

Cataloging-in-Publication Data is available
from the Library of Congress

ISBN: 978-1-4683-1245-4

Manufactured in the United States of America

For Pippa

What I tell you in the dark, speak in the light.
Matthew 10:27

I

I jump in at 09.20 on Monday 30th September 2013, just as he's hooking the noose of his belt on the back of the door. There he is all solemn and tearful, a toilet cubicle at work the last thing he'll see on this earth, when suddenly I come surging through, like that, in a heartbeat. It's a full take. There's no way of describing it, other than to say he just switches off and lets it happen. For weeks now he's been praying for something like this, retreating to the seclusion of this stall, these tiles hard against his knees. He wanted strength – each time those words, *Give me strength*. And I tried my best to oblige, burning on him every way I knew how, showing him he's not alone. But it wasn't enough. Today he simply asked for forgiveness. *Have mercy on me, Lord, for what I am about to do* – that kind of thing. Yeah well, sorry – but no. I can't just let him bow out like that, not now, not when he's so close. There's a bigger picture here. He may not be able to see it, but I can, and I'm afraid sitting back and training the vine hasn't worked. It's time for me to take the plunge.

It's a massive shock, of course. I mean, it was never going to be a smooth transition, not after all this time, but I'd forgotten just how overwhelming it is. The creatureliness of a frame, the fluids and the flesh, the pressure of all that blood and electricity: it's a lot to feel at once. And the noise – it's everywhere. Inside you, thrumming, beating noise, then all around, from every direction.

So it turns out another guy was in here washing his hands and he hears me. He goes to find somebody, telling them there's a person in the bathroom having a fit. By the time it gets round to the maintenance man kicking in the door of my cubicle, I'm starting to get a handle on things. That's to say, I'm fully aware of it happening. There they are, both of them standing above me – the handwashing guy, who tries to talk to me in a shocked sort of way, and the guy in the overalls, who hangs back and says very little.

I'm naked at this point, my clothes are in ribbons, and I've wound toilet paper in a big turban around my ears to try to deaden the sound. I must have been feeling way too hot because I'm kneeling at the bowl splashing water all over my body and I'm panting, like a dog does on a hot day.

Anyway, there's a big commotion and I end up wrapped in a blanket, with the toilet roll turban still on (I bit the guy's hand when he tried to remove it), and I'm led away like that, out of the bathroom and across the fifth floor of the office. Every mouth is pretty much hanging open, and lots of people are holding some temporarily forgotten object in their hand, a phone or a document or something, as they watch our little procession pass by. No one says a word.

It's disturbing how little time it takes for them to be satisfied that I'm well enough to be sent home, alone, in a cab. There are three other people present when this quasi decision is reached in the privacy of a meeting room still thick with the smell of new carpet (having gobbled up some smaller PR outfits, Abel-wood has moved in with the other superagencies that straddle the line between Westminster and Soho).

The first of these three people is an oriental woman from Human Resources – her name is something like Pim or Pin. Then there's a silver-haired man called Nicholas, who is in charge. And lastly there is the unnamed security/maintenance man who brought me here, just sort of hovering in the background in case I start biting or shouting again.

I'm very absorbed in drinking tea, especially in tracking the hot bolt all the way down my throat and into the pit of my belly, so I'm not really listening to much of what they're saying. Which is fine because they mostly seem to be talking about me as if I'm not there: while I am undoubtedly the subject of the conversation, its real agenda is a kind of risk assessment exercise, with the hidden question of what the comeback will be if I freak out, top myself, maul the taxi driver and so on.

Eventually I am asked, almost as an afterthought, if I would like to see a doctor. I shake my head. I then try out my normal speaking voice for the first time, to ask if I can borrow some money – the tracksuit I have on (I am wearing someone's spare gym kit) has empty pockets.

By way of an answer, I am handed a plastic bag that contains the wreckage of what I was wearing, including my wallet (but not, tellingly, my belt) and I am told that the cab will be on account so I needn't worry about that. I am also assured by Pim/Pin that I needn't rush back into work, that I should take my time with it. They can take care of my accounts while I'm gone. She keeps using my name, tacking it on to the end of her every utterance. The softness of its monosyllable, Will, lost in the mouth of this robotic stranger.

In the taxi, I find myself growing increasingly impatient with the gentle cinemascope of the view. I want to be out there, amongst it all. I ask the driver to pull over but he refuses to deviate from his instructions. So next time we stop at some lights I just open my door and get out.

I stride off down the street, ignoring the vague sound of the driver calling behind me. I remove my headdress as I go. The air is sharp and clear against my skin – one of those autumn days – you can almost taste how blue it is.

But it's not long before my progress slows and pretty soon I've reached a near crawl – literally, in places. There's just too much to see, out and about like this, at large in the world. I keep stopping without meaning to stop, if you know what I mean. And people keep looking, while pretending not to look, in that way city people do. Like now, here, in this warm current of air wafting up from … I'm not exactly sure, beneath the ground somewhere, some ventilation outlet connecting the hidden tunnels of the tube trains to the open world. It's intoxicating. Layer on layer of scent, old things rotted down and burrowed out, mixed in with the new life, the films and residues of daily passage. I snort it up in greedy gulps, hands on knees, pulling the life into me.

I am that I am, to plagiarise a line from His Nibs.

'Morning,' I say, in celebration of this fact, to a man coming out of Russell Square station.

Mor-ning. Such a great word, gorgeous mouth-feel. I say it again. Up it comes, rolling through the throat and into the tongue muscle. Thought to flesh.

But the man has gone.

Shame. I would have liked to talk to him, touch him even. When you've been benched for as long as I have, you just want to get involved. You want contact.

Eventually, reluctantly, I drag myself up from my stoop, straightening my spine vertebra by vertebra – acting it out in miniature: the Rise of Man. What you fondly think of as evolution. Ha! I love that: like you did it all yourselves somehow. One day, you're grunting about, Version 1.0, on the make, pulling your food out of trees and holes, then a few million years later you're doing your shopping online and launching satellites.

Wrong.

We're the ones who unmonkeyed you. We whispered it all to you, about the light and the dark and the rain for your rivers, about all the things you could and could not do. It was a simple two-hander: the Big Man and the Bad Man. And you felt its truth.

But now … now it's all been forgotten. The story of how much we love you has been lost in all the noise, it's become just another –

'Sorry,' I have to say to someone with whom I've just collided (my fault – eyes were half closed for a moment there).

But he, the object of my collision, seems to want more than that.

'Watch where you're fucking going,' he warns me. He's a cockney. Not the chirpy sort, the hard man sort.

'Sorry,' I repeat. 'I will.'

Evidently, though, I don't seem as apologetic as I should be because he continues to glare at me for a few seconds longer. There's a rheumy pinkness to his eyes, his mouth is a stubble-surrounded slot from which insults emerge.

'You tit,' is the one he chooses to end our encounter with.

As he passes, he shoulders me so hard I nearly fall over.

But it turns out to be just what I need, the physical jolt of it. It shakes me awake.

I am here for a reason – no more dawdling, no more sermonising. I must finish what Will began.

I set off again.

As I walk I force myself to ignore the chorus of things that are crying out for me to touch them, taste them, fondle them with my itchy fingers. Instead, I focus my attention on Will. I make myself remember his agonies, the tears he spilled, the help he so desperately craved. And I remind myself too how I nudged and prodded him, the tenderness with which I coaxed him – it's excruciating how close he came. But you can't blame him. This situation he had, a guy like him would get eaten alive trying to take it public. I probably should have realised that a little sooner – he just wasn't built for it. But I'm here now, so let's see what can be done.

This time on earth I tell myself, working the words loose with each footfall, *it's like water in my hands.*

At a busy road everyone is waiting for a break in the traffic. I wait with them. Next to me a young woman stands with her child, its hand in hers. I smile at her, she smiles back.

Every drop is precious.

I make short work of the next few miles. On only one other occasion do I fall prey to distractions, as I'm passing a queue of cars at the lights on Bishopsgate. Music is belting out from one of their windows.

'Forget about the price tag ...' the singer chants '... Ain't about the cha-ching cha-ching.'

Away to my left, the spire of St Helen's winces up over the rooftops, a barrage of holy ground standing fast against the floodwater of greed. The usurers' towers are massed on the horizon behind it, a glinting tide of steel and glass.

I find myself slowly beginning to move to the music, sliding back and forth on the soles of my trainers. I reach up into the sunlight, my fingers a silhouette.

Across the street three young men call out to me – *Oi Oi! Nice dancing mate!* One of them is filming me with his mobile phone.

I pull myself together and hurry on. I speed past pubs and office buildings on Houndsditch, pushing east, away from the privileged centre. After a couple more miles, my legs grow heavy and uncooperative – at one point I even wait at a bus stop for a few minutes but the grid of digits printed on the timetable threatens to suck me in. I could dwell for hours on numbers, the way they twist and thread their helixes into you. Those same spirals that spin down through shells and pine cones and whirlpools are tucked inside you too – but you already know that.

Again I resist. Again I press on.

It is nearly midday by the time I reach Stepney, a hinterland of poverty that hangs out of Whitechapel like a stillborn. This is where Will calls home, among the exhaust-blackened terraces and the tower blocks. There is something timeless about this place: suffering distilled through the generations. Marks of weakness, marks of woe.

I've seen these kebab shops, these strip-lit grocery stores I don't know how many times as I've watched Will come and go – this scrub of parkland shoehorned between the buildings. There's nothing pretty about any of it, and yet I find myself irresistibly drawn to it. It makes me nostalgic for that other time I jumped in. Those golden few weeks that preceded my infamous Mistake. I came to feel right at home among the poor and the destitute back then – so much easier to read life there, I found, with the frills torn away and people just being people. And He understood that – I could tell – He appreciated what I was trying to achieve down in those fly-blown dustbowls, with everyone writhing over each other in their blind litter, desperate to get a touch of me. Or at least, He understood it right up until it turned sour. After that, He saw nothing but His own fury.

Appropriately enough, it's a homeless woman who rouses me from this thought. She scuttles out from some corner and grabs hold of my arm.

'I know you,' she shouts, even though we're only a few inches apart.

'No,' I tell her, 'you don't.' I try to move off but her determination to hold on to me forces me to stop.

This is not good. I need to get rid of her, pronto. This kept happening last time – loners, lunatics, vulnerable people as they're now known, they've always been the first to sense us. And if you're not careful, it can really throw you off your game. I ended up with a slipstream of them following me into every temple, on to every mountaintop – and it wasn't just me either: Simon, Barnabas, Paul especially, a lot of those early guys really struggled with it. I don't want to sound callous but it's not exactly what you want when you're trying to sell The Word to people, to have some comet's tail of derelicts and misfits.

I shake her loose. But she keeps up with me, beetling along at my side.

'It's you!' she yells again, this time really drawing out the *ooh* part of *you*.

She's strangely hard to describe, as these people so often are – she's filthy of course, and wild looking, but that's about all you can say for certain. Her hair could be any colour really and she could be literally any age between twenty and sixty. It's impossible to tell, the lives they lead. Her hands, though, are bony and strong.

'Alright, you got me,' I tell her. 'It *is* me.'

At this, she stops dead in her tracks. Her lips are moving silently, her eyes are darting around, looking at everything but me.

I'm going to try to do it the nice way – I owe her that much (she *is* right, after all). 'Look,' I say gently, 'come over here.'

I lead her to a small alleyway where another homeless person is asleep – unconscious is probably a better way of describing it – in a drift of rubbish bags. People occasionally flit past but no one is paying us any attention. She just stands there in front of me, eyes lowered, entranced by her hectic, fiddling hands.

In a whisper, not wanting to break the spell, I ask her to look at me. Which she does, stupefied with wonder. I crouch down next to the sleeping form at our feet (on closer inspection I see that it's a man). He doesn't move.

'This,' I place a hand on the man's shoulder, 'is where you can serve me best. You must help your fellow man.'

'Get off,' he mumbles from the depths of his stupor.

I stand up to face her. She continues to watch my every movement, rickety but intent, like a mangy hawk.

'My sheep hear my voice,' I tell her, 'and I know them.'

Very slowly, I reach out my hands to her, open palmed – *noli timere*. She allows herself to move in a fraction closer. I tell her how He loves her, how He loves all His children, that the poorest in body are the richest in soul. I woo her with my words, nearer and nearer, until finally I am able to draw her against me in an embrace. We remain like that for several minutes, and as I hold her, her aroma reveals itself to me like a deeply held confidence. At first there is only the citrus astringency of urine but, little by little, something far more complex emerges, something unknowably sad – the peaty sweetness of loneliness and decay. I rest my cheek against her grease-dampened head and lull her softly. Then, as the last of her spasmodic movements twitch into stillness, I lay her down in the plastic next to the man and kiss the blackened knuckle of her hand, which still clutches my sleeve.

'You must release me now,' I almost sing to her.

She settles back into the plastic. The man's body adjusts soundlessly to accommodate her.

'Be on this earth,' I tell her as I leave. 'Every second is a miracle.'

By the time I reach the top of Will's street, I'm beginning to feel good. Better than good, in fact. I feel more – can't think of the word – than I've felt for a very, very long time. All I know is that jumping in like this was the right move. I'm sure of that now – it's something I can *feel*, on a cellular level. (Complete! That's the word I was looking for. I feel complete again.) It hasn't been easy, though, doing it like this, against the will of the Big Fella. The last thing I want to do is defy Him but it was a split second thing, you couldn't even call it a decision – more of a reflex really, quick like a cat. And now here I am.

It's a two-storey terraced house with a flat on the ground floor and another above. There are buzzers for Pryce and Sherwin (Will's neighbour – her angry fist comes knocking late into the night, her notes come skidding beneath the door – his pacing, she says, is like a herd of elephants).

Inside is an entrance hall whose floor has been polished to a neck-breaking gleam. A small table by the door bears a stack of letters, all of them for Will, all of them bills. Luckily, though, Ms Sherwin, the stacker of envelopes, the polisher of floors, is not here to visit her disapproval on me. Even so, I take the stairs two at a time. All I want now is to get inside and get on with the job.

A couple of minutes later I'm sitting on Will's sofa, his laptop booting up on my knees. As its fan wheezes and its innards tick into life, I find myself surprised by these familiar surroundings, how different they are in the unfiltered light of reality. The hysteria of all these bible pages, for one thing, taped to the walls like that, scarred by Will's highlighter, annotated by his looping scrawl. Or his mattress, his duvet, his pillows, all of them dragged through from the bedroom and deposited here in the hope that the murmur and flicker of the television might hold some promise of sleep. It all just seems a little unhinged, looking at it this way. I hadn't noticed that before, when I was watching him do it all. I must have got caught up in the moment, I guess. Caught up in the person. It's hard to explain.

The screen flashes on. Okay, this is it. I know it's on here somewhere because I watched him put it there. I watched him stay late at work one evening, waiting for the others to leave. Then once they'd gone, I watched him travel around the office like an insect, sucking data into a memory stick. Too smart, too painstakingly cautious to email something like that, he carried it home in his pocket, vigilant at every step, needing to be certain no one was following.

So why is nothing happening? There was a blank white screen, inviting the expectation of something more, except now all I have is a neutral background that looks nothing at all like Will's desktop. And some stupid video offering to help get me started.

Please no. Surely he hasn't.

He *has*. He's stripped it. He's wiped his computer.

In a desperate attempt not to believe this, I whip the cursor around the screen, clicking on this, clicking on that, but everything I open launches itself for the first time, oblivious to a time before Will lobotomised the system.

I almost hurl the thing at the wall. How could I have not noticed this?

I slump back into the sofa, sending the computer clattering to the floor. He must have done it last night. He must have known what he was going to do today. He was getting ready, covering his tracks, eliminating all evidence of –

'Wait!' I actually shout this, springing back to my feet.

Wait. There's still the memory stick. That dear, darling little memory stick of his. He took it back to work and he left it there, an insurance policy squirreled away in his desk. He must have forgotten about it, or else he just switched off this morning and stopped caring about the details, one foot already off the stage. Either way, it's still there for the taking.

'Yes!' I complete a hugely satisfying air punch as I collapse back down into the sofa cushions.

My weight causes a pile of papers to topple from the armrest and subside against my leg. I pick up the edition of last week's newspaper with Natalie's article in it. Will has left it folded out at the harrowing picture of a cloth-masked doctor injecting a baby whose arm barely seems wider than the needle. Above it the headline reads *Bleeding the heart of Africa.*

I've read it several times already, like I was almost physically there with Will as he devoured the words over and over. But actually holding the pages between my fingers like this, it makes the whole thing seem even more real. The suffering is less abstract when you can feel the story next to your own skin, as if yours are just the last in a long line of hands upon hands upon hands. It suits her writing too – it's like it's meant to be touched. There's a lean muscularity to her prose – the news and nothing more, every word weighed for its content.

I worm down further into the cushions and hold the slightly trembling pages above me. She tells the story with glorious economy. Big Pharma the immediately familiar villain of the piece, except this time she can reveal that its clutches extend further than we ever knew. InviraCorp – the name slips like a serpent into her text – one solitary company but with a root structure so vast that it curls through every corner of HIV care in Africa: the distribution of medication, the bribery of corrupt officials, the eventual dizzying profit hikes. InviraCorp – she keeps repeating it, showing how it's everywhere, an unseen force in the lifecycle of these antiretroviral drugs as they are shipped across a continent ravaged by plague – she uses that word. Children born with a death sentence, whole communities annihilated, while this one corporation looks calmly on. Enormous wealth leveraged from the pit of human misery.

It is the perfect beginning. I crumple the pages down into my lap. Now it's up to me to make sure she finishes the story – Will couldn't, but I can.

I rise from my seat and stand with my back to the window, washed in dusty sunlight. On the opposite wall, I watch my shadow, still and dark, sharpened by His light.

I must go now. I must retrieve the putrid secrets that Will extracted, whose poison nearly killed him, and I must bring them to Natalie. In her hands they will be delivered to the world.

I swap the tracksuit for one of Will's pressed suits and a freshly ironed, cellophane-shrouded shirt. In the bathroom I splash my face at the dank font of the sink.

I will uncover this truth, intact, a still-beating heart of darkness.

I watch my hands straighten Will's tie, smooth down the lapels of his suit. I like this smile of his, how it sets his jaw with new purpose. One of God's own soldiers now.

'Apokálupto,' I tell my reflection in a whisper. *It shall be revealed.*

It's a whisper that remains on my lips as I retrace my steps back out into the daylight, and as I glide through the streets in search of wings to carry me toward my destiny. At a mini-cab office I blurt the address to one of the men who is sitting there playing dominos. He nods and takes his coat from the back of the chair, and still without a word, he leads me to his car. A sturdy charioteer. Together we speed through the traffic. Nothing impedes us.

I shall deliver this vile grub of truth to her.

Am I speaking these words? I cannot tell. The man's eyes watch me in the mirror but they do not threaten. They understand, just as He will come to understand this purpose of mine. It opens in me like a bud – a hidden quick that senses change. The long, hard remission of winter is coming to an end.

2

Back here again.

This building is a Möbius strip of corporate collusion. Corridors turn back on the same corridors, offices reveal the same set pieces of huddled talk. Lone figures at phones and computers, connected to unseen others. I hasten through, and each one that sees me works the same script, affects the same show of casual greeting. Only when I have passed do they begin their excited whispering. And who can blame them?

It's going to be hard to justify my presence here, so soon after this morning's events. Even before today the coals of suspicion have been smouldering. Since the InviraCorp story broke last week, the account has been locked down. Low-level execs like Will were immediately shut out of the files. They must suspect a leak – Will was convinced that they knew he was passing information to Natalie. He barely slept these past few days. The morning her article appeared, the partners were in at dawn, having received early word on the wires. By midday, Invira-Corp's top people were beginning to arrive from the City office. By late afternoon the rest had made it, all the way from the European production facility, rumpled and irritated by hours of travelling. Will watched them come and go – we both did – but no one discussed what was said. Not that they needed to. Damage limitation is all that matters at times like these. Everyone knows that. Bring out the janitor with his piss mop and his bucket. Deny, deny, deny.

The young lad whose job it is to push the demeaning little mail cart around the office has just said something to me. I didn't catch what it was but the tone of it sounded like a well-meaning enquiry about my health. Now he is standing there, open-faced, waiting for some kind of reply. Others who are pretending not to have noticed watch their computers in silence, also waiting to see what I'll say.

'Okay, thanks,' is what comes out. I move on before he tries to prolong this inadequate response into some kind of conversation.

I need to settle down a bit. I've got myself all tensed up, worrying about that memory stick. It dawned on me as I was travelling here that it's not exactly hidden in the most convenient place – Will was alone in the office when he stashed it. So I'm going to have to choose my moment to get the thing back. It's going to take a little patience. I can't just be climbing all over everything and causing another rumpus – the last thing I need is for the security guys to eject me from the building. It was bad enough just now on the way in here, the basilisk stare I got. But they couldn't argue with my pass (although it still didn't stop the guy at the desk asking me, *Would you like me to call up for you, sir?*). I mustered my most imperious look and proceeded wordlessly past him. I could feel him staring, though, as I waited for the lift to come. Everyone listened to Will's shoes nervously tapping on the marble floor.

Predictably enough, word of my arrival has travelled, so that by the time I reach Will's part of the office, there's a small welcoming party waiting for me. The man at the head of their group is Alex, Will's immediate boss. They are, without realising it, standing in a loose diamond formation. It's perfectly natural. Birds do it, bees do it, even shysters such as these do it. Short-range repulsion, alignment, long-range attraction – look it up. It's everywhere. Particle physics, cellular robotics, ants, birds, fish, people. Not me, though. I just push right past them and sit down at my desk. No one else is moving. They're just staring at me. I should probably make an effort to seem a little more professional. I pick up the phone and look as though I am about to make an important call. But before I can think of a number to dial, Alex comes over and hovers at my side.

He is a sorry excuse for a young man (which is what he is – no more than Will's age, possibly even younger). His flaccid, unexercised body presses against his shirt. His face, with its quick, piggy eyes, is that of a sly old spinster or a murdering nurse.

The others hang back in their headless diamond, watching for his cues.

'Hello, Will,' he says, in a voice that makes me instantly dislike him. 'Is everything okay?'

'This isn't really a good time, Alex.' I show him the phone, which unhelpfully starts to make that dim honking noise phones make when you've been holding them for too long. We both look at it. I put it back in its cradle.

He says, 'Why don't we head into my office for a chat?'

'Do I have to?'

'No, of course you don't *have* to,' he lies, then immediately trumps it with an even bigger lie, 'I'm just worried about you. I'd like us to talk things through – I want to make sure that you're taking all the time you need to help you recover from…' he peters out here, suddenly aware of the watching eyes and listening ears and the fact that he doesn't have a convenient euphemism to describe what happened this morning. 'To recover,' he corrects himself, deciding to snip it off there.

I shrug and rise to my feet. *Dissembling serpent. I will tear your house to the ground.*

'Thanks,' I say to him, 'I appreciate that.'

It's the only way to tackle these people, whose livelihood is untruth – by telling lies of your own. The curse of the modern world, if you ask me: lies, lies and more lies. Truth has lost its value. Time was, you could have gone in hard with something like this and come straight at them, swords swinging, trumpets cracking the heavens. And they'd have had no doubt that it was God's righteous anger they were seeing. People were more open to us back then – maybe because they were closer to it all, the deaths and the births, the blood and the spit – they felt the rhythms more. My kind used to stun their souls to the surface just by showing up. It was like fishing with dynamite. A sight to behold. But not anymore. We just don't have that kind of presence now – modern societies are far too busy being amazed at themselves, it's side-lined us. These days if we want to get something done, we have to do it remotely – the touch behind the touch – just like you with your drones and your fourth-generation warfare. No one bothers with jump-ins or any of that old school stuff anymore – it's just not worth it. No one, that is, except for throwbacks like me.

As I follow Alex to his office I feel an almost overwhelming urge to smite him down, to slap the lies clean out of his mouth. There's something so profoundly callous about the back of him, the uniform pinstripe of his suit, the perfectly squared off hairline. I can barely contain my ire. Will's spirit was crushed into dust by these people and their banal, workaday evil, and yet on they go into further iniquity. My eyes bore into the rounded hump of his shoulders.

Will understood it – he saw how avarice is choking this world. And as his understanding grew, his panic mounted. The briar of greed everywhere around him, rooted in every crevice and corner – he simply couldn't cope with it. A blinding swarm – that's how he saw it – the swarm intelligence of countless moneychangers, the flit and crackle of their wings eclipsing the sky, always devouring.

The locust has no king. I watched him say it this very morning to the woman, Stella. The leader. He stood up in the meeting, everyone except him quiet in the aftermath of Stella's announcement, her carefully packaged messages about InviraCorp still hanging in the air. But he dared to tell this appalling truth to her, to all of them, his pointing finger shaking before him.

Watching him after that I realised something had reached an end in him. The way he stumbled in the corridor, those last few steps to the bathroom, holding on to the walls like a passenger on a ship. Minutes later, I was in there, snatching him up.

We've now reached Alex's office and he is holding open the door for me. 'Okay Will,' he says, 'in you go.'

The way he is trying to dominate me with this rote-learned conciliation is making me surprisingly angry. Sympathy as strategy, manipulation beneath a pelt of kindness… I'm sick of seeing it. It's an insidious form of oppression and I've watched its creeping rise in the world with mounting despair. It's perhaps not surprising, then, that I'm starting to feel like I want to gouge out his eyes or thump his gut – but really, who am I kidding? Even if it would change anything, this body couldn't withstand a fight, not even against a house cat like him, and especially not against the thick wrists and sloping shoulders of the security apes. No, there's simply no way. And besides, it must be at least a week since Will has slept more than a few hours in a night. Even the walking I've done today has exhausted me. In fact, a nice sit down may be just what I need.

And so in I go. The dagger of my enmity will remain cloaked a while longer.

He puts a guiding hand on my shoulder. 'Okay Will,' he says again. There is an almost professional patience in his voice – I am a simple but troublesome child passing through his care.

I shrug him off.

Just know this, I tell him silently as I pass. *There shall be no covenant. No mercy either.*

•

I find that if I lean back in my chair, I am able to see past the guy who is talking to me and get a clear view through the window behind him. Several hundred yards in the distance the steel skeleton of a new building is being slowly hoisted and lowered into place. Tiny men are busy operating the cranes or standing and watching the cranes or walking to where there are other machines and more tiny men. Behind them is a bright blue sky. It's really quite poetic in its way.

'Are you still with us?'

This is directed at me but I choose to ignore it because I'm not yet done with my looking out of the window, and anyway I would have thought the answer to that was self-evident.

Even so, the man who is talking to me – mid-fifties, stuffed toad-like and wet-lipped into his suit – has moved his head so that it now interferes with my line of vision, and the concert of tiny men is replaced by his jowly face. His name is Oliver, he is one of the in-house lawyers. Not just one of, in fact: he is their elder. A Son of Zenas.

'Every word,' I tell him cheerfully. It's not an exact answer to his question, which I've already forgotten, but it addresses the spirit of the thing.

'So, Will, what I was saying is that we cannot of course *make* you go home if you do not want to be off work and if you are, as you have stated yourself to be, in perfectly sound ...' he describes a little shape in the air with his finger '... health.'

He then waits for a short while, as if for a response from me. Was that supposed to be a question?

'Was that a question?' I ask him.

'What?'

'What you just said. It sounded like a statement but you,' I imitate his funny little hand gesture, 'seem to be waiting for me to say something.'

'Is there anything you would *like* to say?'

'About what?'

Nicholas, one of the managing partners, has had enough of this. Perhaps he thought it would be easier to get rid of me.

'Don't mess us about, young man,' he snaps. 'Okay? We're in a very delicate situation here.'

His little miss just-so assistant who's been taking notes during all of this doesn't, I notice, write that last part down.

I should probably mention at this point that there are also a couple of other people in the room besides Oliver and Nicholas. There is Alex, of course, the orchestrator of this little impressment (no sooner had the advertised chat in his office begun then these various players began to drift in, one by one). There is also one of the security guys sitting, like last time, near the door – but he's not the one I dealt with when I jumped in, or at least I'm pretty sure he's not, it's hard to remember exactly. And there's Karen, who is from Human Resources. She is standing over by the window (not the one I was looking out of) where the sunlight has drawn the shadow of her body into tight focus beneath her blouse. Unsurprisingly, Will's loins are stirring at the sight of her – I should probably look away, and yet I can't help resenting that thought a little. Why should I be tyrannised by my own flesh? It's a cruel paradox, this body of yours – the mind always straining to take flight and explore its own bounds only to be constantly conscripted in the service of your earthly needs. This carnal divining rod, always twitching, forever pointing the path to debasement, I remember it from last time – the determined effort to ignore it. It's exhausting.

I refrain from putting my hand down my trousers and guiding the thing under the waistband of my boxer shorts so it's not digging in quite so much. The reason I don't is that Oliver here, and the others for that matter, are watching me with great attention. I am certainly not going to give them an excuse to send me home if they can't find one for themselves.

Returning to Nicholas's point, re the messing about in times of delicacy, I tell him, 'My view of the situation, Nicholas, is that *I* am the one being messed about here. So why don't you just let me get back to work? As I keep telling you, I'm fit as a fiddle.'

'Fine,' he says, although clearly it's not. 'But if you are going to insist on being here then I must tell you ...' he ventures a quick glance in the direction of Oliver who inclines his head as if to confirm that yes, this is, unfortunately, our position, '... that I shall be permanently removing you from the Invira-Corp account. I do this as a matter of routine based on the events of recent days – as you know, we are experiencing acute difficulty with this client and they have asked for a completely fresh team on the account.'

He checks that his assistant is committing each and every one of these solemn words to record. She is.

When her pencil stops, he adds, with visible reluctance, 'This is not, in any way, a measure of your fitness to work.'

Her hand springs back into life, the words lace across her pad in a filigree of corporate compliance.

'The moving finger writes,' I observe, 'and having writ, moves on.'

'Be that as it may,' Nicholas says, with an arctic smile, 'you may rest assured that there will be a full review of the handling of the InviraCorp account. No stone,' he almost hisses at me, 'shall remain unturned. And if, my lad, it transpires that –'

'Thank you, Nicholas.' This interruption is the first thing Karen has said. Everyone turns to look at her. Will's slackening member starts awake like a sentry caught drowsing at his post.

'Will ...' she makes a feline movement from her seat on the window sill and slides into one of the empty chairs opposite me '... I think every one of us in this room is acutely aware of, and a little exercised by,' she glances at Nicholas, 'the damage that recent press coverage has caused our agency. It comes at a critical time for our business and, as I am sure you realise, the reputational risk is worn by ourselves as much as InviraCorp.'

'As the apologists for black-hearted wickedness?' I venture.

She scans my face for a second, not unkindly, just genuinely curious. I think she's wondering if that was a joke. When she sees it wasn't, though, her tone becomes less conversational.

'As Nicholas has stated here for the record, Will, the Abelwood Board and the managing partners have launched a formal review into the InviraCorp account. The terms of reference are to ascertain how this very grave breach of client confidentiality has occurred.'

I decide it'll be in everyone's interests (well, mine anyway) if we stop pussyfooting around like this.

'It wasn't me,' I announce, clear as a bell.

She doesn't like that. None of them do.

'For the avoidance of doubt, Will,' she stammers, 'no one was suggesting that you were in any way ...'

'Cut the crap,' I tell her. My turn to interrupt.

Nicholas starts with, 'Look here, young man ...'

I silence him with my hand.

'For the record,' I address this directly to Nicholas's mousey little assistant, who seems to have gone into temporary paralysis, 'I shall state this as plainly as I can: I was not the one who leaked information about this agency's client to the press. Sorry,' I beam at them all, 'but I'm not your man.'

Technically, of course, this isn't a lie. It was Will. Although, admittedly, there was some gentle encouragement from me – okay, there were some coruscating transfusions of raw spiritual plasma from me – but what do you expect? This is serious business.

Since no one else looks like they're about to speak any time soon, I decide to do some light probing. I'm certain that Nicholas knows about the real problem – but I wonder who else does.

'In some ways,' I continue breezily, 'you've got off pretty lightly so far. I guess you'll just have to hope that whoever's doing the leaking doesn't have access to all the dirt on InviraCorp. I mean, that would be an *unholy* mess – if you know what I'm saying.'

Well, Karen and Alex definitely don't know – they're almost as nonplussed by what I've just said as the security guard. A little disconcerted, perhaps, but in the dark, for sure. Nicholas, on the other hand, and his proctor are ashen-faced.

Good to know.

'Okey-dokey,' I clap my hands together, 'I think this little conversation is now officially over. Time to get back to work.'

Several documents have been laid before me during the course of this meeting, explaining the agency's various contractual responsibilities. I leave them sitting on the table.

I'm the first to leave the room but Karen is following close behind. With a light touch to my elbow, she suggests that we go to her office for a quiet chat. I glance over at Will's desk. His computer is up and running, I notice, and there's a cup of coffee next to it. Just as I am wondering who this might belong to, its owner appears, a nondescript man with all the pallid, socially inept hallmarks of an IT worker.

'Not right now,' I tell her.

I march across and demand to know who he is and what he thinks he is doing at my desk. He begins to form an answer, which he directs at my shoes – the first words are *I have been told to* – until Karen arrives within safe interrupting distance.

'It's just a routine part of the review,' she announces in a pitch-perfect Reasonable Voice.

This seems to be her principal function, applying the company whipcord to the frayed ends of other people's ramblings.

'Anyone,' she warbles on, 'who's had any involvement with the InviraCorp account will be getting a file audit in the next twenty-four hours. It's nothing to worry about.'

'I'm not worried.'

It's true, I'm not. He's not going to find anything on there. My fingers, though, are itching to get hold of that memory stick. It can only be about five feet from where I'm standing. But I need to just relax and bide my time. He's not going to find that either.

'How about we let him get on with his job?' She half turns, to remind us both that we had in fact been heading off for that quiet chat she wanted.

Will's colleagues have given up trying to feign a lack of interest in all this. They are openly staring.

'Fine. Whatever,' I say, as much to them as to her.

We end up climbing four flights of stairs to get to her office. I'm not sure why. Perhaps she thinks the lift will trigger some violent reaction in me. Or perhaps, looking at her, she's just one of those athletic women who likes to bound up flights of stairs to keep her calories-in, calories-out ledger in the black. As I'm thinking this, I realise that to my extreme annoyance I've lapsed once again into a lustful trance. The spell is broken, though, when a man passes us on his way down. I scarcely look at him, but it's enough. His hands are all that I really notice – thin, finely haired claws protruding from his suit. They remind me of a hermit crab feeling out of its shell. He disgusts me, and when my gaze flicks back to Karen, she disgusts me too. The flex of the muscles in her calves as she walks, the scent of her as she heats up from climbing the stairs.

'Here we are,' she tells me as we arrive at a door with a large number nine on it. We walk through into an altogether more serene environment than the floor we were just on. The offices up here all have closed wooden doors, no more of that glass and open plan; the 'all in it together' look has vanished, this is very much the 'shut up and mind your own business' floor. The carpet's thicker too. It's all nice and hushed.

This might have been where I was taken after the jump-in, come to think of it. It has more of that new smell, of which there is only a whiff downstairs where everyone has been traipsing and sweating and stressing a lot more.

'Just in here,' she guides me into her office with another delicate touch to my elbow. By the looks of things she's probably the boss of what she does, which is pretty impressive – I reckon she's only about mid-thirties.

She shuts the door behind us and we settle ourselves in the casual seats rather than at her desk, so we remember that this is not in any way a formal interview.

'I like what you've done with the place,' I say.

By way of reply she pats the swanky leather arm of her chair (one of those wing-backed ones) and shifts her legs, which are tanned and ever so slightly shiny and crossed in a way that makes her skirt drift up to about mid-thigh level.

There is an awkward silence.

She's the first to break it. 'Can we talk about your health?' she asks me gently, 'Off the record.'

'My health? Oh you mean what happened this morning?' It doesn't come off sounding as casual as I'd wanted. It just sounds high-pitched. Nevertheless, I soldier on. 'That really wasn't anything to worry about. It probably looked *way* worse than it was. I have this blood sugar thing – I really ought to keep a better eye on it.'

'Will.' The way she says it is more like *Oh Will, Will, Will ...*

I raise my eyebrows, all innocent. *What?*

I love this part, the physical pantomime of conversation. The off-the-ball manoeuvring, as it were. It's such fun. Easy to overdo, though. I bring my eyebrows back down again.

'I want you to think about the last time you had an episode, Will. I hope you'll remember that we did everything we could to support you through that.'

An episode – that sounds interesting. Although not surprising of course (by the time someone's ready for a jump-in it usually means they're right at the feathered edges of what would normally be considered reason or sanity). That said, I *have* been lucky with Will – and I mustn't lose sight of that. It's rare to get such a solid bind on the first go. Most people fry out on you pretty much as soon as you jump in. It's just too much for them to carry. When I think about the amount of attempts I had to make last time, before I eventually hit on The One, and that was with all the proper support too.

So yeah, all things considered, I've landed on my feet with Will. He's a sturdy vessel. Could be a little tougher physically perhaps – but that's just splitting hairs. He's strong in the head, where it counts.

Anyway, back to this.

Karen is still talking. She has parked (as I think I may have just heard her phrase it) the subject of my health for a moment and is digressing into a little spiel about the company's duty of privacy to its clients. That, she emphasises, is at the core of our offering. Again, her phrase, not mine.

'Oh really?'

'Yes, Will,' a single, sincerely vertical groove appears above her nose. 'Really.'

We both mull this over.

'Did Oliver give you some papers downstairs?' she pipes up after a minute or two. Glancing at my empty hands, she decides he can't have done. 'Not to worry, I can print them out for you.'

She goes off to her computer and clicks the mouse around a bit, the printer on her desk rattles out a couple of sheets.

She brings me a document with the words *client confidentiality* in its title and lingers at my side while I leaf through it. She is clearly of the view that I need some help finding the salient passages and decides to perch next to me, on the arm of the sofa. Her hair brushes against my suit as she leans down to look over my shoulder. I get an apricot waft of women's shampoo.

'There,' she says, her voice so close to my ear, her finger resting lightly on the page I am holding. She is pointing to some subsections littered with quasi-legal language. She then slinks back to her chair and waits for me to read it.

After a suitable stretch of silence, she gives an exploratory nudge.

'Penny for your thoughts?'

On a whim, I decide to actually tell her.

'I was thinking about Azazel.'

'Is that a contact of yours?' she asks hopefully.

Well, yes, actually – used to be. The late, great Azie. But there's a limit to how truthful you can be with people – I have, at least, learned that much since my last go-round.

'No,' I tell her. 'He was one of the *Grigori* – a Watcher.'

'I don't …'

'An angel – from the Old Testament.'

Oh God her expression seems to say.

Quite so.

'But watching wasn't enough for Azazel,' I explain, 'he needed to get involved – you know?' She doesn't know. 'He needed to get down to the ground floor, in the mix with mankind. Of course, he was repeatedly told not to,' (by me too, by the way – we *all* warned him it would end badly), 'but he did it anyway, and he showed the people of the earth a thing or two – he taught them how to do all kinds of crazy stuff.'

I leave a dramatic pause, during which she glances at the door.

'But that wasn't the worst part of it – he had another, far more disruptive agenda.' I lower my voice to a conspiratorial near-whisper. 'Azazel harboured a bit of a soft spot for the ladies – or come to think of it,' I chuckle, 'quite the reverse in fact. He spawned dozens of these semi-angelic children – massive creatures, hundreds of ells high – and they just went raging around the place like gigantic toddlers, uprooting things and destroying everyone's stuff. You'll have seen a reference to them in the Old Testament – the mighty men. No? The men of renown? Still no? Well it was a big deal at the time, and it basically left God with no choice – He had to reboot the whole thing.'

I shake my head ruefully. A sad day for us all.

'That's when He pressed the button on The Flood,' I tell her. 'Washed it all away. Back to zero. And as for Azazel – he got his too. Slung into a bottomless pit.'

(That last part's not *exactly* right, but it's not like she's going to know. Anyway, it captures the spirit of the thing.)

I lean back, making it obvious that I've finished.

She doesn't move a muscle.

'All in all, a bit of a watershed moment,' I quip.

Apparently, though, it's not as funny as I think it is.

I gaze out of the window behind her desk. We're on the same side of the building as Alex's office, which means the tiny men are visible to me once more, this time from an even more impressive elevation.

'Why did you tell me all that, Will?'

'Mm?'

My attention is no longer in the room. There really is something about those little guys. It's mesmerising.

'What was the point of that story you just told me? Do you think we at Abelwood are "fallen angels" …' she air quotes this with her fingers '… or do you …?' She doesn't know what might be a suitable end to this question. She looks to me for help.

'You asked me what I was thinking about,' I mutter absently. 'So I told you.'

Again a little pause. I'm still looking out of the window, but it's no longer the pleasurable experience it was downstairs. Something's not the same. Is it the sky? I can't quite put my finger on it. It might just be this new angle – it makes them look more ant-like, a little sinister even.

'Do you mind me asking,' she begins, then carries on regardless of whether I mind or not, 'if you have had the chance to see a healthcare professional, after what happened this morning?'

'A healthcare professional.' I repeat the admirably circumspect phrase to myself. 'Could that mean a psychiatrist?' I wonder aloud.

'It could mean a psychiatrist...' She floats this confirmation in a tone so gentle and trustworthy that for a second I feel a little disarmed, like I could confide in her some of my real problems, the things that are corroding the real me. I need to stop looking at that building.

'No, Karen, I didn't.' I put my attention fully back on her. 'I was just tired, run ragged by work – I've been under a lot of stress and strain here.'

She's not crazy about that answer; she'd like to edge it back round to safer ground. She has a stab at it.

'Yes,' she says, 'work can certainly be demanding. And that's why we would be keen for you to perhaps speak to a doctor and see if there is anything that can be done to help you achieve the right relationship with stress, for example.'

'Did you just say "relationship with stress"?'

'Yes.' There is not the remotest trace of embarrassment. 'We would like to see if we can help you manage that. We have worked through this kind of thing before, Will – and we did it *together*. We just need to know if you have been involving any other ... parties ... in the agency's business ...'

But I can't keep my attention on what she's saying. There's a problem with the tiny men. A few minutes ago, they were in the process of guiding into place two girders, right on the top of the structure, but now they've stopped midway through and left the I-beams hoisted at an angle across each other. The sun is firing them from behind, catching the hard flashing edges.

It's a perfect crucifix, flat against the sky.

A message from His faithful retainers, of course – some little poodle of His, busily arranging the landscape. There's nothing they love more than a bit of good old-fashioned censure.

But why does it have to get so bloody personal? I mean, okay, fine – I get it: I shouldn't be here. I understand that. But you'd think that after all this time they might let up a bit. But oh no, they just can't help themselves. They never miss an opportunity to taunt me with that thing. And yes, I *do* know how that sounds, by the way. But you'll have to trust me on this, it *is* them. I know a sign when I see one.

It must be driving them crazy, me being down here, but He's obviously not too concerned about it. If He was I wouldn't even be sitting here. He'd have just delved in and squashed this. He could even cast me out if He had a mind to. But He hasn't. And not because He's not keeping an eye on things either – I mean, come on, it's *me*: of course He's got wind of it. Even a recluse like Him will have heard the news that I'm off the reservation again. Anyway, they'll have made sure He knows, you can count on that. Every last detail.

No, I think He's waiting, and watching. I think He's actually quite intrigued to see if I can pull this off. He's the big picture type, not like those hateful minions of His. They're just petty and spiteful – they're never going to let me forget what happened.

No one holds a grudge quite like a servant. The greatest snobs of all.

'Yeah well, they'll have to do better than that!' These words actually come out of my mouth as I spring to my feet.

Karen emits a tiny squeal. Any pretence of concern for my wellbeing vanishes from her face. She is now looking at me with all the fear and surprise of one who is alone with a lunatic. And no doubt I did give her a bit of a shock, but even so, that's just rude.

Whatever. I have far more important things to be thinking about. I need to get to Will's desk before one of those meddlesome idiots thinks to look underneath it, if they haven't already.

I look calmly down at her and apologise for my sudden movements.

'I need to get going,' I tell her, heading for the door.

She looks like she might be about to start with some more of her HR drivel so I toss in a little parting speech, about the persecutory behaviour I've been victim to today. It hits all the sweet spots with phrases like 'singled out' and 'discriminatory'. I even stretch to a few rhetorical questions, as if I am standing there in all my tragedy before a tribunal of hungry employment lawyers.

She looks massively uncomfortable.

'Stress is not a stigma,' I warn her.

She musters a halfway compassionate smile.

'No one's singling you out, Will.' She seems to think about putting her hand on my elbow again but can't quite bring herself to do it. 'We're just worried about you,' she simpers.

That same smile blinks on and off again in her face.

'So you should be,' I tell her gravely. 'So you should be.'

Right then, back down the silent corridor I go, and back down the stairs, two at a time. My hand slaps the railing, my heels click out an echoing canter.

This time when I arrive at Will's desk, I don't waste any effort trying to look the part. The IT guy seems to have gone, so I just squat down and start groping around underneath the desk, where, to my immense relief, my fingers find a promising obstruction, right where Will left it, near the back and off to the left. But it's stuck too well for me to prise off. I'm going to need some scissors. My work station is part of a small open plan area and a few people have left their own seats to take a closer at what I'm doing. I ask them if they have any scissors, which is their cue to melt away again.

I effect a quick but thorough search of Will's desk. No scissors in any of the drawers.

The door to Alex's office, which was firmly shut, is now wide open. He has come out into the corridor and is watching me.

I ask him if he has any scissors.

He tells me in his 'I'm so very concerned about you' voice that he doesn't think scissors are a good idea.

Nahash. Viper.

Then I spot some, poking out of someone's plastic desktop organiser. I stride over and retrieve them, before dropping to my hands and knees and crawling under my desk. It only takes a few seconds to cut free the memory stick from its duct tape chrysalis but while I'm still under there I take the opportunity of cover to slip it into my pocket. There are two pairs of men's shoes next to my desk now – and if I know the security staff in this building, and I think I do, my guess would be that they like to wear exactly this kind of no-nonsense, shiny black footwear.

'Hello gents,' I greet them as I emerge from beneath the desk, 'just getting rid of some gum.'

I put the scissors down. They are immediately picked up.

Now no one really knows what to do. I stand there smiling.

I call over to Alex, 'Alright with you if I pop out for a bit?'

He just looks at me.

'I'm going to pop out for a bit,' I tell the goons, who seem unsure whether to let me pass or not. They glance at Alex.

He shrugs and turns back into his office.

Right then. Time to get out of this faithless hive.

Just to make sure, the security guys escort me all the way to the lobby, clumping along at my side. I stand between them in the lift. We listen to its rigid cables lower us to the ground. Not a finger is laid on me, not a word is exchanged. At the big glass doors, they watch me step out on to the pavement.

It's a massive relief to break the hermetic seal of that interior. Back in the open, I realise just how oppressive it was in there. It takes me a couple of seconds to get used to it, the rush of all these people again, dozens of them skimming past, heads down, intent on their course. It's like I'm waiting to join a river – it needs to work back through me again, as water passes through the gills of an unwanted catch. When I'm ready, I twitch back into the flow and head north, leaving the shadow of that sepulchre behind me.

But even when I'm well shot of it and am enclosed in the tumult of the tube station, there's still a certain sadness that I'm struggling to shrug off. I do not want to be playing this role. I do not want to be typecast as the Disobedient Son, courting everyone's displeasure. It sits heavy in my gut.

'This is not about me,' I tell myself.

I get a couple of looks, but so what? It's important I have my head straight before I sit down with Natalie and finish this thing off. Or else I may as well just step back into the shadows and be done with it.

'This is not about me trying to clear my name.'

I am jammed into one of those lifts that transport people from the surface down to the trains.

'I am doing this for the common good. For all humanity.'

Deep! Deep! Deep! go the doors of the lift as they slide apart, sluice gates for this flow I'm in.

It is only now that I realise, down in this burrow, that I've forgotten to call Natalie to tell her I'm coming. Never mind. Let the news arrive unannounced. Let it come worming through the ground to her, surfacing at her threshold. A gift from below.

I reach into my pocket and close my fingers over the memory stick. It pulses in my fist, like there's blood in it.

My wrong shall at last be righted. You'll see. I shall cut the monster's heart from its chest.

I am still in the crowd, still in the current. Among you all.

I'm going to straighten this all out.

I've got this.

3

Mind over matter – that's what people say – I know: I've heard them. Wise people, movers of men, writers, philosophers, orators whose words have dropped like balm. In fact, they've said it so many times, in so many ways, that it's solidified into a Truth. This mind, this brittle consciousness of which mankind is so proud, makes you better than the rest. Is that it? Nothing left to learn from God's other creatures, with their base occupation of the flesh. *Cogito ergo sum*, as one Frenchman so grandly proclaimed.

Well sorry, but I'm calling you out on that.

Take this last half hour as an example. At any stage through-out my journey, I could have allowed myself to get bogged down by the spectres of the past, the myriad little reminders of my failure that had been left scattered for me wherever I cared to look. Even the name of my destination, for crying out loud: King's Cross. It would have been *so* easy to do – they wanted nothing more than to see me buckle under their jeering attention. But I resisted. Not by *thinking* my way out of it, though – that's my point. By doing precisely the opposite: I just let it go – I shifted into neutral and I glided it out. I spent that time sheltering in this body, where neither reason nor memory has jurisdiction.

So when I'd get a glimpse of a brash black cross tattooed on some bloke's arm, say, flexing in his repulsive milky flesh, I'd simply rest my head against the window of the carriage – against the cool-to-the-touch glass with its backlit scratches – and I'd let my eyes do some lazy looking. I'd watch the quick slick of world rush past, let the pressure drain out of my head. Same when a dinky little cross came winking its light-darts from a woman's neck chain, or just now, up in the world again, when I glimpsed through the window of a bookshop the yellow and orange spines going down the shelves, and the red ones ripping across the top – a flaming cross, the worst kind. I just did what I'm doing right this minute –feeling every little flex of my skin, letting every molecule of air open itself up in my lungs, outside in, swelling the alveoli, putting the vermilion of oxygen into my blood and pushing it out into the rest of me.

From the tip of your nose to the prints on your toes, so much territory to keep track of – it's absorbing stuff. Although, don't think for one second think that I find it easy tuning out like that. Because I don't. No words can describe how I hate that stupid shape springing out at me from everywhere the whole time, like it's a symbol of hope. There's nothing hopeful about it, not for me anyway. Not for anyone who's been splayed across it and left for dead.

Anyway. Enough said.

I'm here now, and there's business to be done. I'm right around the corner from Natalie's office but I'm not managing to get her on her landline or her mobile – just the cicada buzz of office background on both, overlaid with *You're through to Natalie Shapiro, please leave a message.* So I did – the same one twice – telling her I need to speak to her now, in person, that I'll wait for her in The Lamb. (What? That's what it's called – I don't get to choose the names.) It's the pub she and Will met in last time. And I must say, it looks a lot better in the daylight – more cheerful, not as grubby as it seemed when I watched them have their clandestine drink here last week. The hanging baskets are still dripping from a recent watering, and there's no gaudy neon sign shining out from next door (the Sunny Side Up 'tanning salon and social club', whatever that's supposed to mean). The door, too warped to close without a significant shove, is standing slightly ajar, suggesting that it's one of those pubs that welcomes the early drinker.

Before I go in, though, I decide to cover all the bases and fire off a quick email too. It takes a certain amount of faffing with Will's iPhone to get it done (it's funny, I see these things being used all the time, but actually doing it yourself, skating the fingertips across the screen, bringing glowing fragments of information swimming up to meet them, that's something else). I have to sift through a ton of addresses – mostly journalists and PR people by the look of it – before I find Natalie. The first tap selects her, the second tap sends the mail. I could do this all day, it's so satisfying.

Inside The Lamb, the first thing I notice is the smell of beer-soaked wood, which I find immediately reassuring. There are two men already at the bar, sat several stools apart, but neither one of them bothers to look up as I walk over and order my drink. The barmaid serves me my whisky then disappears to some unseen task, leaving us to our muffled, stale silence. Outside, the distantly layered sounds of car horns and sirens seem remote and irrelevant. I feel entirely relaxed, and as the whisky lights its small and warming fire in my chest, I am finally able to kick back for a minute and marvel at yet another new sensation. I thought the tea was good but this, it's a whole new level of drama, a tiny sun forming and then silently imploding around my third rib level. A small belch of whisky aftertaste delivers itself into my mouth as proof of what just happened.

It's a good thing, her not being here right away. I needed this bit of down time – pun very much intended. A jump-in takes it out of you, especially if you're not used to it. It was different when I did it last time, I was fresh, I sprang right back into shape. But things have changed. It's been a long, bitter haul. This time, I'm going to need a little rest.

Maybe if I scrunched around in this chair a bit and let this stubborn body just unkink itself, like that – now *that's* what I'm talking about – just get the back to scooch down a little further and the legs can start to flop out to the sides, and the belly, here you go, now I'm starting to get there, the belly just pushes up into a nice little pillow for my hands, and the –

A loud noise, crisp and sharp as a gunshot, brings me jangling up from my slump, stomach churning, head spinning.

Help!

It's such a violent shock that I think I may have actually shouted this word – its echo is still rattling in the corners of the room. The barmaid, unnoticed by me, had snuck to the table next to mine and snapped down her can of polish with a resounding crack.

'You can't sleep here, babe,' she announces, then squirts the table a couple of times, wipes it and moves on.

My heart is beating up in my throat, like it's some creature I'm trying to swallow. I lever myself up on the back of a nearby chair and teeter away to the dimly lit bathroom.

It takes a while before I'm ready to come out again. When I do, there is a man standing next to the dust-thick curtains on the far side of the bar, staring up at the sky. When he sees me emerge, he stares at me instead. He is in his mid-fifties, I would say, about a head smaller than me – he would appear to be another local. The barmaid seems to know him.

I nod in greeting, trying not to look like I've just been resting my head against the greasy tiles in the toilets. I go to smooth my hair with my hand then I remember that Will's hair is clippered down to a stubble. I give it a pensive rub instead.

He is still staring at me. Partly as a way of turning my back on him and partly because, hey, this is my chance to live a little, I go to the bar and order another a drink. A brandy this time. But when I hand over the money, the barmaid doesn't see it. She's looking over my shoulder.

'Simon,' she says, 'you're not going to start getting all arsey, are you? You know we don't put up with that nonsense in here.'

I follow the direction of her gaze. I see what she means. The starey one – Simon, apparently – is standing at my table and is now eyeballing us with what can only be described as a murderous expression. His whole body is trembling with rage. Eyes as lamps of fire, is how we might have phrased it way back when. Countenance like thunder.

He barks something at me, which at first I don't understand, and which is so sudden and guttural it actually elicits a small grunt of surprise from one of the morning drinkers (both of whom, by the way, have now bothered to look at me, and at Simon – they're not fans). The barmaid hops back a half step. He does it again, a little louder, and this time she squeaks in alarm.

'What the shit is that?' asks one of the alcoholics.

'Don't worry,' I tell them. 'It's okay.' I knock back my brandy in one swill. 'It's okay,' I say again.

I see what's happened here. It took me a couple of seconds but I'm there now. Those noises he's making are in fact words, just not ones you'd expect to hear in this day and age.

I reply to him in kind as I walk towards him. The Aramaic feels alien, unwrought, like pebbles grinding together in my mouth. *Calm down*, is what I'm saying to him. *Sit down and calm down.*

He needs a little more persuading. His entire body has gone rigid. His eyes look like they are being forced out of his head.

'She,' I nod my head in the direction of the cowering barmaid, 'is going to call the police if you carry on like this.' But there isn't a word for police, as such, so I have to say *dayan* – judge. This threatens to make him even angrier (he thinks I'm referring to Him) so I just say it in English: 'Police.'

'Do you want her to call the police?' I tack on, partly for emphasis, partly for the others' sake – it's important they see I'm getting things in hand.

He fixes them with another of his radioactive stares, then slowly, stiffly, he sits down. His hands are unnaturally planted on his knees, his head completely still. When he looks back at me I have to force myself to hold his gaze, the sheer tonnage of his disdain is so immense.

'Wherefore art thou here?' He demands to know, albeit not as quietly as I'd like. But at least he's speaking English now, kind of. 'Dost thou forget He forbad it?'

Listen to him: wherefore; forbad. Fusty old fool. I can't stand this lot, with their superior ways. It's perfectly obvious he hasn't the slightest interest in your world – he hasn't been watching you, sucking it all up like I have. He's just pushed in now because I'm here, and everyone knows I shouldn't be. That's all it is. He doesn't care why I'm here, or what troubles could be in store for you. He just cares that I've broken The Rules. And he's exactly the type I'd expect to come and speak to me about it – from the upper reaches, one of His inner circle – a starchy bureaucrat with all the trimmings. As far as he's concerned, our Lord and Master could not have been clearer: no more jumping in for me, ever. And I've chosen to flout that direct order – it's little wonder he's in such a state. He's virtually oscillating in his seat.

'Yeah well, sorry, but it had to be done.'

He cocks his ear towards me. Not sarcastically – I genuinely believe he thinks might have misheard me.

'I *had* to do it,' I tell him again. 'I've discovered something – something important.'

What little composure he had burns off in another flash of righteous anger. He's standing again, the chair upturned beside him.

'Only He shall determine consequence!' he bellows at me.

The barmaid disappears out the back. Now the police really will be on their way. Or worse, some guy with a bat. I need to make this quick.

'Listen – you *have* to listen to me. I need you to explain this to Him: you tell Him –'

He holds up a silencing hand. It's a jerky movement, sudden but mechanical – the body control is virtually nil in these situations (this is not a jump-in, you understand: these types don't do that, far too grubby for them, they just push through to say their piece, then they're gone again).

'Mankind hast paid for thy foolishness once before,' he thunders. 'It shall not be repeated.' Simon's face is contorting under the pressure. It's like the bones are moving around in there.

'Look,' I hiss at him, 'I don't need you to lecture me about the past. Okay? I'm well aware of what's happened. What I'm trying to tell you is I've seen a chance to change things – to make good on all that. It's different this time. I can see what needs to be done.'

He's looking at the glass on the table like it's a potential weapon. He's thinking about smashing it and thrusting its jagged edge into my throat.

'I will not,' I tell him, 'be forced to live under the shadow of that mistake forevermore. You understand? I *am* worth something. I don't care what you people …'

I choke the last few words. I'm getting a bit upset.

His expression has changed to one of sneering contempt.

'Thou art weak and wretched,' he whispers.

Then slowly, intimately, he begins to smile, which feels far more threatening than the shouting.

Still whispering, but reverting to Aramaic, keeping it between us, he asks, 'You do know what will happen, don't you?'

I wipe my nose and cheeks with the back of my hand. I do my best to appear unconcerned.

'He will do it. You know He will.' That hating smile, sharpening the words like a lathe. 'You will be cast out.'

Cast out, *garash*, that phrase in particular, he works into me like a stiletto.

In as calm a voice as I can muster, I say to him, 'You just tell Him what you have heard. You tell Him I'm making amends.'

One last look, then he releases a wordless sound and Simon is left to collapse down into his seat, a puppet whose strings have been cut.

Slowly the bewildered Simon begins to stir. 'I feel ... I don't ...' His pale face is shining with sweat.

I have a quick check to see what the others are doing. The two drunks are still watching us in appalled fascination. No sign of the barmaid, though.

'I need to get out of here,' I tell him, not giving him a chance to process what's just happened. Not, of course, that he'd be able to – in a few seconds he'll have no recollection of it. He has more chance of holding on to the gravity that transfixes him to the earth.

'I must have eaten something ...' he says weakly as I head for the door.

See what I mean?

I go stomping off in the general direction of Natalie's office. I'm trying hard not to think about that vicious old prig and all his threats and his bluster. But the truth is it's rattled me – the way I started blubbing, more than anything, as if deep down I agree with him, that I've lost my right to an opinion, that I'm never again to be trusted with anything.

I swing my foot at a can and send it whizzing into the road. A man on a bike looks up to say something to me, sees my face, then decides against it.

'Woe betide you if you ever make a mistake,' I tell a gaggle of school kids. 'It'll never be forgotten.'

When I'm about ten paces past them they erupt into fits of laughter. Mockery wherever I go.

By the time I'm coming down on to York Way, I've calmed down enough to think about making a phone call. Near the overpass, I stop and find a step to sit on, with a view of the weed-sprouted railway sidings. I get out Will's phone and give *NS Mob* another try.

This time it's picked up on the second ring.

'Will?'

I'm silent for a second. It seems an odd thing to ask. Then I remember that that's my name now.

'Hi, sorry – yes, it's Will,' I confirm. 'I tried you earlier.'

'Yes, I know, I got your message – I'm on my way to you now. I should be there in a couple of minutes.'

'No, don't go there!' It comes out crazy and loud. She goes all quiet on the other end. 'Sorry, Natalie – didn't mean to shout there. I'm having a very stressful day,' I put some of that smiling at my own silliness type of sound into my voice (like a half-sigh but with a wider mouth and a slightly higher register). 'What I *meant* to say was I'm not at The Lamb anymore, I'm right near your office. I was actually on my way to you.'

'Okay sure, no problem.' Clearly I'm free to sound as loud and crazy as I want – Will is a once in a lifetime source and she'll take him however he comes. 'So where are you?'

I look up from the patch of ground I've been studying, where a hairline fault in the tarmac is running at a seventy-eight degree angle to the kerb. (I've been having to focus pretty hard to block out some of the taunts that have been jostling for my attention. One, in particular – two slowly dispersing vapour trails crossed high up in the sky – is still determinedly hanging there.)

'I'm right next to where the road crosses the railway lines, down the side of King's Cross Station.'

Ha! I hadn't noticed that part before I just said it – not only is it the King's cross but it also manages to get station in there too. A station of the cross. Oh bravo!

'I think I see you – sitting on the pavement.'

I get up and peer into the distance. There she is, holding up a hand.

'Hang on,' she says, 'I'll be with you in two secs.'

I spend that time smoothing down Will's suit jacket and brushing the dirt off the knees of his trousers, or trying to brush it off anyway – whatever it is, it's not budging. Must have knelt in something.

When she arrives we shake hands. There is a tiny, almost imperceptible scar on her left wrist.

'Sorry about all the drama. As I said, it's been a strange morning. Things at work are …' I shrug – *what can I say?*

'I can imagine.' When she smiles her whole face smiles with her, if you know what I mean.

She is completely different in the flesh. Her eyes, for example, are the colour of honey – I hadn't noticed that when I was watching. Not the honey you get in a jar, but the kind that Ovid described to you, oozing from the black oak. The luminous kind.

'So …' I go rummaging in my pocket and produce the memory stick between thumb and forefinger '… I have something for you.'

'Thanks.' She takes it and immediately pops it into her bag. 'What's on it? More about InviraCorp?'

'Is there somewhere we can talk?'

'Yes, of course – we can go to my office. There's a café there, we can grab a –'

'Actually, no.' I suddenly feel very uncomfortable at the thought of being cooped up inside again. I think I'd rather stay out here in the open. 'Do you mind if we just walk? We can walk and talk.'

'No problem – whatever you feel most comfortable with.'

I wonder how often she finds herself in these kinds of situations. She seems very relaxed.

'Let's head up that way,' she tosses her head back slightly, meaning *behind us.* 'We can get down to the canal. The towpath goes all the way to Camden.'

Walking next to her I find myself thinking about my darling Maryam. I don't know why – they look nothing alike, there's none of that dusk in Natalie's skin. Maybe it's just the sense of having an ally, a soft womanly companion who will bear witness to my suffering.

'It must be difficult for you,' she says, right on cue. She is looking past me, at the slow trains approaching and cautiously departing the station. 'But you're doing the right thing.'

Actually, I think it's the way she *sounds* – or the way she's saying what she's saying, if that makes sense. It carries the tiniest echo of my little Magpie. *You are my lamp.* How I remember the way she pronounced that word, *noohra*, lamp. And now this woman's words are running into me the same way, that same cool stream into the darkness of me. It really does show, though, just how much you miss when you're only watching. I'd never have been able to pick up on something like this just by looking on – things have an antiseptic quality to them when you're off site, as it were. It's like looking at a photograph. No, actually, not like a photograph – it's like the world's coming at you through an old television set or a … You know what? It's not really like anything. I guess that's the point.

We've been walking for a few minutes now and I've yet to say a word. We've just passed the monolithic headquarters of Natalie's newspaper and are about to turn down on to the steps that will take us to the canal. She is patient, also quiet at my side.

'I don't really know where to begin,' is all I can think to say. I really don't. It's kind of overwhelming now that I'm actually here. Also, I'm feeling profoundly exhausted again. I'm not too sure that walking was such a good idea after all. I might look for a place to sit down.

'Why not start by telling me what's on the USB you handed me?'

It's very gently put, like how you are with someone you know is trying their best but just isn't quite managing to get there. I wish more people would talk to me like that.

'Okay, look: InviraCorp isn't the story. It's part of the story but it's not the really bad part. You need to follow the money to get to that …' I put a hand on her arm. 'Do you mind if we stop here?'

The here in question is one of those heavily vandalised benches you tend to see at the side of canals. It has the look of a structure that someone has recently been murdered on. I flop down. She perches a little more gingerly on the edge. Next to us the canal is motionless, the colour of old silver.

'Do you have any idea,' I ask her, 'where it's coming from? The money, I mean – the tens of millions that fund InviraCorp's manufacturing and distribution?'

She looks slightly exasperated by this question. It's obviously something they've been hitting a dead end on, just as I knew they would.

'The company's run through offshore vehicles – that's all we've managed to find out. You know what these places are like – it's impossible to get any information. So what are you saying? Is it government funding or …?'

'No,' I wave that suggestion away. 'I wouldn't even …' What? Wouldn't jump out of exile for something as footling as that? 'No, it's much worse than government money. It's the church. And not just any old church – the Roman Catholic Church.'

I give her a second or two to start working through the gears.

'The same people,' I continue, helping her along with it, 'who spend all their time ...'

She jumps in and completes it for me '... telling people in Africa that using condoms is a mortal sin. The same people who are fuelling the HIV pandemic.'

'Exactly. With one hand they're allowing the disease to flourish, with the other they are milking enormous profits from its treatment.'

'Can you prove this?'

I glance at her bag. 'What I've given you there gives times and dates of meetings between key players at InviraCorp and members of the Vatican administration. Signed minutes of board meetings, placing those people together. Also, you may have noticed that the Vatican Bank decided to publish its accounts for the first time a few weeks ago. Some bullshit PR stunt to show the world how transparent they are ...'

I shift forwards in my seat a little so I don't have to look anymore at a jagged acrostic in the graffiti across the water from us. *U fall*, it says.

Her attention is riveted on me.

'... well, before I decided to send you that data last week, getting the ball rolling on InviraCorp, as it were, I printed off the Vatican accounts – the full version. There were offshore assets referred to in the annexes that I happen to know are trust vehicles for InviraCorp profits. But of course, if you were to look at those accounts now, you'd see that all mention of any offshore money ...'

Again she completes it for me '... has been removed.'

I smile and sit back again in my seat. 'Yup.'

She had shuffled round on the bench while I was explaining it to her, one leg tucked under the other, so she could look at me straight on. Now, though, she sits round like me, staring at nothing.

'This is a lot to take in,' she says.

Then she gets up and turns back in the direction of her work. 'I'm going to need to have a good look at what you've given me.' She wants to be getting on with this now. Every moment that passes out here is a waste. 'I'll need to take it to my editor.'

When I make no move to follow her, she tells me, 'Will, you're going to have to come too.' I must look a little lost because she goes back to her gentle voice. 'I'm going to need you to stay close.'

So I go with her, docile as a child.

'Bloody hypocrites,' she says as we start climbing the steps.

I make no reply. I'm just pleased to be leaving the accusing graffiti behind us, and that glowering crow I saw just now, fixing me with its cocked head, putting a little of its darkness in me.

'If this is God's work, I'd hate to see what the devil can do.'

The devil. Now there's another of my foolish utterances come back to haunt me. A few passing references to the *ha-satan*, that was all it was, and the next thing I know everyone's spinning yarns about the devil.

It was just a metaphor I feel like yelling, although in fairness, she looks like she already knows that. There are people, though, I would like to yell it to – countless congregations of them. It's amazing really, when you think about it – the dark prince, the hoofed avenger, Old Itchy Scratchy himself … there really is no end to their nonsense. They'll be talking about drinking my blood next – oh no, wait …

'There is no devil,' I tell her. 'It's just people doing it to themselves.'

When we get to her office this precise point seems to leap from every page as I sit in the reception area leafing through the day's paper while she goes off to arrange somewhere quiet for us to talk.

When she re-emerges, my mind is fizzing with thoughts I'd like to try to get across to her (it can be a little over-stimulating reading through the news on a global scale – I find, anyway). There are so many different things happening at once and yet the common themes that bind these events are surprisingly few.

'Okay, I've got us a meeting room,' she tells me, before I have time to begin talking about the article I was just reading.

Then by the time I've finished filling out the information in the visitor book, I've pretty much forgotten what it was I wanted to say to her anyway. That's how it is, I guess – the business of getting things done always pulls it back into a nearer focus. Who has time for the big picture?

Not me, not us, that's for sure, as we're whisked up the escalator surrounded by the light and glass and busy people of the atrium, where the bright autumnal sunshine is allowed in to fill every corner. Even as we move away into the guts of the building, the corridors remain bright and wide. You get the feeling that there is more than enough oxygen for the truth to survive in here. No need to be afraid that it'll be suffocated in a closed circuit of rooms and tunnels, like what I saw at Abelwood, the cloistered stage for Will's creeping paranoia.

'In here.' She shows me into a small meeting room. 'I'm just going to fetch a laptop. Do you want a drink of anything?'

'I'm fine thanks.'

I sit down in a chair that turns out not to be as comfortable as it looked.

She puts a hand on my shoulder. 'Thank you, Will.' The heat of her hand radiates through me, softening me with its understanding. 'Thank you for everything.'

When she's left the room, the afterglow of her touch remains. Her scent too, like a summer orchard. I find it deeply comforting. All this time, I've longed for physical contact. Abandoned like that in the shadow of His disappointment, I felt so little warmth.

If it hadn't been for you, for my watching of you, I would have cracked.

But it pulls too. I'm here, and I have no right to be. Will showed me something I couldn't turn away from. Not the worst thing I've seen, not by any means, just the last in a very long line of things.

Everyone has their point they need to reach. That much we know. It's a knowledge we all share, a knowledge we have drawn from the earliest light of His universe. Electrons clamour for the nucleus, their nature drives them to it. And yet, not all of them manage it. Some find themselves jostled to the perimeter.

It is here, too distant from the nuclear centre, that they become susceptible to detachment.

All that's required is a conductor strong enough to pull them away.

4

She closes the lid of her laptop and rests her elbows on the table. The tip of the memory stick continues to glow hopefully in the machine's side.

'I don't think there's enough here – not yet,' she adds, wanting to keep it upbeat.

Looking at the pieces Will has scraped together, I have to agree with her. It's suddenly all seeming a little thin.

'But it's a starting point – an *excellent* starting point,' she reaches across and folds her hand over mine. 'We just need to work it up a bit.'

I can barely be bothered to speak. I'm beginning to wonder why I even bothered at all, to do any of this. I can't begin to imagine what it's going to cost me with The Boss.

'What would it take?' I mutter. 'What more do we need?'

'Look, Will,' she gives my hand a little joggle, like you do with the mouse of a sleeping computer, 'none of this has been a waste of time. This is invaluable data – we just need to attach some hard evidence to it, that's all.'

Her hand is alive on my skin, a part of her on a part of me. The contact is working its way through to me. There's that Maryam vibe about her again. It's a kind of *We can do this*, with a bit of something else added in. Something thrilling.

'I'm going to need some material that's concrete enough to satisfy our lawyers.' She smiles apologetically, as it seems to me anyone should at the mention of a lawyer.

'Primary material you mean – direct from the source?'

She sighs. 'Ideally, yes – but I don't see how that would be possible.' This is obviously a familiar cul de sac. We know what we know but proof isn't easy to come by. I can relate to that. 'Unless you know someone on the inside? In the offshore side of the operation?'

I do a kind of non-committal thing with my eyebrows. *Maybe I do.*

She perks up a bit at this.

'If you could get me solid proof, Will, that those trusts in Jersey really are paying out to the Vatican, then ... Let's just say we'd be able to eviscerate them with something like that.'

Eviscerate, now there's a word you don't hear very often. Nor, for that matter, do you come across the thing itself anymore, or very rarely anyway. Horrible business – seen it done a few times.

'That, to answer your question, is what it would take. Something on that scale. I can't file on what you've given me here. Don't get me wrong, it's compelling stuff, but at the end of the day, what's in these accounts, what you have references to in all those emails, they're just offshore assets – they could be for anything. They don't *prove* anything. I mean, *I* believe you, one hundred per cent – I'm with you on this. But as far as my editors are concerned – as far as the lawyers are concerned – it could mean anything.'

She removes her hand from mine.

'If we tried to run with this – even supposing the lawyers would green light it – InviraCorp would knock it out of the park in a second. You know that better than I do.'

I grin at her. 'You mean some PR asshole would get to work on it with his asshole PR messaging?'

She looks a little uncomfortable.

'I'm *joking*,' I tell her.

I push back my chair and get to my feet.

'Look, if it's proof you need, I'll get you proof,' I find myself saying. 'Don't you worry about that. Just sit tight and wait for me to contact you. Tomorrow, I declare, plucking a time out of thin air. 'I'll have it for you tomorrow.'

'Will, hang on for a second.' She's up on her feet too. 'Just slow down. How are you going to …?'

'Seriously, don't worry about it. I can fix this.'

Can I? I have absolutely no idea. All I know is I want to. More than anything I have ever wanted. I already have the door open and am halfway out of it.

'O-kay.' She says it in that slow, decoupled way that means it is in fact a fair way off okay. 'But don't you think it would be a good idea to hang around here, just for a little while longer? I want to bring the news ed in on this, maybe even the boss. I'd like you to be there.'

'No, you do that,' I tell her, more or less over my shoulder. 'I don't have time for any more talking.'

She follows me out.

'Will?' Her left hand is on my arm, the lower part, my forearm – is that a word? It muddles me, her being so close. 'Be careful.'

I nod.

'The substance of things hoped for,' I whisper, like it's the only secret I know. 'The evidence of things not seen.'

And with that I'm gone. Back out in the world.

I don't like walking these streets. If anything, the situation is getting worse. There is almost nowhere I can look.

At a clogged roundabout I come across the ghastly sight of workmen in the road, besmirched with filth, standing expressionlessly in their hole as if wakened from death. Blinking in the pit of their grave. It has the quality of an omen, a scene from one of those Tarot cards – one of the bad ones. *Il Giudizio*.

Don't stop, don't look. That's the secret. Just shake it off and move on.

Around the corner from Will's flat I get a text message from Natalie.

Ed meeting @ 5pm, it says. *Will call after. We can make this happen.*

Yes. Exactly. I tuck the phone back in my pocket. We *can* make this happen. I step off the kerb.

Something hits me, hard, slamming me face first on to and off it in the same second.

The next thing I know I am sitting up on the tarmac with a circle of strangers looking down at me. My face is warm and wet. Blood is dripping on to the front of my shirt. My nose is beating like a bull's heart.

'I couldn't miss you!' a semi-hysterical Indian man is gabbling at me. 'Vy don't you look?'

Someone, a woman from the circle leads him away, speaking to him quietly. I hear him even in the distance, saying, 'You saw him stepping right in front of me.'

'Don't get up,' a voice tells me. One of them, a cuddly looking woman, has squatted down next to me. 'Stay where you are until the ambulance gets here.'

'I don't need an …' *ambulance* gets lost in my swooning effort to stand. I reach a wobbly half-crouch then sit back down hard on the ground. 'Okay,' I concede, 'maybe I should just …'

'Don't get up,' she repeats, a little more firmly this time. She puts a half reassuring, half restraining hand on me.

When the paramedics arrive they shine a light in my eyes and ask me some resoundingly clear questions about who and where I am. By this time (it's taken a good twenty minutes for them to get here) I feel pretty much back to normal. The fogginess has burnt off, although a low, menacing ache has set up shop in the mid to back section of my head. And my nose is throbbing to such an extent that my entire face seems to have joined with its pulsating rhythm.

They take me into the back of the ambulance to put some wadding in my nose, or at least one of them does. The other one stays outside, talking to the driver who hit me, the Indian guy, who continues to flit around like a moth.

'You're lucky to have got off so lightly,' she tells me. 'But I'm just going to shut the door while I put the cotton in there. I think I may need to make a manual adjustment to your nose – is that okay with you?'

I nod, pointlessly since her back is turned to me while she pulls the door to. I'm about to say it in words when she turns around again. But I don't. I don't say anything.

'No need to stare like that.'

Her voice has changed, *she* has changed, but it's different this time, not like it was with the guy in the pub. She has none of the rage that Simon (was that his name?) had, and she's actually speaking normal English too, like she's bothered to notice what you've all been up to in the last few hundred years.

She doesn't appear to hate me either, which is a little unnerving.

'He wants you home,' she tells me, making it sound like the most attractive thing in the world.

'Then maybe He should have picked a better driver,' I say.

'You know as well as I do what I'm talking about. He could cut you off any time He wants – but He doesn't want to play it like that. Not with you. He's giving you a chance here. He wants you to be able to come back – while you still can.'

Ah right, so not *entirely* non-threatening then. Still, a nicely phrased, backhanded threat is a far sight more pleasant than being called a fool and a weakling, or whatever it was that last one said.

'But I'm not finished here.'

She sighs and sits down on the fold-out seat opposite me. This is much more like an actual conversation than my previous encounter – this paramedic barely seems to have skipped a beat. You never know, maybe she's used to being puppeted like this. Perhaps she's one of their regular conduits. Wouldn't surprise me, the line of work she's in.

'There is nothing to finish here …' then she tries to say my name – my *actual* name – but it gets stuck in her throat. There's no way that was ever going to work. We both smile at this. It's a little shared moment – come to think of it, she probably did it on purpose. A cunning reminder to me: *We're both on the same side.*

'I'm sorry but there is.'

She shakes her head, in a kind way.

'It can't be easy for you.' She has her hair pulled back in a no-fuss pony tail. Her hands are pink and scrubbed clean. 'And just so you know, not everyone blames you. There are some of us,' she lowers her voice a little, 'who didn't agree with the way He handled things. You've been badly mistreated, if you ask me.'

I lower my head, although strangely not to cry – you'd think this would be the time I would do it. Goes to show, a body has a mind of its own, stores up feelings in its muscles and tissues, only lets them go when it's good and ready. No, my bowed head is to hide from her the traces of a smile. I see plain as day what she is trying to do to me. She doesn't pick up on this, though. She's encouraged by what she sees. Penitence, imminent capitulation is the sense she is getting. I feel at an expert advantage – crucial hours ahead of her in a body, already so much more mastery of it at my disposal.

She leans forward, all friendly. 'I'm curious …' She wants to take this opportunity to ask me some things – a prurient guard walking the condemned man to the chamber '… that Christ thing, how did you manage to …?'

'Mess it up like that?'

She spreads her hands. *Your words, not mine.*

'Because I felt sorry for them.'

That's not enough for her.

'But weren't you supposed to just be … how can I put it? … a bit part? You carry David's crown for a while then pass it on – wasn't that the plan? Get a lineage in power and have things running His way down here, instead of …' words fail her '… this Jesus cult you left behind' is what she lands on. Then she spreads the hands again, the only apologetic gesture she has – probably not much call for it. 'That's what I heard anyway.'

'I'd say that's pretty much the size of it. Except when it came to it, I kind of drifted off message.'

She makes a *You think?* face.

'Fine, totally off the rails then. Whatever. But at the time, it felt like I was helping.' I rub my face with my hands. This conversation is even more exhausting than the walking and getting hit by a car. 'I don't know what else to tell you,' I say into my hands.

And it's true, I don't. Two thousand years of raking it over and still I don't know more than that. I had no idea the Jesus thing would go viral like it did – it didn't seem so important at the time. Who knew it would drag on for so long?

The door opens and her partner starts climbing in. 'How we doing in here?'

'Just give us a second, Rob.' I can't see her face but some sign passes between them – they must get tricky customers all the time. 'I'm fine,' she adds. 'We just need a couple of minutes here.'

'Sure, no problem.' And he's gone again.

'Look,' she says to me, 'I don't have time to be chit-chatting with you. The fact is He understands why this is stirring you up so much – of course He does. What happened back then was a disaster, no one's disputing that. Far from it – it's galling for us all, the way they've taken to heart all that babbling you did – but He needs you to stop it now, okay? Whatever it is you think you're doing, you're going to need to back off. Others will take care of this for you.'

'Oh will they?' I get myself ready to leave. 'No, I'm sorry, but this is my mess, and I'm going to clean it up. I can't sit by and watch anymore. I'm tired of just *watching* all the time. I'm so tired of all of it.'

'You stay *right* where you are,' her voice commands me, under new strain, about an octave deeper. 'You callow brat.' Here we go. 'Is it not enough that you poisoned the well once before with your mindless promises about heaven and eternity? You do realise what you've done, don't you? These people are shooting for another life now, thanks to you and your jam tomorrow fairy stories.'

'Yes – *exactly*. Why do you think I'm here?'

She fixes me with a desolate stare.

'I really don't know. But what I *do* know is that you should not be here. And you know it too.'

'The hand that errs,' she mutters as she rifles in one of the equipment drawers, 'is not the hand that heals.'

She holds out to me some vials of morphine and a large sealed syringe. 'Use these. Return yourself to Him. Throw yourself upon His mercy.'

'No.' I stand up, like a giant in this confined space. 'I must find an ending.'

She makes a gesture I'm not sure how to describe. More than a shrug, less than a shudder.

'An ending is exactly what you will find. He will show you no kindness if you refuse Him now.'

So this is it.

Do I say it or think it? I cannot tell. No matter, there are no words left to speak. It is a mutual kinesis – not just me, but Him too. Another hand must set the fire in this dry straw.

'He will put you in the earth,' are her final words to me.

That's what they call it, when He casts one of us out.

'*Lama sabachthani*?' I croak. Forsaken again. Godforsaken.

I stumble out of there and push past her partner. He doesn't seem especially surprised to see me leaving like that. People in sudden aggressions, refusing help, it's part of his job. Mine too.

The way back to the flat is a blur. Houses, doors, railings, fences, people peeping out of windows, a dead something under a bush – it all goes scudding by me. A wet trim of fallen leaves runs along the side of the pavement. Its musty stench of rot and damp is still in my nostrils as I open Will's door.

Inside, it's the most I can do to reach that sofa again. I am suddenly overwhelmed by fatigue. It is choking in my throat, aching through my limbs. My entire frame is working to a new gravity, like it wants to be way down there somewhere, in the earth's core. All around me is the detritus of insomnia. How long since this body last slept?

The most I can manage is to roll down on to the floor and crawl over to the mattress. Lying on the sheets, I blink slowly. Curtain down, curtain up again: I see the carpet and the small pile of books beside the makeshift bed, Aquinas's fat face in there. I blink again, but this time my eyelids will not open. There's nothing more I can do.

It's been a proper, old school Monday. Lundi. Lunes. Howl at the moon day.

I take a deep breath. All sound shuts out, leaving only the slow, steady beating of this heart, telegraphed to me through the springs of the mattress, remote and rhythmic. The drum call of a forgotten outpost.

5

The moment I open my eyes, I feel the change.

I pat my body, checking for what I do not know.

Can this really be it? The dark descent?

Are these *my* hands now? My flesh? Or am I being tricked by imagination? This sudden feeling of being fastened here just another fluke sensation.

Reason shakes her head.

I raise myself up on watery legs. A constriction in my chest tightens my breathing then lets it go again. I hear the air rasping in my lungs.

It is night and the room is in shadow. Swatches of streetlight stripe the carpet at my feet.

'I'm going to be sick,' I say into the stillness of the room.

I vomit a few chokes of nothing, bile and water. I take a few steps forward, then vomit again as I hold myself up against the doorframe.

A low, persistent pain in my nose has been woken from its own sleep and is now establishing itself in new positions, behind my eyes and cheeks. I am burning up, the shirt on my back is wet through.

'I am planted here now.' My voice is gasping, faraway, explaining this to me. It understands better than I do.

I sink down to my hands and knees but even the weight of this proves too much and I roll over on to my side, legs tucked up against me, stunned as if by birth.

She was right, He has put me in the earth.

A spasm of panic begins in my abdomen and stabs its way

through to the rest of me. My teeth clench shut. I grip my knees tighter and close my eyes. Animal sounds come, not from me but from within this body. Whatever was left of Will is being displaced and released as my occupation completes itself.

'There is nothing to fear,' I tell myself in a hoarse whisper. 'He has put me to matter.'

Saying these words aloud gives me pause, and for a second the panic, the tension in my body, the world itself spinning on its axis, all seem to stop. This obstinate reality sits, unblinking, in my path.

I say it again, trying to believe it this time. 'He has put me to matter.'

I look around me. Little seems to have changed. The colours perhaps are off, washier than before, but that may just be the lightness in my head. Inside, though, I have been transformed from the centre out. The cupped light at the heart of me has been snuffed. All connection to Him has gone dark. Signal lost. There is only this heavy coat of flesh.

'There is nothing to fear,' I repeat.

And I'm right about that, I know I am. It is entropy, pure and simple, an irreversible process that cannot be gainsaid – it requires only acceptance. I am a part of its governance now, slaving to it with the other beasts. I have taken my place alongside the people, the cattle, the creatures that walk and those that roam free by feather and fin. I am in the care of Nature.

I exhale a long, whistling breath.

'I am alive in His world.' These words settle me. My pulse begins to slow.

All His miracles are tethered to me now. I think about the almanac of the seasons, the crops that rise and are cut, the tides that push and pull as the veiled moon slowly bares its face. I think about the violence of birth and the surrender of death. I smell rain rising from hot ground. I hear snow creaking underfoot. I think about the roosting bird that comes only because it knows it should, or the cellar spider that makes his silent dance from life to dust in the bounds of a single day.

'The bee has one sting, the primate has two thumbs, the octopus has three hearts, the dragonfly has four wings ...' I make a list of these things, softly into the carpet, on and on, until my voice becomes so heavy that I am unable to carry it, and there is no longer anything left, no thought or word, that can stop me from sinking into the black, currentless quiet of sleep.

What follows is as intense and crippling as any illness. The sun rises and sets on two days before my fever breaks. I sleep and I dream and I wake and I sleep and I dream and I wake.

The first time I open my eyes, it has been raining. Drops are still clinging to the window frame. They tremble there for a long time before letting themselves go. Such pressure at the surface of things, it makes me sad. Water curled in on itself. The molten earth forced into a sphere.

Another time, I wake to find I am on fire, being shaken in the grip of a delirium. I cannot think straight. Everything in me has been burnt down to a bottom ash of dry protests. I call out to Him, in the old way, crying for Him to take me under his wing.

After that my dreams become a series of sweaty, tangled elisions. More visions than dreams really, acid-sharp in detail and all of them charged with the same regret – images of Jesus that lash and fork like plasma. On the last day, the deepest of them all is dislodged.

It is from the later time, when I had haunted him down to near nothing. I watch it play out, eyes open, as if it is projected on the white wall in front of me. I am there, back on the stony ground of the desert. Christ's legs painfully thin, the bones in his feet sharp against the sandal leather, but despite these diffi-culties I journey for days, battered by the sun and kept from sleep by the frozen night. I fast, I thirst for as long as I can, until finally I collapse. That night, the night of my collapse, I wake with a start, a deep ache of cold in my bones. The sound that woke me is still there, whispering between the rocks, but I see nothing. The air is a swarming gloom. I search for a stone, something, anything I can use as a weapon. But there's nothing. When I look up, it is beside me, silently watching, as big as a man. It is reared up and tensile, almost still, just its head moving very slightly from side to side, the way serpents do when they are ready to strike. I am so afraid that I begin to weep. That's when it too begins to make noises, quietly at first, soft like my weeping, then louder, unnatural sounds.

As I sprawl on my back, it moves on top of me, its appalling weight on my chest, its tongue tasting the air between us.

The fever leaves me scoured down like whitened wood in the shoreline. My lips are salty and dry.

I must have water.

Bent in a slow walk, I take myself to the kitchen tap. I drink and drink, and then I drink some more. The water swishes painfully in my belly. It has, I realise, been days since I have eaten.

I go to the fridge and heave open its door. It's a picture of neglect but there are a few things that are still this side of rotten. There's an open tin of spaghetti hoops in tomato sauce, there's a block of dry and cracked cheddar. I also see some kebab meat in a grease-soaked wrapper, and a carton of grapes shrivelled on the stalk. I sink to the floor, not knowing where to begin, but my body does not wait to find out. It moves independently of all thought and volition, seizing what I need.

I dip two fingers into the spaghetti hoops and shovel them into my cement mixer mouth of lamb and cheese. I add in a tomato I find lurking at the back of the shelf. It explodes between my teeth, juice runs down my chin and drips on to the floor. I bend forward and suck up the little rusty pools, then I take four more huge bites of cheddar. Finally, and only when I absolutely have to, I get up and go over to the tap for more water, cradling my belly on the way, as if it's a bomb that might go off.

I continue like this for some time, stopping occasionally for my gut muscles to cramp and flutter beneath the strain. When I've finally had enough, I wander down the hallway to the bathroom, taking the grapes with me, vacuum popping them into my mouth like a tennis ball machine in reverse.

I draw myself a hot bath and slip down among its crinkling bubbles. I let my thoughts rise away from me like the wisps of steam that curl off my arms as I hold them up in the pale afternoon light. And as I lie drowsing in my tub, it softens, this light, to the glow of evening. It is beautiful to watch, a little sad too, to hear the tap drip-dripping its count into the water at my feet. Time tugging at the edges of me, pulling me along. Every second is now being taken away, grain followed by grain. Moments I shall never have back.

I haul myself out of the bath and stand steaming on the mat, pink as a ham. I let myself dry naturally, the dripping from my body fast at first then slowing to a delicate, hesitant pace, like those raindrops at my window, each one drawing so painfully close to letting go. It is intoxicating, the slowness of it. Nature's speed. One element banished by another, just as I was – the creeping change towards a new state.

As I dress myself in Will's pyjamas the light outside continues to change, smudged by the dusk. On a whim, I decide that I want to go out there. I feel strong enough after the food and the bath, and I want to do it now, before it gets dark. There is something at the moment, about the dark, that I do not like.

I pull on a coat and shoes and go clumping down the stairs. The sound brings Alice Sherwin to her doorway but, on seeing me, she doesn't say whatever it was she was planning to say. She just shakes her head and goes back inside.

The daylight is almost gone. As I come to the edge of the park only the top windows of the high-rises at the far end of the playing field catch the fire of the setting sun. Yet again, I have to stop. It's not weariness this time that makes me keep pausing, as if to catch my breath, nor is it that same exhilaration that I felt during those first few hours after jumping in, that marvel at the firing of my senses. This is the reward of beauty – I don't know how else to describe it. For longer than it should be possible, I have watched, only watched. I have seen the way people struggle with the task of fitting their lives to the perfect, impossible circus of beauty that whirls around them. Some manage it, many – most – do not. But for all my watching, I have acquired nothing more than a kind of clinical wisdom, the ability of a psychiatrist observing a patient, to predict what will and what will not work, who will or will not succeed. What good, though, is this truth when it is not grounded in experience? That is what I have lacked all this time. Real knowledge. Knowledge born from life – not from a brief intervention in your lives or from endless observation, but from joining with you. And here is my reward – this great beauty that lay hidden from me for so long. From knowing in my gut, the way you know it, that all this huffing and puffing will lead us to the same vanishing point, I am able to see the world afresh. I turn with it now. I too am fixed to its workings.

These leaves that lie scattered beneath the trees, the map of their veins is drawn from the same skein that puts the blood-shadowed lines in my own flesh. Their creases, too, are the same. I pick one up and hold it next to the skin of my palm – time folded into all matter, marking it. I am matched to this now – a part of life, no longer apart from it. Each moment flurrying like a snowflake, distinct from the last but impossible to grasp, dissolving on impact. I relax into it. This is right.

Along the path from where I've decided to sit a small band of derelicts and drunks are performing their evening routine. They move as a single entity, orbiting the bottles and cans arrayed on the wall of a nearby flowerbed. The choreography is repetitive and precise, binding them together in a series of small shuffling engagements. Starless planets locked in alignment.

Needless to say, now that I am thrown in with mankind, grounded so to speak, not one of them notices me. I have become just like any other. I am all but invisible.

Some distance beyond them, a game of football is proceeding against the failing light. The players are too distant to be anything more than shapes, line drawings of form and movement. Occasionally their shouts rise up off the flat ground and reach me, mixing in with the isolated bark of a dog or a snatch of music. At one stage, two young men lope past, hoods up, both on their phones. The one nearest to me shakes his head at whatever he is hearing and makes a kind of hiss-spit noise. It's a well-practised gesture, so much more economical than words – the equivalent of which, had he been forced to use them, would be something like *I have nothing but contempt for you and/or what you're saying.* I make a note of this useful device.

It also reminds me (him being on the phone, I mean) that I had agreed to speak to Natalie on Monday afternoon and it must now be … Wednesday. Yes, that sounds right – I glance up at the sky, as if I'm expecting it to be confirmed there. Perhaps it would be if I knew where to look. Mercury's day.

She must be wondering what's happened to me.

'Is it Wednesday today?' I ask one of the homeless guys who happens to have strayed within earshot of my bench. Like he'd know, but I have to work with what's to hand.

He looks me over, one eye squinted mostly shut, the other doing the work of two, writhing around the socket like it's trapped there and wants to be out.

'You bunk out then?' he slurs.

I make what I'm pretty sure is my *What?* face.

'What?' I say, to leave no doubt.

'Hospital trousers.' His good eye is ranging up and down my leg.

His swaying is beginning to make me feel like I too am moving. Like the ground is slowly undulating beneath us.

'Oh – right. I see what you mean. No, I'm just wearing pyjamas,' I inform him, as nonchalantly as it's possible to say that to a stranger, in public. 'I live nearby. So anyway,' I steer us back to the point, 'do you know what day it is?'

He either doesn't understand the question or doesn't know the answer because what he says is, 'Have a little syrup, mate.'

He holds out a plastic bottle containing a few fingers of something roughly consistent with motor oil. In a gesture of invitation or impatience, he gives it a sharp little shake. The liquid slops malevolently.

'It feels like a Wednesday,' I tell him as I take the bottle.

While we've been talking, the sodium street lights along the path have clicked on, turning our clothes, the grass and his mystery syrup into different shades of the same kind of no colour.

I take a swig. It goes down like a bad oyster steeped in something medical.

The bottle is then immediately reclaimed and the eyebrow above his watching eye waggles inquiringly (by the way, I can now see that it's the whole of the left side of his face, not just the eye, that's hanging in a lifeless sag).

'Heh?' he wants to know, meaning *How was it?*

I am not confident I can speak at this precise moment so I opt instead for an enthusiastic nod. The motion makes me feel sick and dizzy.

With this act of kinship now between us, he is moved to sit down on the bench with me. It's more of a controlled subsidence than a conventional sitting down. He all but keels over onto me. The bottle, however, rights itself in his hand, gimballed like a ship's instrument. Muscle memory from years of falling and fighting while holding a drink.

My bones, cold and heavy as steel a moment ago, seem to be warming up. From deep in my stomach a syrup-tainted belch releases itself. I let it go discreetly through my nose with that *umph* sound nostrils make as a gust passes through.

This seems to remind him that he ought to drink some more. With unexpected deftness he raises the bottle in one swift movement so it's standing vertical on his lips and drains the lot in a single open-throated swallow. He then lets his weight redistribute itself, partly on to the wooden bench-back, partly on to me.

I want to get up and leave but my legs say no. The thought then comes swimming through to me that, even so, I really must.

Natalie. I need to speak to Natalie.

My attempt to move brings him sharply back to consciousness.

'Heh!' he says, except it's not the warm, interrogative *heh* of moments ago. This is a more threatening *heh*. 'Doing?'

I understand this to be shorthand for a longer question.

'I need to go,' I tell him.

'Why you even here?' he's properly awake now, eyeballing me.

'Good question. God question,' I add, releasing, again through the medium of my nose, a little laugh. This time it's more of a quacking, trumpeting sound. It makes us both start a little.

I do want to go, genuinely I do – in fact, I must, as discussed (ha! that rhymes) – but I also want to sit for a few more seconds on my soft syrupy seat, maybe say some more things with my loose lazy lips.

We both lapse into a further silence for what could be two or twenty minutes.

'I'm here because it's what I've always wanted,' I tell him when I'm ready. I like saying the words. 'Always,' I repeat. Particularly that one.

His head lolls on its limp-stemmed neck. 'Eh,' he says, gently this time, leaving off the first, hardening *h*.

'Why now?' I shrug. 'Can't rightly say. It's not like this thing of Will's,' I wave expansively to include the tramps, the footballers, all the houses, but meaning of course the Church, far from here, in their gold and incensed bunkers, 'is *that* bad.' I look at him. 'It's pretty small potatoes. Po-tay-toes,' I say. We both have a quick giggle. It's a funny word. '... compared to what I've seen. All manner of unholy horrors,' I suddenly turn a bit serious here, so does he. 'All manner,' I reiterate gravely, 'carried out in *my* name. And I just sat on my hands.' I show him what I mean but the hard wood hurts my knuckles so I take them back out. 'For centuries ...' his head nods at my words '... for centuries, I did nothing. But!'

This *but* snaps us both to attention. We look at the finger I have held up to accompany it.

'But,' I resume, 'it was happening all the time. I just didn't know it. I kept trying to *think* my way out of it – you know?' It's a rhetorical question. I've stopped looking at him now. I'm looking at myself, back then, whatever that was like. I'm already forgetting how the other way felt. This earth pull is so strong, it pushes everything else out. 'Except that never works, trying to think through a problem. All you do is mangle it up, bend it so far out of shape with your thinking that you don't even know how it looked to start with ...'

I trail off then immediately find I need to start up again. It's a bit like being sick. So much so, in fact, that I find myself checking the ground at my feet to see that I haven't been. I haven't.

'The *process* is what counts. Catysis, catalystis, cataly, sis.' I can't say it. 'Change moves through you,' I say instead, and prefer it, because it's a better description of the way it seems, like you're the ecosystem in which changes form and evolve. 'It crept up on me, like stuff does.' I do look at him now. Both eyes are shut, a thread of saliva has run from his open mouth and now swings softly from his chin. I tell him anyway, 'Every person on earth has experienced it – and it was no different for me: these things grind away below decks, down in the engine room, just a growling you can't recognise as thought, but then one day it gets spat up into your conch, your conchuss, your conscience-ness …' My tongue, slow-witted mollusc, apparently unable to perform that trick either '… your mind. Fully formed. Obvious.'

I get up and start staggering off. This time he doesn't notice me leaving, he just flows into the space where I'd been sitting.

'The truth,' I continue to burble nonetheless, 'always comes at the most trivial moments. Like Paul,' I smile to myself at the memory of that lunatic, 'riding along on his horse, clippety-clop, drowsing in the dust, swaying in the saddle, probably daydreaming about throwing stones at poor old Stephen … and then boom!' I shout that. And why not? Because that's how it is – *boom!* 'Everything changes. The gears suddenly bite, and off he goes. Off he *went*,' I correct myself. 'New life, new name, new truth. Just like me.'

At the top of Will's road, an old man is opening the door to his house. I stop to watch him. He has to put down his two shopping bags so he can get his key in the lock. I don't need to see his hands to know that they are thin-skinned and mottled. His trousers billow about his legs, which can scarcely be wider than the bones that support them. He has the small head and big ears of a nocturnal creature on the listen for predators.

I want to speak to him, share some words of fellowship, but there is nothing to say. The affinity between us, he the forward traveller down a road I myself have just set foot on, is too complex for language. Besides, it is only I who am new to this. To him, it is all he's known. Killing time. Days, glowing bronze or streaked with rain, happy, sad, unnoticed or dull, that conspire to kill you with their passing, one by one, until finally the last of them comes, death-laden, in a dawn like any other.

6

What I should be doing is sleeping, recovering, getting warm again, but I'm not, I'm speaking to Natalie. Will's phone is tight against my ear, radiating its heat, thawing my frozen emotions. I have been explaining to her that I fell ill on the day we last spoke.

Sorry – did I just say *thawing my frozen emotions*? If so, apologies for that. A touch of tramp syrup and the hyperbole soon kicks in. So anyway, I've been telling her, with an increasingly tinny edge to my voice, that I have not been at all well. But, investigative journalist that she is, she knows a cover story when she hears one, so I'm now midway through a fumble on her latest question, which wasn't even really a question, it was one of those statements that hopes for contradiction – *You don't sound like you're okay*, is what she said.

For some reason, I'm going completely off beam. For some reason? Listen to that. I really must learn to give myself a break – it's always been my problem. Anyone else would be telling themselves it's a miracle to still be functioning at all after everything that's happened. Not a *miracle* miracle, obviously, but you know what I mean.

'Look, just so you understand,' I'm telling her, 'I'm not The One. I can't emphasise that enough. There *is* no One, there never *will* be a One – it's just something people would like to believe. It's back to that whole narrative thing again,' I explain, as if we've discussed this many times before, 'mankind's fatal weakness for a tidy story, like there's always going to be that One, the hero to usher in the right ending. But the truth is I don't know how this is going to end. No one does.'

'Will, are you sure you're okay? You're not making much sense.' Worrying that might be a little harsh to one as fragile as myself, she immediately adds, 'Please don't think I'm looking to you for all the answers on this. What you've given us already is –'

'But I *can* get the answers – it's not that. Sorry, sorry to interrupt, but I just want to be clear about what I'm saying here. I *can* get you the answers, that's really not a problem – I'm simply trying to point out that …'

What? What am I trying to point out? That I'm not the second coming of Christ? I think she probably assumes that. Seriously. What am I thinking? I'm not, that's the point.

'Never mind,' I tell her.

'Look, I really don't want you to think anyone's putting pressure on you, Will. I don't want you to …' she runs into a dead end, unable to summon a tactful phrase for the sort of freaking out she thinks I might do. 'What I mean is, if you can get more information easily and,' she leaves an emphatic pause here, 'legally, then yes, great, of course I'd love to see it. But if you can't, then please don't feel like it's expected of you.'

Like last time I jumped in, you mean? Shooting my mouth off to try to meet that constant expectation, that tireless need for reassurance, to be told that there's something more than all this, that there are many rooms in my father's house and other assorted nonsense. Some of that was forgivable – at the end, especially. It was just the pain talking. (Try it some time: getting flogged to within an inch of your life then left dangling in the wind, birds pecking at your head while you get freeze-frame jointed by your own miserable weight – it *hurts*, it makes you say things. It was just unfortunate for me, for us all, that people were properly listening.) The other stuff, though – my *I'll be back* shtick in particular – that's on me. That was a huge error of judgement. But the trouble is, once you start down that path, reassuring people, telling them little stories to make them feel better, you can't stop. It's like trying to fill a bath with the plug out. What you end up with is a lot of disappointment and thwarted expectations. It's probably hard to imagine now just how bitterly let down they all felt by my failure to come back to earth and gather up all the good ones. Time has passed, and most people seem to have forgotten about all that now, and for those who haven't there are still the fanatics and the zealots, the televangelists making a tidy little business out of the waiting game. But you should have seen them back in the day, the ones immediately after Jesus, waiting and watching for my magical *parousia*. Talk about a slow-hand-clapping audience.

Anyway.

'I've just got a thing about this,' is my colossally inadequate summary of all that. I try to weave in a phrase that I've heard bandied in Will's work place, 'I've got a thing about managing expectations. Expectation management,' I summarise, trying to make it sound more like a formal Thing.

Nothing from her. She's at a bit of a loss now.

'Okay, look – let me tell you what we need to make this case.' What am I, a policeman now? I need to ground things a bit. 'Let me run through the information that will more than satisfy your lawyer. Information that I can get for you.'

'Okay, sure.' She sounds tired.

I take the phone away from my face and look at the clock. It's 20:09. Of course it is. A two and a nine, a couple of little zeroes wedged between. What else but a hard eleven to root me in the loneliness of this moment? I know I said I wouldn't get sucked into the numbers, and I'm not about to start, I'm just saying it couldn't be clearer: eleven, or *ainlif*, as I still think of it. *Ain*, *lif* – one, left. Just me.

I put the phone back to my ear. 'Quickly then.'

I have produced a pen from somewhere, in a drawer I didn't even know I'd been looking in. I've moved to the kitchen, it would seem. I start sketching on the wall, making a diagram of my plan.

'Okay, so you have the Vatican Bank.'

For this I draw the hated shape, except that here, like this, a cross actually looks right. Dark axes of power.

'They want to invest in InviraCorp ...' I draw a long line almost to the skirting board, far enough down for me to be crouching. There I mark a black circle. 'But they can't just do it directly or else everyone would know and ...'

'They'd be writing my story for me,' she chimes in.

That's good, her engaged voice is back. She's finishing my sentences again, like the other day down by the canal.

'Exactly,' I tell her. 'So they have to use some offshore location – in this case Jersey,' I draw a big fat pound sign midway down the line, 'where they set up a little cluster of trusts,' I stab at the pound sign with the pen point, making the cluster, 'administered by faceless trustees, for the benefit of undeclared owners.'

'And you think you can get the details of these trusts?'

'I know I can.' My pen hovers over the dot cluster, I know no such thing. I believe it, though, to the point of knowing. Quite the model man I'm becoming. 'All they are is conduits, these places. No money is kept there, it just flows through, but what they do hold is records. Details of where that money is headed and what other money it will send back.'

'What do you mean *send back*?'

'Well ...' my pen quickly sketches another line, shooting off at a tangent '... the money doesn't just go straight from the Jersey trust to InviraCorp, it goes via another one of these offshore places – let's say Cayman for argument's sake.'

I intend to draw a palm tree but it comes out looking like an anchor – that'll do just as well.

'From there, it goes to InviraCorp. But, and this is the important part, the profits also come back. That's what the trustees are there for, to ensure that the right people are benefiting from the different income streams. So when the money they ushered out of the holy coffers has doubled, tripled, septupled itself, they then divert it right back in.'

I delve a little more into the granular detail, talking her through the twists and turns of these structures, all the while etching in my words until my diagram has become labyrinthine, Escheresque in its conundrums. It now covers the whole of the wall space between the door and the fridge.

I realise it has been several minutes since she has spoken. 'Are you still there?' I ask.

'Yes, of course. I'm just trying to keep up.'

'Don't worry if it's all a bit much to take in. We can go over it again at some point – this is just to give you a sense of the situation. It's really not an uncommon set-up. In fact, pretty much every business runs its money through these places – it's all perfectly legal. It's a standard way that companies have come up with to avoid paying their dues. That's just how people are – how they've always been.' Darwin had that cold, I want to add, but I don't because I don't want to come off sounding too certain, like some kind of evolutionary biologist, secular zealot type, which obviously I'm not. I just happen to know what I'm talking about. 'But this isn't about tax avoidance. This is about something much, much worse than that. This is about a cabal keeping their secret, about the vast market they have created. First they sentence the God-fearing masses to death with propaganda about contraception, then they portion up life itself, in the form of hopelessly inadequate delay drugs, and they sell it back to the miserable wretches as they die in their ditches.'

I pause, not for effect but to recover my composure. It's made me pretty angry saying all this. With myself, as much as with them.

She breathes a rush of static into my ear, the phone like an exotic shell that's trapped the sound of a warm and perfect sea.

'You should hear what they have to say about it.'

There's the sound of her fingers tapping a keyboard.

'Are you still at work?' I ask.

'No but I can access it here, the comment they sent last time. I only used part of it in the piece I wrote but there was a phrase in there that …' The sentence is left hanging while she scans through her email folders.

'Here it is.' She reads, '*InviraCorp is part of the solution in the global fight against HIV, not a part of the problem* … Okay, that bit I used but this: *InviraCorp is a politically and religiously neutral organisation.* I didn't bother with it. It wasn't relevant, or at least, it didn't seem relevant at the time. Now, though, it makes perfect sense why they would want to drop in a phrase like that.'

It has Alex's fingerprints all over it.

'Cheap spin,' I tell her, 'will not be enough to get them out of this mess. Not once you have the evidence to dish the full dirt. Besides, InviraCorp is not the real target here. They're the small fry. We're hunting for the big prize.'

I have in my mind a spear held aloft in the leaf-filtered light, silent footfalls taking us deeper into the wood. The beast sulking at the mouth of its cave, surrounded by bones and scattered trophies of shields and helmets.

She, meanwhile, is still busy on her computer. I can hear her typing again, the sound a modern hunter makes.

She's forwarding to me a few bits that I might find useful, she tells me. She then starts again to address her nagging feeling that I may be biting off more than I can chew – if only she knew (am I doing it subconsciously, I wonder, this rhyming thing?). She's worried about me, just like my little Mary Magpie always was (with good reason it turned out, but this is not the same thing at all). I tell her, for the last time, that I'm absolutely fine. That I'll be in touch in a day or two. Then we hang up.

I decide that what I need to do now is go and look at myself in the mirror. The physicality of this body has become much more centre stage with me since I got dropped by the Big Man. I kept noticing, for example, during that conversation with Natalie how different parts of it would light up and react to things she was saying, to changes of temperature in the room even – it's non-stop. But whereas before all of that was just stuff I noticed, as you might come to grow familiar with a car you are driving, say (maybe a little more than that, but you see the point I'm making – there's a separateness), now it's actually a part of my intellectual landscape. My thoughts, my feelings, all of it, have become attuned not only to this body but also to the atmosphere around it.

Strange though, because the face that confronts me in the mirror shows no sign of the self-possession and calm that I feel inside. Its appearance is agitated and gaunt. Older too, I fancy, from when I last looked, just after my bath. Vital minutes, a matter of hours even, have been confiscated from me since then.

'Need to shave this stubble off,' I mutter as I start looking round for the things to do that with.

It's not something I've ever tried before – as you may recall, JC had a big glossy beard, not to mention lovely thick hair and dreamy brown eyes (you can see how he got on the shortlist for possible frontmen) – and, I have to admit, it's not quite as easy as it looks. But bit by bit I get the hang of it and pretty soon I'm enjoying the rasp of the razor (particularly during the parts near to the bottom of each ear, when the rasp becomes richer, more of a rolling something heavy across gravel sound). It's hugely rewarding to see the bristle-flecked globs dropping into the sink and being washed away by the running tap.

The mirror itself forms the front of a cabinet and when I'm finished shaving I open it to reveal an inner pharmacopeia. I have a closer look at a packet of pills I find stuffed towards the back of the top shelf, dated October 2010, exactly two years ago – *Olanzapine, atypical, prescription only, one tablet three times daily*. This must be what that HR woman had been referring to in our meeting this morning. No, hang on, was it this morning? Can't have been. Whenever it was. She had alluded to some previous episode – I'm sure that's what she had called it because I remember thinking at the time how amusing the implication was, that anything out of the ordinary must surely be part of some series of events. This constant suspicion that there are other, less reliable, more frightening forces at play in the world whose episodes must be suppressed at all times, whatever the cost, lest they develop into a series.

There can and will be only one reality. Words to live by in this quick-killing time.

I pull out from the olanzapine box a leaflet warning of possible side effects: tremors, fever, akathisia, confusion, uncontrollable twitching, uncontrollable eye movement, sores, itching, swelling, numbness, loss of vision, loss of speech, loss of balance – it goes on. Much more interesting, though, is the way in which these ailments are announced, between brackets, in a thick slab of text separated from the rest. It is only as I run my eyes down this list that I suddenly understand something about my own situation, so strikingly similar in structure to what has been neatly contained between these curls of ink. Finitude, in a word. In order to understand this mess of mine, I had to bracket it in mortality – inception on one side, death on the other. Just as mathematicians set numbers, I have delimited my own troubled bio into something a little more time-constrained. It makes perfect sense. Chunking is, I believe, what the computer geeks who are building your future like to call it. (On a side note, it is also occurring to me that I could even use this method to explain, at some later stage, the wider mysteries of the shape and substance of His universe, as in the formulation { } or the empty set. By definition, of course, a set cannot be empty, it cannot contain nothing, so this formulation can therefore be used to express the substantiation of nothingness, which is the key to understanding and, ultimately, embracing the natural genius of His design.)

I'm getting a little hot again.

My armpits and neck and hairline are damp with sweat and my vision has become what I can only describe as melted at the edges. It's not an aggressive heat like before, with the fever, but I do still feel like I need to simmer down a little. Maybe I got too cold outside or maybe it's a lingering after-effect of the syrup. Either way, my mind is over-processing, which in turn is running the body too fast and too hot. I need to watch out for that. It's no different to a petrol engine or a computer in its casing. Everything needs fanning.

I shove the box back in the cabinet and take out something that should help cool me down: a blister pack of yellow and turquoise capsules, fifteen mils of slow-release Valium. Every morning I watched Will rise raw and nervy from the sleepless hollow of his mattress and pop one of these into his mouth. It always seemed to help him calm down; worth a try now, then. Without it there'd be little chance of sleep, and sleep is what I need right now if I'm to head out of here tomorrow and fulfil my promise to Natalie.

I crack one of the pills into my hand and wash it down with a slurp from the tap. I wait a few minutes, then I decide to take a second one. No point going at it half speed.

Back on my mattress I notice on Will's phone that there are new emails, must be from Natalie, she said she was sending some, and several missed calls, voice messages too, from the last few days. I dial in to pick up the messages. Two are from HR

Karen, executing her corporate responsibility of pretending to care if I'm okay. The others are from Natalie, pre-dating our conversation just now, and essentially irrelevant, but I listen to them anyway. I lie down with the phone between my head and the pillow. I am supremely comfortable.

They all say things like, *Will, hi, it's Natalie Shapiro. Give me a call when you get a chance.* The two later ones also include phrases like *hope you're okay* and *surprised not to have heard from you.*

Each time, her voice flitters through me. That Maryam thing.

I start thinking about her (Mary). Lazy thoughts, drifting through like music from a distant room. My dusky little temptress. Not, by the way, that I ever touched her, not like that, but I drew great strength from her physical presence. Even when I was making a spectacular mess of everything, she was there for me. It was love in its purest form – but just like everything else, it has been sullied by my celebrity. I find it hilarious that people assume the tabloid mentality is something new. When I think of the generations of prurient Christians who've pored over every last scrap of information, each tiny detail they might be able to construe as evidence of the brief and frankly inglorious life of Jesus. They're no different from the gossip mongers who drive your princesses to their deaths or hound your politicians to ruin and despair. All celebrity is toxic, and my little Magpie became tainted by association. And whenever I'd start to think that maybe finally it was all dying down and her name might actually be left to rest in peace, they (and no, I'm not being paranoid – it *was* them) would throw some new morsel into your path. The spite never dies. They would roll back a stone, say, like they did in Nag Hammadi, and expose some faded tractates. Who was it with that Egyptian stuff again? … I lose track. Philip? Or was he in with the Dead Sea codices? Whatever, it's irrelevant where they happened to 'turn up', the fact is that the maunderings of Philip … It was him, by the way – of course it was – prancing

Hellenophile, always sounding off just out of earshot somewhere. Anyway, where was I? Yes, Philip and his codices, too boring for the fire that destroyed the others (there was some cracking stuff in that earthenware pot they found out there, incidentally), were idly tossed into your path so we could have a fresh bout of speculation about Mary and me, based on his nincompoopish observations (with a few key phrases mysteriously nibbled out, naturally). What was it now? *The Saviour used to kiss her often on her* – then a strategic blank, neatly excised – by ants, I think was the consensus of the archaeologists who unearthed it. *On her what?* People wanted to know. *Kissed her where, Philip? Do tell.* And so on it goes, with the ant-eaten blanks eagerly filled in by a gormless fraternity (because it *is* only men who care about this stuff) of Madonna/whore obsessives.

Ants – I ask you. My poor sweet Maryam, she deserved better. She was no angel, I'm sure (join the club) but whether she was an actual working prostitute before I met her, who can say? Certainly not that old masochist Philip. She never spoke a word to me about any of that, not about her life in Magdala, not about what she did when she wasn't with me, and I never thought to ask. Why? Because, to be perfectly honest, it couldn't have mattered less to me. And nor should it to anyone else. Shame on those who care. What *does* matter is that we found each other and we shared something, something transcendent. Everyone else can just go ahead and think what they like.

I extract the phone from where it's wedged in my pillow. The moment I lift it up, it goes dark in my hand, a candle that's just blown out.

'*Mē mou haptou*,' my mouth says, addled and sideways.

My thoughts are woozy, scattered on a warm wind. A zephyr. I say it, *zephyr*, blowing the sound warm and soft as the thing itself, through my teeth and into the pillowcase. I hum a tune I heard once – *zefiro, zefiro, torna, zefiro*.

One half-open eye shows me Will's electronic appliances winking their little lights of standby from the shadows.

I am the commander of a vast army, gazing out at a blackened horizon, where signal fires send messages of victory and allegiance.

I am change.

I am love.

So eager was I to be awake that not even the ballast of those pills could hold me under for long. I watched the sunrise from a cold, hard perch on the kitchen counter, my legs drawn up against me, inspecting every detail of the street beneath my window. The transfusion of colour into the monochrome dusk, announcing by degrees the presence of a crimson Coke can in the gutter, the sharp blue lettering on the side of a parked van. Even the smudged brickwork and roof slates of the houses revealed veins and glints of new shades. Brought to life from darkness. I wept a little – joyful tears – at the sight of this new day being born around me, for me, with me. *Fiat lux.*

Now, having stepped out of a long, hot shower, that joy has hardened into something more substantial. An earth-riveted certainty of belonging surges through me now as I roam through these rooms, towel around my waist, still beaded with water. My chest is full, barrelled, armoured with light. My arms are knotted twists of sinew. My mind is a limpid pool.

I stop and howl at the top of my lungs, like a wolf does, chin up, mandible jutting. *How-how-hoooo!*

It is so intoxicating to be in this second then tilted into the next and the next. I keep on moving and howling and growling and beating my chest, until I decide to stop on the kitchen lino and sprint on the spot. The room shakes with my efforts and the house keys and water glass drift on these vibrations towards the edge of the table.

That's when I realise that I need music. This energy must be structured, it must be guided. All I have to do is dock Will's iPhone into the little speaker cradle and … voilà!

What comes blasting out is simply delicious. I have no idea what it is called but its languorous rhythm soon builds into something more assuredly percussive, pulling me away from the snake-hipped gliding of my first dance into an atavistic trance. It is while I am stomping in this ape-like funk that I hear the sound of Alice Sherwin hammering on my door. Almost immediately, as if responding to this intrusion, the music reverts to its early tempo, sleek and sinewy, and I find my body mirroring the change, unjointed, eely in its contortions as I slither and slide towards the door.

The cold draught that comes with the opening of the door makes me realise that I must have lost my towel somewhere in the flow of my dancing. Unabashed, and unable to remain still, I continue gyrating. The Sherwin woman seems unable to find her words. The most she has yet managed is the syllable *I*. Shimmying a half step towards her, one hand at waist level, the other reaching for her shoulder, I invite her to join me in my celebration of music, of life itself.

She draws back but does not, this time, turn away. She looks determinedly at my face, but in a way that avoids any contact with my eyes. Her attention is focussed on a spot in the centre of my forehead.

'You are ruining my life,' she says so bleakly that it stops me in my tracks. It is a sentence shorn to the bone.

The music continues to pound but I find myself suddenly motionless in the doorway. Her face is arid, drained of all expression.

The door remains open as I hurry back inside and stop the music. I pick up my towel from the floor and re-skirt myself. She is still there, a dry cactus of hatred.

'I am so sorry,' I tell her as I approach, respectfully this time, cautious of the despair I/Will have been causing.

I want very much to hug her. There is something profoundly vulnerable about her primly belted dressing gown. Perhaps my expression or my stance betrays these thoughts because she takes a definite and exaggerated step back from me. A parlour game in reverse, with me, the shamed and chastened Mr Wolf, left to drop my head and stare at the splay of my toes on the floorboards.

She says, 'I am keeping a diary of your behaviour.'

I have no reply. It is clear that she is beyond my reach.

'For the police,' she states tonelessly, for the record, before departing the scene.

I find my tongue again only after she has gone and I have heard the vague sound of her own front door being quietly closed.

'I'll make it up to you,' I promise.

After that, as I am looking through the rack of Will's suits, deciding which fabric might complement which shirt, taking my time with it (the textures so delicate on the fingers, the cut of the cloth so sharp, the stitching so close and precise), I am still saying this under my breath. *Make it up to you.*

In between mouthfuls of breakfast (the remaining spaghetti hoops, chocolate biscuits, a quarter wedge of lemon) I convert it into something more like a little song. *Making it, making it, making it up.*

It is only when I realise I have wasted a full hour on all of this that I decide to continue in a more organised silence. *Tick, tick, tick* says the watch on my wrist as I sift through the papers next to Will's printer. I saw something here on that first day, I'm certain of it, some mention of Jersey. *Tick, tick* as I continue to look.

'Silence,' I tell it. But it doesn't stop.

Tick, tick.

I unstrap it from my wrist and take a closer look at the dial. I shake my head at the offending hand mindlessly ticking its way around.

'Time is not there to be minuted,' I say.

And yet still it persists, tick after entitled tick, bossing the day into pedantic little units, warehousing the accumulated hours in a swivel-roll of calendar numbers.

'No – I don't think so.' I tell it, with a bitterness that surprises me.

I march through to the kitchen. I am not here to count off the days. Time is a gift, a thread that is quietly drawn from us. I lay the watch out on the table.

'We each contain our invisible spool,' I remind it. Delicately, I smooth flat the platinum links of its strap. 'None of us knows that the end has slipped free until the very moment we are undone.'

I turn it a quarter-rotation clockwise so that it is precisely in line with the grain of the wooden table top, then I lean down and remove my shoe.

'It is a miracle, a living mystery.' I raise the shoe high above my head. 'It should not be debased into units. People's lives are more than just the sum of hours and weeks.'

I smash its face in with three quick, powerful blows.

I watch its second hand, curled upwards by the impact, quiver in place, paralysed above a silver seven. I stare at it for I do not know how long. Until I am ready to stop.

7

I am on the train to Gatwick, looking out of the carriage window. I have been doing little else since we set off from the station, trying to absorb every little detail as it speeds by, so much so that my eyes are now beginning to ache. I decide to rest them and turn my attention instead to this piece of card that I have retrieved from my jacket pocket and am now holding in my loosely laced fingers.

I turns out that I was right, I *had* seen something with a mention of Jersey in Will's flat, it just hadn't been anything useful, and nor had it been among the papers next to his printer – it was here, on this card. That stuff he had printed out was just junk. I can say that with such authority because I spent a good hour looking through it all (there were two precarious stacks about a foot high). It was nothing but reams of pointless conjecture and guess work spewed out from various websites, about the lives of Jesus' so-called apostles (always makes me laugh, that, with its suggestion they were somehow there to help me, which they most certainly were not; they were there to serve their own, highly individual needs) and, a little creepily, about Mary too (that's to say, *my* Mary, not JC's poor disturbed mother who trailed round telling everyone that God himself had planted an infant in her womb). It was quite striking actually, seeing it all pulled together like that, my supporting cast, I mean – it made it a lot easier to see how I wound up dangling on that cross. They weren't exactly the most baggage-free crowd, let's say, with their broken lives and their histories of violence and mental illness.

But as I said, I was barking up the wrong tree sifting all that junk. In the end, I found the word Jersey in a small print address right at the bottom of this stiffly formal invitation, which had been taped to the door of the fridge. *Our new address: La Fin de Chasse, Rue de Châtaigne, Grouville, Jersey, JE2 3GF*, it says. I had to do a sweep of the whole flat before I spotted it, using the soft eyes (not really looking, if you know what I mean, just letting the brain do its CPU thing), and there it was, stuck to the fridge, virtually engulfed by all the other scraps that Will had collected together and taped up there. An invitation to a reception at St John's College, Cambridge, to commemorate the retirement of one Augustus Lemprière. So hardly worth searching for, then, let alone stuffing into the pocket of Will's jacket, which is what I did nonetheless. But now that I'm reading it, I'm naturally a little curious, as to why, for example, Will still had this invitation taped to the door of his fridge when I see here that the party was in June last year. Perhaps he meant to go and felt guilty for not getting around to it, kept the card there to remind him to write or send a gift. I guess I'll never know. What I can find out, though, thanks to the magical tablet of this iPhone is something about Augustus Lemprière.

He has, it turns out, earned himself a lengthy Wikipedia entry. He was a fellow of St John's College before retiring last year to the Channel Island of Jersey, the place of his birth. There are other scant biographical details – he has a wife, children, a brother, Ernest, also listed by Wikipedia, who acquired the rank of Lieutenant General in the British Army – but the bulk of what is written about him focuses on what is described variously as his influential, pioneering and seminal research in biomathematics and, in particular, molecular set theory. The Lemprière model of wide-sense chemical kinetics is described as the foundation on which much of the current mapping of individual molecular events is based. A man, in other words, who shares my own enthusiasm for numbers in nature.

Given that the good professor's field of work involves concepts I already understand perfectly, there appears to be little need for any further online trawling. I suppose I could try to discover what Will's connection to him might have been (I'm assuming he was either a student of his or perhaps a family friend) but it doesn't really seem to matter much. If there was ever a need to know anything about Will, that need has now gone. It went when Will went. This phase of his existence is mine to live now. And besides, I'm finding there's just too much else vying for my attention inside the carriage. I shove the invitation down the side of my seat, to be forgotten.

Most of my fellow travellers are suited up like me (I'm wearing Will's black two-piece, by the way, with a black silk tie, crisp white shirt and a grey overcoat). But as well as us business types, there are a good number of tourists in the mix too. The large, noisy family of Thais sitting across the aisle from me I find particularly interesting. And apparently the feeling is mutual, at least as far as the head patriarch is concerned. He has been unabashedly staring at me from within his creased and shrunken face for some time now.

Finally he decides to ask me a question, in Thai. Wily old bugger can see that I'm taking it all in (unsurprisingly, I'm quite the linguist), he just needs to check. What he asks me is whether I think his granddaughter is old enough to be married. This is what they have been discussing, in between making openly rude and offensive remarks about a couple of the other passengers. One in particular, a Brit with pursed lips and ruddy cheeks, who has been the subject of much speculation – is he headed for Bangkok, same as them? Another filthy pig for the whores, no doubt. When will the King sort it all out? That sort of thing.

But all of them are now looking at me in expectant silence, wondering if it could really be possible that a white-skinned office drone such as myself can have understood anything of their conversation. I fire back with a short reply, being careful to mirror their speech – they are southerners so they speak a language that I think of as Dambro, as opposed to formal Thai. I've heard it a great deal in Bangkok, where I've often had cause to look over the years, as you can imagine. Although, interestingly, it's not always straightforward putting the knowledge into practice – a few times, for example, I tried to make Jesus speak in Greek but his palate was resistant to it and it just ended up making him sound ridiculous. But Will is adapting well to the oriental sounds – he has the right shaped jaw for it.

I say, 'You should be more careful what you say in public. You never know who might be listening.'

One of their party, a girl of about Will's age – the granddaughter in question – actually yips with surprise when she hears me speak her language. The old guy loves it, though. He falls about laughing, saying *I knew it! I knew it!* At this point, most people in the carriage have a quick look to see what's going on, including the possible sex tourist, whose eyes I meet for a fraction of a second. It's enough to know that they had been right about him. I tell them as much, referring to him with the country phrase they had used – literally, 'farm pig', which I rather like, mostly because of its suggestion that there is another, fancier kind of pig. Anyway, we all have a good laugh about it.

As I'm laughing, Will's phone starts to ring in my jacket pocket, except that I don't realise right away that it's his phone (he has it set to vibrate, rather than actual ringing) and so there are an alarming couple of seconds when I think I might be having some kind of convulsion. It's an odd sensation, that buzzing, if you're not used to it (and odder still if you're still acclimatising to the ticks and twinges of a body – no two are the same – there are always little surprises tucked away).

It's Will's mum. She calls quite often, if the last few weeks are anything to go by, but the conversations never seem to last long. So I answer it.

I don't hear the first few words of what she says because the driver chooses this moment to make his announcement that we are approaching Gatwick Airport. I get up from my seat and start walking up the carriage (much to the disappointment of the Thais, who've still not had the explanation they deserve).

'Where are you?' is what she's now saying.

'I'm on a train.'

'Did he say Gatwick? Are you going to the airport? Billy, are you sure that's such a good idea?'

Bit of an odd question. And Billy? Really?

'It's a pretty good idea if you're going to get a plane, Mum.' I'd wanted that to sound light-hearted, not peevish and wearily sarcastic, which is how it came across.

'Dr Bund' – Bun? Bunt? Bundt? It's hard to catch the sound of it exactly – 'told your father and me that it wasn't a good idea for you to travel on your own at the moment.'

She sounds really worried, like I should be saying something to calm her down. But I'm more interested in finding out about this doctor.

'Dr Bund said that?'

'Dr Bundt,' she corrects me. Who knows what she's saying? 'When we all saw him together, when you were at home last time. Darling, you remember.' She says it like *please say you remember*. She then lowers her voice, 'After the incident,' she intones that word like it's some embarrassingly exotic practice she'd rather not have to refer to, 'at Rebecca's house. When you got yourself in a bit of a pickle,' she all but whispers.

A pickle? I thought episode was good, but pickle ...

'And anyway, where are you going in the middle of the week? Why aren't you at work? I thought you said you were coming to help your father decorate the church for harvest festival this weekend.'

Wait. What?

'What?'

'You said you would help Dad with the church decorations.'

Will's dad is a priest?

Ah. I think I might have said that out loud. In fact, I know I did because she has now started to cry, very quietly, like people do at funerals.

'I was *joking*, Mum.' But that sounds feeble, even to me.

'Oh Billy.'

I really wish she'd stop calling me that.

'Listen, I'm only going away for the day. Just over to Jersey,' I divulge stupidly, 'for work,' I add, even more stupidly.

But then, actually, is it really that stupid? I can't imagine Will's colleagues are going to be tracking down his mum and pumping her for info. Also, it seems to settle her down a bit. She stops crying anyway.

'You're there with people from work?' she asks hopefully.

'Yes,' I lie. It seems the kindest thing to do.

The train is slowing down and there's a bit of a crowd behind me. I step through into the little hallway.

'Oh,' she sniffs loudly. 'Oh I see. I'm sorry, Billy. I don't mean to … You get back to your work trip then, and we'll see you on the weekend. Will you come down on Saturday morning? Just text me the time, Dad can come and pick you up at the station.'

Who knows where I'll be by Saturday morning?

'Will do. I'll see you then.'

But she's not quite finished.

'Billy? You are remembering to take your tablets, aren't you? Only Dr Bundt –'

'Of course I am.' Number three in my liar's triptych.

'Oh good. I hope you don't mind me asking. I just worry about you ...'

'You don't need to worry.'

'I'm your mother, worrying's part of my job.' She's much chirpier now. 'See you on Saturday then. Love you.'

'Love you too.'

Poor woman. And poor Will. It's the worst part of suffering, to see how your pain spreads to the people who love you.

I slip the phone back in my pocket, which is a feat in itself. There's barely room to move in here now. Everyone has squashed into this tiny space, with their smells and breath and chatter. At the other end of the carriage I can hear the Thais faffing about with their luggage – they're a squabbly bunch, more like chickens than people.

As I step out on to the platform at Gatwick I reflexively check my surroundings for signs of His disapproval, but am not surprised to find that there are none. Throughout the day I have been watchful, before that even, after my conversation with Natalie yesterday, during my first outing in the park, and yet not one sign have I seen. It seems odd, not to be opposed, to have been stripped of my well-worn role of Disgraced Son. Even His minions appear to have forgotten me – no more sport for them in the mocking crucifix, no more scolding cameos. The abandonment is total. And yet, Paranoia still whispers to me now and then, as it is at this very moment, that surely there must be a reason for this, that He knows something I cannot yet see. They all see it, a fatal crack in my future, a flaw that will see me subside into failure.

No. I shake my head free of this thinking. I must stick to the evidence of my eyes. It is simply that I am forgotten. The moment I was born into this world, I died in His eyes. He, they, none of them, have any further interest in me. For them, mortality is an early form of death, no longer worth watching in any detail, just part of a seething, faceless whole. And that is precisely how I need to stay: invisible. From here on in, I must keep to the cover of humanity, and accomplish my work in the shadows.

All around me, I see evidence of His absence. The billboard ads that litter the airport concourse – Lust, Greed, Pride, Gluttony: I've crossed off four of the Big Seven after just three minutes of walking. This is the people's terrain, where His reach is incomplete, confined only to those spired strongholds I mean to attack, and the forces they mobilise. I can hide here from His judgement.

And so when the airline girl asks me at the check-in if I have any baggage, I simply tell her no.

'I have nothing,' I say. 'Just me.'

8

As we descend upon Jersey and the rattling tube of our small aircraft banks to line itself up with the runway, I am given a tilting vista of the island. The coastline is perfect, its hems of greenery and unspoiled sand touch a glittering sea. Large houses sit like jewels on their abundant pillows of land. Only money, and lots of it, can keep a place looking so good at this fatigued stage of the human race.

In the arrivals terminal, corporate drivers wait with their cardboard signs, messenger bees buzzing back and forth from the moneypots. With me on the plane were the men for whom these signs are intended; also alongside us were other rich men's wives laden with London shopping, returning home to rest before drawing more from the well. One such woman has, like me, not had to dally in the baggage hall and has swept through into arrivals more or less alongside me (while studiously deleting the fact of my presence from her consciousness, if you know the type I mean). I have no bags – she has a few of those stiff paper bags with rope handles from fancy boutiques. She is sour with the stench of emptiness. A genuine sadness washes over me as I watch her walk out towards the car park and recede into the distance. I hate to see life squandered like that, body and heart hardened by the thrust and parry of securing a moneyed husband, and for what? Trinkets, personal trainers, house, car – stuff, just stuff.

Speaking of the quest for money, it occurs to me that I need to pay a visit to the cash point. I find one in a quiet corner of the arrivals lounge, which would have been a perfect setting for the channelling exercise of extracting Will's PIN from the muscle memory of his fingers. Unfortunately, though, I was forced to have a stab at that earlier this morning, in the loud and echoing concourse of the railway station when I was buying my train ticket. It doesn't do much for your powers of concentration to know that there is a queue of time-pressed commuters at your back – not to worry, though, I got there in the end (third time lucky – but still, a win's a win).

I am pleasantly surprised by the oddly colourful notes that come out of this dispenser – it's like real money, just a bit more fun. Some of it even has pictures of Jersey cows. *So that's what a cash cow looks like*, I nearly say to the gentleman (he deserves the term – hand-stitched gloves, perfectly parted hair, Windsor tie knot) who has ambled up to take his place at a respectful distance behind me. But I keep my thoughts to myself and confine myself instead to a cordial nod in his direction – a gesture of thanks, really, that his subtly cologned presence (nothing floral, more like an old sandalwood box with a squeeze of lime) has chased away the stench of that offshore slut creature.

It takes no time at all to get into St Helier, or Town as the taxi driver calls it. I ask him to drop me at Maritime Plaza, which turns out to be a sizeable development of new buildings, some of them apartments, some commercial, abutting an equally spotless marina with nothing but white speedboats moored in it. Behind, out in the bay, is a sunlit castle. All of this, combined with the apparent absence of any people (there is not a single soul in sight), makes for a vaguely dreamlike effect. A favourite phrase drifts into my mind, *the beached margent of the sea*. It's pleasing to say, and I repeat it happily to myself as I walk across the plaza towards the Spyre Group building. This is my target – the trust company through which the Vatican's assets are channelled. All I need to do is find a way of getting in there and excising that very particular portion of its carefully guarded data. It seems easy enough – what I mean is there's nothing special about it from the outside, just your typical modern office block, four storeys of chrome and glass with a down-ramp to a basement car park. I sidle past and have a furtive glance through the entrance – a couple of girls are sat behind the reception desk, one is talking on a headset, the other is sending a text message. Neither of them look at me as I pass.

I decide the best idea for now is just to hang back and look for an opportunity. It's gone one o'clock, the offices are steadily disgorging themselves of hungry workers. Too busy at the moment. From the window seat of a nearby café I watch the suits go back and forth in a stuttering stream. I keep my eyes glued to the Spyre Group building, waiting for something useful to happen. I am on my third coffee by the time it does. One of the receptionists, the texting one, not the headset one, has appeared. It's well past lunch now, and at first I think she may just have come out for a cigarette. But no, off she goes, beetling straight past me across the once-more deserted plaza. She must be off on some errand. This is my moment. When she's well out of sight, I pay up and wander over there to make my move. If I've learned one thing in all these centuries of watching it's to keep a plan as simple as possible, and this is no exception. All I do is rush up to the front desk and tell the headset girl that there are some kids skateboarding down the ramp into their car park. She looks predictably shocked at my battered appearance (this bruising around my nose is making everything a lot harder – people already see me as trouble before I've even opened my mouth, I can see it in their faces) but she looks even more outraged at what I've just told her. As I hold the door open for her, she races out to take a look, not even waiting to see if I am following behind her. Which is good, because I'm not. Instead, I'm stuffing a security pass into the pocket of my jacket, an act which, even though it takes just ten seconds to complete (seven to locate the pass on her desk, three to get it in my pocket), she very nearly catches me doing.

'Did you see them?' I ask affably when she walks back in.

It's clear from the way she's eyeing me that I have the look of someone who has only just stopped doing something they shouldn't have been doing. She bustles past me.

'There was no one there,' she tells me, while scanning the surface of her desk – she shows no sign of noticing that one of the passes has gone. 'I'm sorry, I don't think I caught your name.'

'Oh don't worry,' I tell her, as I breeze back towards the door. 'It's not important.'

Outside, I set off at a nice brisk pace in the direction of the marina. I have to say I'm feeling pretty pleased with how smoothly that just went. A quick glance at Will's phone tells me that it's a little after three. Got some hours to kill, then, before I can try to inveigle my way back in there. *The cover of night*, another phrase that pops into my head. Yes, I like that – it has the right feel to it. Not the cold brilliance of the stars, but a blanket that can be pulled over, close and tight.

When I get to the long sea wall that shelters the marina from the open water of the bay, I see that the tide is a long way out. I smell it too, a deep, reeking mud scattered with weed, some of which has clumped, brown and friable in the autumn sun, while other strands trail in the slow-running rivulets left by the tide. The wet earth left naked for the air to touch, and then releasing the essence of that touching for me to draw into myself in long breaths that pull down to my stomach, filling me from the centre out with the layers of life and matter that have been churned into the shore.

I watch a beaten-up old Land Rover splash out through the pools and streams towards the castle. As it nears the unmetalled strip of causeway that runs between castle and beach, it cuts across a slightly raised, drier bank of mud. The tracks of its tyres show darker here, almost black, beneath the chalky grey of the surface. I want desperately to get down there, to delve my hands into these fresh scars. I want to rub myself with it. But I won't. Even amid the beauty of this open space I am still aware of watching eyes – the houses and offices that overlook the bay, all of them filled with people.

I start walking. I need to keep myself moving for these remaining hours of daylight. I turn to the East, as Barnabas did in his desire to see and hear for himself the masses out in Antioch who were already beginning to sing out Christ's name to Paul's mad conducting. It seems incredible that the starved ravings of those men could still hold fast in a world like this, could still have a place among these modern buildings, these lanes of cars, this bright emerald of a traffic light showing through the branches of a tree. Even then, there was something faintly ridiculous about their snarling sermons, that dogged stance they had, leaning into the crowds as if into a strong wind. Their desire to die, for that is what it was – with my face, Christ's face, in the air before them, egging them on.

But I never hid from that responsibility. I accepted it and I pulled it into me, a sharp grain that century by slow-dripping century became smoothed like a pearl into my own dream of death. I see that now, so clearly, in the ebb of this perfect after-noon. Guilt wears you down, steady and forceful as a tide, and leaves you dreaming of peace. And when you see that peace will never come, you begin to dream of silence instead, the deep and lasting silence of an ending. But it has taken until now for that ending to begin. It happened the moment He cast me out. My final second of life was released into the air, to start wending blindly, inevitably towards me.

I have now reached the coast road that exits the town to the east and follows the contours of a peculiar landscape. The rocks that have been exposed by the sea have a low, lunar geography, pitted with craters and volcanic pockets. They cover almost all of the empty beach in a single mass. Here and there, where breaks open up like tiny canyons pushing into the edges, terns step daintily on the sand, dipping and pecking in the collected pools of seawater. In one place, a man digs small trenches with a garden fork, occasionally stooping to collect whatever he is looking for and dropping it into a bucket.

After about an hour of walking (although, it must be said, I stop a good many times to look at the view or simply to rest) I come to a small roundabout where there is a chance to head inland. A sign indicates that Grouville Church is somewhere along this narrower road. I had planned to continue my tracking of the coast but something in the name of this church makes me stop and choose this way instead. A short way along it, I find myself passing a yellow telephone box, which I notice has a direc-tory sitting on the little shelf next to the phone. I decide to check to see if what I'm thinking is right. I open the directory to *L* and run my finger down the listings. There are a few Lemprières but the first of them, Mr and Mrs A, does indeed have that word, Grouville, in the address. I key the number into Will's phone.

It rings for a long time. I'm almost ready to hang up when a woman's voice comes on the line, so formal and slow that at first I think it is an answering machine.

'This is Will Pryce,' I say when the voice has finished. 'I used to be a student of Professor Lemprière's.' It's my best guess. 'I just happened to be in Jersey for a meeting and wondered if perhaps ...'

'Oh yes, of course. When did you say you were planning to be in Jersey? I can let him know that you –'

'No, sorry,' I cut her short, 'I meant I'm actually here now. I thought perhaps I could drop in and say hello to the professor. But if it's not a convenient time then ...' I let the line lapse into awkward silence.

'Not at all,' she says, with undiminished formality. 'I'm sure he would be very happy to see you, Mr … Price, was it?'

'Yes, that's right. Will. Will Pryce.'

'Why don't you drop in for a sherry this evening, say around six o' clock?'

I instinctively glance at the bare wrist where Will's watch used to be. But anyway, I don't need to see the time to know that her suggestion isn't going to work. I have a couple of hours to kill right now. By six I'll be on my way back into town for phase two of my plan.

'I'm afraid I'll be heading back to the airport by then,' I lie. 'I was really just thinking that perhaps he might be free now to … um … see me.'

This conversation is becoming a little awkward. I'm clearly colouring outside the lines, etiquette-wise. Perhaps I should just ditch it. It's starting to feel like it would be less frosty out here.

I'm about to put a quick *maybe next time* end to this when she pipes up with a stoically cheerful, 'Of course, that would be lovely.' And then, warming to it, 'An impromptu guest – what fun!'

'Great – I'll head over now, then. How do I …?'

'Oh just tell your taxi driver it's the first left after the Hollyside farm shop in Grouville. The name of the house is *La Fin de Chasse.*'

'Lovely. Thanks very much.'

'I'm afraid it will just be a simple tea,' she tells me before hanging up.

Her mention of tea makes me realise how thirsty and hungry I am. As I'm walking, looking out for someone who can give me directions, I feel the hunger gently shifting in my gut, a creature quietly dreaming in there.

A man sweeping leaves in his driveway for a fire I can smell but cannot see tells me that the Hollyside farm shop is just up the way, on the corner with the main road. With the sweet acridity of burning leaves still clinging to my hair and clothes, I continue walking, realising that I may in fact be on the right road already. I start looking at the names of the houses. There are long intervals between them, with hard rutted fields and sparse hedgerow filling the gaps. At one point the road narrows to a lane and I am forced to climb up on to the bank so that a tractor is able to pass. The driver looks at me, in my suit, ankle deep in grass and nettles, without thanks or curiosity.

Sure enough, I eventually come to a wooden sign that says *La Fin de Chasse*. It announces the beginning of a muddy driveway lined with mature chestnut trees, many of which have been pollarded down to little more than hefty stumps. In a dip, about two hundred metres away, I can see the roof and upper storey of a house. A thick ribbon of smoke is rising up from the chimney, suggesting a fresh load of coal has just been tipped on the fire. As I get closer, I can smell that it has. All this burning in the countryside – man's proof that he is here, making known his Promethean arts.

The door is answered by a lady whose face and attire perfectly match the voice I heard on the phone.

'Oh dear,' she says, looking first at my nose and then down at my shoes – following her eyes, I see they are covered in mud. 'You ought to have told the driver to come right to the door.'

She insists on taking them from me so she can clean them up. She tells me to wait where I am, that she'll be back in a second with some slippers for me. As I am standing there in my stockinged feet, a figure emerges from the dimness at the end of the hallway.

'Is that Will?' He has a gentle, mellifluous way of speaking, as if he's reciting a poem to himself.

It is a dark, long corridor of closed doors, so it's only as he gets near to me that I am able to see him properly. His eyebrows and hair are a pure white, and his long limbs seem frail as twigs. But there's a brightness to him, in his step, in his eyes particularly. He grips me by both shoulders and holds me out before him, frowning, as if at a possession he can't quite place.

'Will,' he says, 'how the devil are you?'

'I'm well, thanks,' although it must be patently obvious that I am anything but – my own body seems only marginally sturdier than his.

Before either of us can say more, Mrs Lemprière returns with the slippers.

'Rosie is bossing you around already, I see.' He says this to her, rather than to me, but with great affection in his voice. And her face, when she smiles back at him, is transformed into an expression of almost girlish adoration. I see now that she is a good many years younger than him.

'You get back to the fire,' she says. 'I'll bring you some tea in a while.'

'Molly-coddled is what I've become, Will,' he sighs happily as I follow him back down the hallway into the gloom.

He leads me into a study lit by a couple of lamps and the light from an open fire. It is nearing dusk and the curtains are not yet drawn. A desk next to the window overlooks a wide lawn that sweeps down to yet more chestnut trees. Black pools of shadow are beginning to form at the foot of the trees. My own reflection is cast faintly on the glass of the window as I look out, a suited figure, ghosted and indistinct as a daguerreotype, but not out of place here in this room among the musty books and the pictures, many and lopsided, with their peeling gilt frames. The mantel clock ticks softly behind the hisses and cracks of the fire, not officiously like that smashed watch, but with a fuller, more melodic tone. There is wisdom in its faded ivory face, as if it knows some larger secret about the hours it sees passing.

'Have a seat.' The chair he is pointing to is one of two angled towards the fire. The material on its arms and back has been worn to a lighter colour by the many others who have rested there.

For a few seconds we both seem content to look into the fire and forget the other is there. The bright caverns between the fused lumps of coal burrow off into a world where no living thing can follow. Resting above them is a log, blackened and just on the edge of being consumed. Licks of flame are up the back and round the side of it. Just a moment ago, as I stood by the window, it was hissing, making a kind *feeesh* sound as the last of it moisture was forced out into the open; now it has accepted its fate and lies still, in charred resignation. The silent glory of no return.

'So to what do I owe this pleasure, Will?' It's not a challenging question. He says it with a look of wry curiosity, as if this is perhaps not the first time Will has turned up announced at house. His eyes, though, are not to be fooled. They notice everything.

'I had a few hours to kill after a meeting, and …' I decide to venture a little more guesswork '… I was sorry to have missed your retirement party. I wanted to catch up.'

'Yes, yes of course.' He returns his gaze to the fire. Still watching the flames, he asks, 'So what business brings you to Jersey? The last I heard from you, you were off on your travels.'

'I work for a firm in London now – public relations, that sort of thing. We have a client here. It's not very interesting.'

'So why, I wonder,' and now he does turn to look at me, 'would you be doing it?

I shrug. 'Good question.'

'Simple question,' he corrects me.

'The good ones always are.'

I smile at him, wishing we could go back to our comfortable silence staring. But he's not going to be fobbed off.

'How are you, Will?'

A *how are you?* at this stage in a conversation is not a nicety, it is intended very much as this one was said, to find what is wrong.

There's something about him that makes me want to tell the truth, so I do.

'I've been through a pretty hard time recently, but I'm on the mend. Better than that, actually. I'm moving towards some kind of understanding, I think.'

'An understanding? Oh dear,' he says, reaching across and patting my arm with his liver-spotted hand. 'Oh dear me. It's worse than I thought.'

Behind us, the door opens and the tinkling of crockery announces the entrance of his wife. She places the tea tray on the small table between us. There is a plate piled high with fruit scones, a bowl of strawberry jam, and a block of rich yellow butter. The teapot and cups have a faded design, washed away by decades of use. I can just make out the lines of horses hitched to a chariot.

He sees me looking at it. 'Phaethon,' he says, his eyes shining in the firelight. 'Take note.'

His wife pours the tea, putting a little milk in mine and a slice of lemon in his, for which she uses a tiny set of silver tongs that were resting on top of the sugar bowl.

'The jam is from last year,' she says. 'We had more straw-berries than we knew what to do with – such a long, dry summer, they ripened beautifully.'

She rests her hand on his shoulder for a moment, as if sharing the warmth of that memory.

'Thank you,' I say, but she doesn't seem to hear me. Neither of them does.

When she has left the room, the suspension of our conversation continues as he sips his tea and I demolish three scones in a row. The power of suggestion perhaps, but I fancy I can taste the sun-clotted blood of that summer still swollen in the fruit. And the deeper notes too, of dust and hay, the earthy dankness of dewfall.

'Still with us?'

I realise I have been chewing with my eyes closed.

'This is exquisite jam. Are you sure you won't ...?'

'I'm getting too old for afternoon snacks. It's satisfaction enough to watch you make such short work of it. Rosie will be pleased,' he chuckles.

The tea is delicate, some kind of China blend. It has a sharpness in the aftertaste that makes you feel parched for more. It reminds me of rue, a flavour that cropped up a lot during my JC tour of duty. As I lean forward to put my cup back on the table I notice just how many books there are on his desk, several of them with little paper markers sticking out. There are pages and pages of notes too, in ad hoc little piles.

'Looks like you're working on something.'

He waves the suggestion away. 'I'm more interested in this "understanding" of yours. Tell me about that. And tell me exactly how you came to be working in a job that is not very interesting. You,' he adds, 'of all people.'

And so I tell him everything I know, using whatever words I have to hand that might straddle where I have come from and where I find myself now, in the soft collision of this young man's mercurial sprint and my own granite-faced marathon.

He thinks about it for a long time afterwards. His expression is hard to read. Eventually he says, 'And your health? I say this as one whose prostate has swollen to the size of an onion and whose skin hangs about him like a loose-fitting garment, but Will, my boy, you do not look well.'

'I could do with a little more sleep, that's certainly true. But –'

He doesn't want to hear my buts. 'Are they the same worries as before? As when yours and my paths first crossed?'

I'd like to hear more about that. This occupation of Will has left me with a kind of vested interest in his past, as the new owner of a house might want to hear tales from the neighbours of how that line of fresh slates on the roof was because of a lightning-struck tree or how the hatch door to the cellar was boarded up after a farmhand fell down there and broke his back.

'Why, is that how I seem? What was I like then? I can't even remember.'

He finds this amusing. 'The hurry of youth,' he says. 'So busy reinventing yourselves you can't remember who you were just five minutes ago. But trust me, you haven't changed as much as you might think.'

The day has vanished, unnoticed, as we have been talking, and now blackness is pressing on the windows. I feel safe folded away here in this pocket of stillness, with nature's dead growth burning at my feet and our two hearts, one nearer to death than the other, still beating in our chests.

'I have never known of a student to switch to Mathematics in Part II of the Tripos, Will. I am fairly sure it has never happened, except in your own, very particular case. I remember the day you came to see me – I had been told simply that an undergraduate student from the faculty of Divinity was asking to speak with me. I assumed you had some crackpot bible code you wanted to discuss, and then you showed it to me,' he smiles, shaking his head, 'that vast body of work you had already completed, on the Riemann hypothesis, no less – some of the modelling there ...' Again he shakes his head. 'You have an extraordinary gift.'

He laughs quickly, at another memory, just coming to him. 'Do you remember what you said to me?' Fortunately he leaves no time for a reply. 'I asked you if this had been part of your guided study and you said to me, "I've been doing it for reasons of my own". Reasons of my own, that phrase always stuck with me.' And yet something about the phrase also burns off the genial atmosphere of reminiscence. When he speaks again it is with none of the humour of before. 'But you always were a troubled boy, Will. And those reasons of your own worry me a little. It worries me that whatever made you turn your back on mathematics and the tremendous opportunities that were there for you is also the same thing that sent you off bumming around for all those years and then into this job about which you care so little, and perhaps even brought you here today.'

He pushes himself up out of his chair, his elbows shaking slightly under the strain, and fishes another log out of the basket. There is a small shower of sparks when he tosses it into the grate.

'Forgive me,' he says. 'I have spoken out of turn.' The poetry has gone from his voice, he just sounds weary now.

He walks slowly over to his desk and brings a handful of papers back to where we are sitting. He hands them to me before lowering himself into his chair.

'It's a biography of Turing,' he mutters. 'Something I always meant to get around to, but research was always in the way. Now, though, I have the luxury of leaving it to others to clear the way for the future.' He doesn't look as though he considers it a luxury.

The papers are numbered typed sheets, seemingly the first few chapters of his manuscript, with what I assume to be his spidery handwriting in the margins, adding in, striking through, correcting these initial thoughts in irritable bursts. *A genius of such violent intensity that it was to shape the thinking of a future generation* is one phrase that I read. This strikes me as an old man's undertaking, something drawn from the embers.

'I look forward to reading it,' I lie. 'When's it going to be published?'

'When I find the energy to finish it. That's the trouble with tenure – you only leave when you're too tired to carry on. Which is when you realise you're too tired for anything.'

'You didn't speak out of turn,' I tell him, to his slight surprise. He probably thought we were done with the serious part of our chat, but there's something I want to say to him. It feels important. 'You were right, in many ways. I did turn my back on Divinity – but the answer wasn't in numbers either. They are descriptors, and that is all. There is no understanding of God's design through numbers, merely a description of it.'

He seems a little exasperated by this. 'But is that not enough, Will? Is it not the responsibility of each man to describe only what he sees? Not to purport to understand those things he cannot see?'

The new log is hissing on the fire, not yet ready to be burnt up.

'Yes, but I *am* able to describe Divinity, I *have* seen it.' Unfortunately, this is where I am forced to break out from the rather convenient cover that Will's academic career had left for me. 'And I am going to provide a proof that will show what it is *not*, at least, even if there is no language, no ready means for me to show what it *is*.'

'You're not making sense. Are you trying to say that a mathematical proof can demonstrate –'

'No. I mean actual proof. Evidence that will demonstrate in very clear terms just how completely and utterly wrong the so-called spokesmen for God are. The church – I am talking about the church, and their endless toxic promises, their murderous lies.'

My hands are shaking. Rosie, who must have entered the room while I was speaking, is looking at me with undisguised concern. I realise now that she knew perfectly well who Will was when I called here, she just didn't want to be reminded of him. He clearly has a history with this man over whom she is so protective, and she is not about to let things get out of hand now.

This is confirmed by the professor's face. He is giving her a *Just hold on* kind of look – *I've got this.* Reluctantly, she perches on the arm of his chair, when she would clearly rather be telling me she will phone for my taxi and that my shoes are clean and waiting for me by the door.

'But Will, surely you can see that this generalisation you are making is a poor basis for any proof, mathematical or otherwise. There is good and bad in everything – you know this – your own father is a priest, is he not?' I nod, he spreads his hands, as if to say *Well, there you go.* 'There are always fluctuations – you cannot isolate an entity en bloc. You cannot …'

His trailing off is taken by Rosie as a sure sign that all of this has gone quite far enough, and that it is now her turn to speak.

'Mr Pryce, I will speak frankly if I may.' Her husband shrinks a little into his chair. 'We must make no pretence about the…' she searches for a word '… deleterious effect of the stunt you pulled at the college.'

'I …' I don't know what it is that I am going to say but she does not allow me the chance to find out. She has clearly been bottling this up and now is its time to come out.

'No, I am sorry, but I will say my piece.' She glances at the professor, who has turned his face to the fire. 'You stood on the stage at an important symposium – perhaps the most important of Gus's career – trusted by the faculty, vouched for by my husband, and you denounced him, his colleagues and their work in the most extraordinary terms.' She says the word in two parts, extra ordinary. 'And then you disappear without a word of explanation. No, I am sorry, but you do not get to come barging back here – what makes you think you have the right? Because you sent those absurd postcards to my husband? Was that supposed to be some form of apology? After everything he did for you ...'

He is patting her leg and telling her that's enough now. She is still glaring at me, watery-eyed. In the silence that follows she gathers together the tea things and walks out. The clock continues to tick, indifferent to how long its seconds now seem. It was a mistake to wander in here like this, unsighted.

Interestingly, though, the professor seems rather pleased to have it all blown out into the open. He is looking substantially more cheerful.

'In my desk,' he says, meaning me to go over there. 'Bottom left drawer.'

What I find there is a bundle of about twenty postcards held together with an elastic band. They are from various locations in and around Thailand. *Ko Pha Ngan – Party Island!* one of them proclaims over the psychedelic backdrop of a multi-coloured full moon.

'I never showed them to anyone,' he tells me without turning around. 'Only Rosie has seen them – as you know.' He does a funny thing with his voice there, something complicit between the two of us, letting me know that she worries, that she loves him but that she does not speak for him.

I turn the pile over and start sifting through. Each one is densely packed with writing, symbols mainly, interspersed with tight mathematical notation. In some instances, when the proof cannot fit on a single side, the cards are numbered, one of three, two of three, and so on. At a glance, it appears to be advanced number theory, *abc* conjecture by the look of it.

'Have you checked these?' I am still standing at his desk. My reflected self out in the window's darkness also looks up at him.

'There are imperfections, but as far as I can tell, they are correct. I would need to show them to colleagues, get other opinions, to say for sure.'

I look at the postmarks. They span a range of three years, the most recent of them from April 2010.

'So why haven't you?'

I am back in my seat now and he is looking at me with something like paternal affection.

'Because they belong to you, my boy. They are not mine to show.'

I don't know what to say.

All I can think of is, 'I'm sorry. I wasn't myself back then.' Both, at least, are true.

After that things settle down, he even invites me to stay for some supper. *There is no plane, is there?* he asks at one point. At his suggestion, I go to find Rosie. She is in the kitchen at the back of the house. It has an ancient granite fireplace, large enough to burn the limbs of trees, into which an AGA stove has been installed, with a row of copper pans hanging from the lintel. It smells of baking. She is chopping vegetables on the worktop, and barely glances up from her task when I enter the room.

'I'm sorry if I was rude,' she says as her knife *rat-tat-tats* on the chopping board, 'but he took it badly, what you did. Not that he'd ever admit it, stubborn old goat. I just don't want you getting his hopes up with more talk and promises. He takes it all so seriously. I don't think you realise how much.' She puts down her knife and turns to look at me, wiping her hands on her apron. 'He genuinely thought you were some kind of genius. Maybe you are,' she adds, not meaning it as a compliment, 'but that is no reason for you to be unsettling him again now. He has aged a lot in the last few years – as I'm sure you have noticed, genius that you are,' this is accompanied by a halfway conciliatory smile.

She returns to her chopping without another word. I stand for a few moments not quite knowing what to do or say. When I make to leave she doesn't look up, but says, 'You may as well hand me that large pan, if you're staying for supper. I presume that's what he sent you in here to tell me.'

And so we eat a meal together, a simple vegetable soup with bread rolls that were baked this morning. A half bottle of red wine, already open from the night before, is shared among our three glasses, and weighs me down with a blissful fatigue. We talk of this and that. He speaks for a long time about how much the college had begun to change by the time he left. She discusses the felling of a tree in the garden that had become a nuisance and a terrible worry in high winds. They both agree that high winds have become a feature of recent years. It is all very restful and I soon feel my eyes beginning to droop. Rosie is the first to notice.

'I think perhaps your chess game will have to wait until morning,' she says. All pretence of me having to rush off anywhere to catch a flight was dropped some time ago, by us all.

With a belly full of hot soup and red wine, the thought of a cosy bed in this quiet, enchanted house is more than I can resist. I allow myself to be taken to a room up in the eaves, a space that has been whittled into the ancient timbers, and I say my good-nights. I sink effortlessly into the downy embrace of the duvet.

As I lie there in the dark, I start to think about what he said to me, how this Christian myth has brought as much good as bad. I know in my heart, from all that I have seen, that he is probably right. It would be foolish, wrong even, to condemn the whole thing – *en bloc*, that was his phrase. Imagine the cost to those millions, for whom the radiance of Christ is all they have, the only gift of hope with which to warm themselves, their children. Or to those who set their courses by Christ's star in circumstances too horrific to imagine.

Why race to tear down a structure that has so much good in it? He's right, I must slow down, take a breath, step back …

These thoughts begin to cradle me towards sleep. I feel the warmth of my cover – so *this* is the cover of night, I smile in my drowse – like the glow of that hearth downstairs. I visualise him and I hear once again the comfort of his words as he spoke to me – to Will, *my boy* – and I know that it is not too late for me to salvage something from the wreckage of this young man's life and to live it out with grace and humility. My hair could also whiten, my body could curl as the professor's has done, dry as a leaf. I too could be surrounded by the spoils of a life lived in observant inquiry, my books, my memories, the echoes of those I have known, the wife that I love and who loves me in return. The promise of completion that was never to be with my Magpie. Someone to grow old with, to die with, whose love could carry me into the ultimate quiet that awaits all nature's work.

I am free. Free to live as I choose.

9

A small sound wakes me. It is deepest, coldest night. The moon, high and bright in the sky, lights the room. A silent parliament of strangers sits on the floor around my bed, packed tight against the walls, all the way back to the door, eyes wide, watching me. Mothers with sunken cheeks and loose breast skin hold the awkward parcels of infants hollowed out by the disease. Men, dark skinned, white-eyed, stare in wordless accusation, their arms folded like sticks, missionaries' wooden crosses hang on strings from their necks, the hard corrugation of their ribs tight against their skin.

Sick with dread, I remain absolutely still, alone with their silence. Then comes that sound again, the sound that woke me, still a long way off, but getting closer. It is the sound of a mob, baying for my blood. I can smell the dust and heat of Jerusalem, the sweet decay of Pilate's breath.

I open my eyes, not suddenly in horror or surprise at my dream, but with the familiar oppression of guilt reinstalled in my body. It has permeated me like a gas, suffocating the hope that nudged me to the borders of sleep. Now it is my evening spent at the fireside, the soft persuasion of the professor's words, that seem like a dream.

I dress in the dark and move as quietly as I can through the house, taking great care not to rest my weight on a creaking board. At the front door where my shoes were taken from me, I find them, cleaned and polished on the mat. My coat is also hanging there. It occurs to me that I should leave an explanation as to why I am about to run off, ostensibly for a second time. But what would it say, this note? How could it possibly explain my trajectory through two millennia?

No, this departure must be silent, in the dead of night. There can be no explaining it. *Vanishment*, I think to myself as I slowly turn the door handle. A term the good professor would understand in his own way – a return to zero.

Outside, a persistent, cold rain forces me to tilt forwards and draw my coat tightly around me. The whole way back into town, I barely look up, nor do I spare time for a thought except for the dogged visualisation of where I must get to.

But when I finally do reach the plaza I find it looks very different at night, and not in a good way. While some of the office buildings are still brightly lit, despite being empty, the Spyre Group building is completely dark. I stop at the doors of the reception to cup my hands against the wet glass and peer inside. I can just make out a baseball cap and what looks like a bunch of keys that have been left on the counter where I stole the pass from. I hadn't reckoned on any kind of security, and the thought that these things might belong to a guard is profoundly unnerving. I wait for a few minutes more but nothing changes. As I walk down the ramp into the car park my footsteps echo ridiculously loudly in the closed space. My stolen pass activates the door that leads from the top of the car park's steps into the office. It beeps loudly as it opens and it closes with a sharp metallic click. I half hope that a light might automatically turn on but it doesn't. I spend an awful few seconds feeling along the walls like a blind man, without success. It is only when I remember Will's phone in my pocket that I am able to light my way to the far door at the end of this long, windowless corridor.

After that, each new room I enter, every turn of desolate corridor, makes the susurration of blood pressure grow louder in my ears. I shake like a wino as handles are turned and light switches flipped on. But little by little, as the building slowly reveals itself to be empty, I start to calm down. When at last I reach the darkened reception, I pick up the bunch of keys and give them a triumphant shake.

'Now,' I tell myself, 'for the hard part.'

Except the thing is, it really isn't. It's disconcertingly easy to get into their computer system. I simply cruise around the building scanning each person's work station until I find someone who has been stupid enough to write down their username and password. Inevitably, the offending Post-it is stuck to a monitor in one of the partners' lairs (one of the few offices that is furnished like an actual room, to the extent that there are pictures and items of non-commercial type furniture in it). It always seems to be the most senior figures who end up letting down an organisation with their carelessness. Maybe that's just what happens when you are isolated from the daily rigours of work. You become divorced from the detail.

I sit down at the desk and crack my knuckles while the computer boots up. On the far side of the room is a rather fancy little drinks tray – dark lacquered wood, a friendly crowd of bottles and tumblers. Next to it is a mini fridge, no doubt stocked with mixers and ice. But not yet. That will be my reward when the job is done. You have to have a work ethic.

In the end it takes nearly three hours of unbroken concentration before I manage to retrieve everything I came for. But still, that's not bad going, especially when you consider the Byzantine structure of this trust, not to mention the fact that all I had to begin with was its name and the name of the beneficiary (which turned out to be one of three shell companies used by the Vatican). But I got there in the end, and what I now have is enough to draw everyone into the picture – InviraCorp, the Vatican Bank, the Vatican's accountants – in fact, it's more than enough. Every last detail is laid bare to me, the files like artefacts carefully arranged on the side of an archaeologist's trench.

I try to access Will's Hotmail account only to find that it is blocked by the firewall – but it's not a major setback. When I logged into the system using this guy's details, it automatically launched the company's email account, so I'm able to just use that instead without having to faff around with more passwords. I open a series of new messages (I was right, by the way: according to his email signature, this guy is a partner of the Spyre Group) and I begin the process of sending the files to Natalie. There are eighteen of them in total so I spread them across several messages, just to be sure that they don't get snagged in this system or hers. I also write a brief covering note so she knows it's coming from me. The messages I title like those postcards I saw earlier this evening: *Proof 1/18*, *Proof 2/18*, and so on. It's good to have a motif.

When I finally come to shut down the computer, my hands, my fingers, the tendons in my forearms, everything is aching from the strain. My neck makes a sickening crunch when I straighten up from my task. And yet I can't help thinking that despite the intensity of the work and the stress of finding my way into and around this building, and despite the professor tempting me from my course, this has all still seemed a little too easy. Not once have I felt His attention on me, nowhere have I registered the warning signs of their disapproval. But then, I suppose, there's no reason why I should. I am, I remind myself, lost to His view now. A solitary pixel. I need to start getting used to that fact.

'You mustn't look for problems when there are none,' I murmur, rubbing my eyes with the heels of my hands.

Perhaps having that drink might make me feel more victorious. The amber glow of whiskey is beckoning – bourbon, Maker's Mark – couldn't be more fitting. I slosh a few fingers into one of the heavy-based tumblers. These glasses, with their good solid handful of liquor, are made to compliment that well-hung feeling of money and power, the surveying of a small empire of funds and cash and assets and liquidity surging through the place, driving turbines of administration and wealth management. No doubt the person whose working days are spent in this office likes to wash back a man-sized mouthful of bourbon at the end of a fat-pocketed day, or perhaps in mutual alpha recognition with a client or cohort of some description. And as I stand here doing the same, I can see why. It's a good feeling. The long day done. The soldier home from the field.

Drink still in hand, I gently horn off my shoes with the tips of my toes and go padding in my socks out across the carpet, for a little bimble around. I end up settling in the largest of the meeting rooms, where a flat screen television is mounted in the centre of the far wall, at the head of the table almost, as if it presides over what goes on here. I find the control and click it on.

The next couple of hours fly by.

The first thing I click on is a news channel. One item features an English clergyman talking about the hierarchy of their church – women, he declares, will soon be allowed to become bishops. In a stroke of staggering genius, the reporter refers to him at one point as the *chief primate* of the church.

'Love it,' I say, raising my glass to the screen before swilling back the last of my whiskey. I think about going to get another but nothing, not even the promise of more of this honey-sweet slugging juice, could tear me away from the television. It's fascinating, it's heartbreaking, it's hilarious, it's gut-wrenchingly tragic, all at the same time. It's you, basically, all packed up in a box.

What comes next is the most extraordinary thing I've seen so far. I have no idea what it is called, nor can I say for certain what it's about, and yet every last detail is utterly addictive. It's like heroin for the eyes. All I can be sure of is that these people – deeply ugly characters, every last one of them – have been forced together in confined and challenging circumstances. They appear to be in a jungle, but again, I could be wrong about that. By rights, it should be a truly dismal viewing experience, except that somehow, it isn't. In fact, it may well be one of the most heartening things I've seen since I jumped in. I love it that people are making programmes like this – it reminds me of the *commedia dell'arte* you used to see so much of, the way each character tells of some dangerously soft patch in the collective soul. It's vital for mankind, I think, to have lightning rods of this kind, to draw people's hatred and despair into a common circuit. Excellent stuff.

But my restless finger soon turns to switching again and I find myself plunged into another kind of drama, slower-acting this one but, as each phase unfolds, more and more disturbing. It's a film, not a high-budget affair – the colours are weak and the way it is shot forces you to look at the characters in an unflattering, pitiless way. A woman is being held captive in a dingy back room. A man, who we never see, who features only as a voice on the phone, relays instructions to her increasingly reluctant captors.

It leaves a bitter taste, this story. It is an unwelcome reminder of the kind of things that corrupted my relationship with Him – the ways in which I used to see Him behaving towards you, acts that sowed the early seeds of doubt and resentment in my mind (seeds I thought had come to nothing but which I now realise had been steadily growing into a choking vine, thriving in the shade of my denial). You must see it too, of course you do – I *know* you do, I've heard it a million times from the atheists and the rationalists – *what kind of God would ...?* and so on and so forth. But the others, too, the triers, the ones who want to believe, they must feel the needle skipping from time to time. How could they not? But then that's where my Suffering Son routine comes in, always invoked to persuade people away from their better instincts, and to swallow down the lump of doubt that perhaps He has it in Him to behave badly, cruelly even.

'Christ,' I say. 'Jesus Christ, what a sorry state of affairs.'

But the cardinals, the vicars, the Zadoks of your age, they can never really explain it away, not so that it doesn't just keep coming back, again and again – the damp appearing each time through a fresh coat of paint. Because there *is* no explaining it, some of the stuff that's gone on. Take Abraham as a for instance. God calls him up, effectively, just like the man in this film, an authority figure suddenly on the end of the line, and He tells Abraham to grab his son, tie him up and then drag him up a mountainside. Once he's at the top, he is informed that he must murder the child. Like any father would, Abraham protests, he begs Him not to ask for so much. It is not until Abraham, demented with grief and horror, is about to push the knife into that delicate ribcage that the instructions are withdrawn. It was just a test, he is told.

Now, you tell me: is that love?

But hey ho – what's done is done. There's no point in getting worked up about it.

I have a last flip over to the news channel, just to sort of cleanse my palate, as it were, and I am immediately told that it is five o'clock and time for the headlines. Well, not for me it's not – it's time I got going. These finance types like to get into work nice and early. It's the same promise of that fat, lazy worm not yet gone to ground that brings the birds down from their trees.

On my way back through the office I stop at one of the windows and watch the bay start to lighten in the pre-dawn. The rain has stopped, the sky washed clean for another new day. Time for me to get outside, maybe even have a little stroll on the beach before I have to head up to the airport. *The sea, all water, yet receives rain still*. Amazing, how many words I have committed to memory. They keep just bobbing to the surface in neat packages, like flotsam from a sinking ship.

I exit the building the same way I came in, dodging the CCTV angles, and I emerge from the garage's up-ramp into a world that is suddenly looking really rather lovely. That very early light is putting its thin blue shade on the bricks and tarmac and the frosted backs of the parked cars. My breath announces the life that is in me with vapour patterns that appear and immediately disperse before my face. Scattered birdsong comes *blitting* and *witting* out from the little hiding places they will always find for their homes. Halyards clink softly against masts. There is no traffic, there are no people – I am perfectly alone.

I walk past the marina and decide that I do have time to go down on to the wet and deserted beach. There's a good mix of shale in the sand, which makes for a pleasing foot-crunch. The tide has not long turned and there's a brackish smell in the air. It feels just right in my lungs, laden with life. After a mile or so of walking, I take the steps back up to the road. The soles of my shoes scrape some of the beach along with me.

From the bus stop where I stand waiting for the first service of the day, I watch a man walk down from one of the beachfront houses. At this distance it is hard to tell his age but his step is lithe and springy. He has a towel rolled into a tidy tube, which he leaves a little way up the beach, where the sand's a little drier. As he reaches the waterline his movements do not betray the slightest resistance to the cold. He wades slowly and methodically up to his waist and slides into the water. He has the air of a man who has done this all his life.

The next time I look he is nothing more than a distant churn of arms and water, just swimming out deeper and deeper, aiming at nothing.

10

It's just before seven o'clock when I decide to call Natalie. She hasn't replied to my email yet, so I thought I'd try speaking to her instead. I'm operating in a bit of a bubble here – it'd just be nice to share the news, feel some of her excitement about it, hear her first thoughts on how she'll be running it (they're bound to want to splash it on the front page, but maybe there'll be follow-up pieces inside, copy filed from the affected countries even). I'd just like to have a bit of contact, is all I'm saying.

But the person who picks up is not Natalie. It's a man, older by the sound of it, and half asleep. At first I think it's the wrong number – I hold the phone away from my face to check – but no.

'Is Natalie there?'

'Who is this?' he wants to know.

'It's Will. Is Natalie there?'

He perks up a bit. 'Ah yes – Will.' But I do not like the way he says *Will*, as if it's something amusing, and I especially do not like the *Ah yes*, with its implication that he, whoever he might be, has been discussing me with Natalie.

'I'm sorry,' I ask him, 'do I know you?'

'No, but I know you.' Again, his tone is insolent. If I didn't know better I'd even say there was a suggestion of something more in it, a threat of some kind.

'Look, are you going to put Natalie on the phone or what?'

'She's not here,' he says, a little distractedly, as if he might be able to see her coming back.

'Well, I'll just stay on the line and …' But he's already hung up.

For a little while I just sit there in the moulded plastic of my airport seat, staring at the phone. Then I redial the number. I'm not going to be spoken to like that. Except this time it goes straight into voicemail. He must have switched off her phone. I have no idea who this guy is but, mark my words, this is not the last he'll be hearing from me. I close my eyes tightly in an effort to expunge him and his outrageous behaviour. How dare he come between me and my darling Mary?

I decide to have a wander around to take my mind off things. I still have twenty minutes until I need to check in and I … Wait, did I just call her Mary? I think I might have done. Apologies for that – I'm sure you understand – blood's running a little high.

But it turns out that wandering around doesn't help. If anything, it puts me more on edge. Airports are unsettling spaces at the best of times – that perpetual sense of unrealised metamorphosis, everyone about to be somewhere else. It's like being in the middle part of an equation.

By the time I reach the check-in desk I'm in a pestilent mood.

'I'm afraid you've run out of battery power, sir.'

I am being told this by the youth who is checking me in. He is handing back to me Will's phone, which has – had – my boarding pass on it.

'Well isn't that just perfect,' I snap at him.

He isn't quite sure what to say to that. My defunct phone is still in his hand.

'Sorry?' he ventures.

'Give it here.' I snatch it back from him.

I am aware that I'm now just standing here, giving him (at best) a withering, (more likely) a threatening look, but I can't seem to help it.

'Stupid phone,' I say. 'Puny batteries, functional obsolescence – these manufacturers have us by the short hairs. Nothing is built to last,' I warn him darkly.

He tries hard to look interested in this, as well as to seem unperturbed by my general behaviour and (let's not forget) my bruised and busted face. But it's a lot to pretend at once and he doesn't make a brilliant job of it.

'Oh I see,' he says, but is then glad to be able to get things back on script with, 'Do you have some ID please, sir?'

'Will this do?' With a flourish I produce Will's wallet from my jacket. His driving licence is in there somewhere.

Poor kid wobbles in alarm at my admittedly rather sudden movement. I should probably try to put him at his ease – but really, what would be the point? I revert to my glowering, and we conclude our transactions in a profound and nearly unbroken silence.

One good thing happens on the way to departures, though: I come across one of those mobile phone charging stations. It's a little box with a coin meter that lets you plug in and lock up your phone while it charges. All I need to do is give it a fifteen-minute burst then I'll be able to try Natalie again (by which time she'll be finished with whatever unpleasant interlude that idiot man was a part of). When I hook it up, my phone makes an encouraging *blip* and shows me a picture of a battery being nourished by green electricity.

I then join the herd and slowly make my way through the various checks and procedures that make people feel less worried about someone trying to blow up or seize control of their plane. I divest my pockets of all their jangly contents – coins, keys, a fountain pen I must have filched without realising from the Spyre offices – and through I go. No criminality detected.

It's not until I'm through the gate, on the plane and in the sky that I realise I've left Will's phone charging in Jersey airport. I've been in something of a trance until this point, looking out of the window at the distant furrows on the ocean beneath us, and so my sudden squawk of realisation comes as a shock to those in the seats around me, as does my accompanying slap to the fold-down table in front of me. It sends my snacks and drink flying up in the air, a bit like when there's a sudden loss of cabin pressure (in this, as with most things, I speak from experience – I have witnessed more plane crashes than I care to remember – when people are suddenly praying en masse like that, and with such fervour, it's kind of hard not to notice them).

The stewardess rushes over to see what the problem is and it takes me several minutes to persuade her that I am not causing an inflight disturbance. Everyone is so serious about flying these days. Even mildly angry passengers are B Team terrorists.

Anyway, back to my problem. That phone is lost now, along with all the information (and, who knows, maybe even a message from Natalie) that was hibernating in its SIM card. Which means … I'm going to need to dig deep. I'm going to need to really focus and see if I can remember Natalie's phone number. It was stored in Will's phone after she called me, so I glimpsed it a couple of times, which should be enough for me to reconstruct it. I'll just need to loosen up a bit first. I ring the bell above my head several times before the stewardess appears (it seems she's much harder to summon when you actually want to see her). I ask her for a whisky but she lies and tells me the drinks service has finished. I shake my head in pity for her and wave her away with my hand. I might even say the words *Be gone*. I certainly think them.

So, first thing to do is take out my borrowed/stolen pen and start jotting down some likely-looking integers. The sick bag is the only blank writing surface I can find in the little pocket next to my knees, so I use that. On a separate sheet (i.e. the sick bag from the pocket of the person next to me), I represent these sets graphically (sometimes I find patterns are easier to see when you plot numbers – it allows their natural shape to emerge). At various points during this exercise, I become aware of the fact that I am humming to myself in the atonal way of someone who is deep in concentration. Perhaps my row companion who occupies the aisle seat next to mine is disturbed by it, she looks as if she may be, but I decide that she'll just have to learn to live with it. I can't break my rhythm at this point just for the sake of a little harmless humming. There are other factors too that make it difficult to concentrate, such as the constant feeling of the stewardess's eyes on me or the leaden muddle of tiredness that is still lurking at the core of this broken body. But I refuse to be defeated by these mundane distractions. I redouble my efforts and hunch back over my work.

It's an elusive process, finessing a number sequence of this sort (by which I mean one that exists only as a shallow indentation in my subconscious). It's done on a basis of imperfect retrieval, rather like having looked through your fingers at the sun or something and then just letting the scorch of that image sail past on your retina for a second. The secret to seeing it is to try not to look at it, if that makes any sense.

By the time the wheels are clunking down from the fuselage and I have been told for the second or third time to *please* put my table in the upright position, *sir*, I have got what I am confident is the full number. You know when it's right because it has traces of the thing it represents – in this case that's the feel of her. I run my fingers across the waxy surface of the sick bag, the tiny pressure points of the numbers caressing my skin, and I get a picture of her, a Braille of her essence, if you like. The same as when you might clasp an item of someone's clothing to your face and breathe it in. Trace elements – we leave then in everything, even our numbers.

On the ground, I flash through the checks and barriers. When I reach the train station part of the airport, I plug a few pound coins into a payphone and wait to hear the confirmation of her voice at the end of this number of mine.

When it is her who answers and not some odious stranger I feel so jubilant that all I can say is, 'It's me.'

And before she has a chance to respond, I dive in with, 'Did you get what I sent you?'

'Yes.' It's a very cautious *yes*. A deflating *yes*. Something is wrong. 'Will, we need to talk.'

There is a scratch of interference on the line, almost like something is in there, scraping its legs against the sheer gut of the cable. And suddenly I understand the reason for her caution. Someone is listening. Some alteration has been made to her phone – that would explain the way it shut off to voicemail before. We are being overheard – she has realised this too and is trying to protect me. She is signalling to me to be careful. I wonder who it might be – maybe it's more interference from His army of flunkies, hounding me even in my mortal frame.

'Don't worry,' I tell her, 'I understand everything. I am coming to see you.'

As I say this it dawns on me that she too could be in danger, that the man who answered her phone may not have been known to her. The urgency of this thought affects me like a drug. I could just drop the phone right now and start running to her.

'You mustn't worry,' I assure her, a little hoarsely. 'Just wait for me at work. You'll be safe there.'

'No, Will, you have to listen to me ...' she begins.

'Not on the phone,' I say with such mastery that I actually hold up my spare hand in flat-palmed authority. 'We must speak in person.'

I cannot risk public transport. I cut a warpath through the station and arrive straight at the head of the taxi rank. A few people complain, including one man who looks like he's employed to ensure that things like this don't happen, but no one actually tries to stop me. I get into the back of the first cab, give the driver the address of Natalie's office then snap shut the little dividing window, to leave him in no doubt that the talking part of the journey has ended. I must have time to think.

It is an incomplete silence that follows, punctuated for the first ten minutes or so as we navigate the various roundabouts and slip roads of the airport by that little click that London cabs make when they slow down and start moving again. Click, go, stop; click, go, stop. I suffer a little during this period with worries about Natalie, and indeed myself. About what might have compromised my mission, *our* mission. Everything (isolated colonies of trading estates and soulless office buildings, interminable rows of parked cars) and everyone (people meeting my eyes with suspicion and malice, from behind the windows of cars and coaches, or shining out from the protective seal of motorcycle helmets) seem to churn in the same conspiracy. But then we break out on to the motorway and begin speeding towards that bright, light office where Natalie waits, surrounded by the computers and the wires and the vast storehouse of expertise that will see our truth sent flashing out into the world. Suddenly the oppression is lifted and in its place comes a surging tide of relief.

Sleep tries hard to push me down, but I push back with all my strength, forcing my eyes open (literally, with my fingers). It takes upwards of ten minutes of fast driving with my window pulled down as far as it will go for me to feel like I have won the battle.

I am awake.

'What's that, mate?' the driver asks over an intercom.

What's the point of a sliding partition if you've got an intercom? Unless it's for the money. Yes of course it is. It's for handing over the money.

'What's what?'

'I thought you said something.'

'No.'

He looks at me in the mirror. He thinks that the damage to my nose was caused by a well-deserved punch. I can see him thinking it.

'Are you feeling alright?' There's not the slightest hint of concern in his voice, except maybe for the interior of his cab.

'Yes. Are you?'

'Okay mate, listen: I don't know what's wrong with you, but you're going to need to pay for this fare. You do know that, don't you?' (He actually says, ya, not you, as in donchya, but we'd be here all day if I started trying to do accents – it's hard enough remembering what language I'm supposed to be speaking.)

'Everyone has to pay,' he lets me know in a marginally less strident voice, probably trying to make himself sound more reasonable.

'Don't you worry,' I say, all chipper. I have no desire to argue. 'I've got plenty of cash.'

I tap the breast pocket of my jacket and wink at him. Except I'm now feeling so horribly weary, just from this short conversation, that my wink is sabotaged by my eyes rolling into my head, just for a second, and twisting up my cheeks, so I end up doing what is probably more of a stroke/fit face.

By the time I get a visual fix on him again, he's staring at the road ahead. There's a traffic jam looming.

'Bit of a snarl-up,' I remark. But he has turned off the intercom.

The rest of the journey seems to take an age. It is simply impossible to hold out against sleep for that long. I sink back into the seat, resigned to defeat, and allow my vision to blur into a soft cataract of rest. We slow down, we speed up, we slow down, and so on, as we are jerked along in the faltering fortunes of an enormous traffic jam, which appears in my sleep-defeated mind as an enormous smoking tail stretching out from the city and by turns lashing and dragging through the dirty greenery of the suburbs.

Oh, we've stopped.

'This is it,' says the intercom voice.

I'm lying down so I can't see him.

'What?' I ask, raising my head slightly. My cheek unpeels itself from the vinyl seat cover. It's very quiet in here. 'Why is the engine off?'

'Because we've arrived. This is where you asked me to take you.' He's a bit short on patience, this bloke.

I push myself up into a sitting position and peer out of the window. He's right, we're kerbside right next to Natalie's office. Just along there are the steps down to the canal, where this contract of ours was made.

'So we are.'

He slides back the thing, opening the money channel between us. 'It's a hundred and eighteen pounds.'

I glance at the meter.

'Christ on the cross,' I say (these little private jokes – we all have them).

'The meter's been on the whole way, son. You should've said if …'

'No, no,' I give a generous wave of my hand, 'that's fine.'

I look in Will's wallet. All told, I count eighty five pounds, plus another three pounds and twenty-seven pence in my trouser pocket. I clear my throat.

'Well, this is a little embarrassing…'

He says something under his breath, which I don't quite catch.

After a bit of huffing and puffing, he asks, 'You work here, do you?'

'No, not exactly. But perhaps there's a bank nearby?' I suggest. That probably sounds a little old-fashioned. 'A cash point,' I add, modernising it a bit.

He shakes his head and starts the engine. 'I'm turning the meter back on for this,' is all he says.

Natalie is not at her desk.

'It's going straight to voicemail,' the woman in reception tells me. 'I'll try again in a few minutes.'

She then looks past me at a cycle courier who is waiting to get something signed.

I move my head so it's back in her line of vision. 'No – you haven't finished dealing with me yet.'

'I beg your pardon?'

'Sorry,' I say to her, and then to the guy behind me, 'and sorry to you too, but I was here first. I'd like you to please try her mobile for me.'

'We do not keep a list of mobile numbers here, sir.'

She is the second person within as many hours to have called me *sir* in that same mutedly aggressive way.

'Well, this is your lucky day, then,' I tell her, 'because I happen to have memorised it.'

Once again she looks over my shoulder – not at the cyclist this time but at one of the security guys who has plodded over from the part of the reception where bags are checked and passes are shown.

'There is no need to be raising your voice, sir.' His *sir* is a different kind – it's like a halfway point between being spoken to and being touched.

'Was I raising my voice? I certainly didn't mean to.'

'Can you please step to one side, sir?'

He puts a hand on my shoulder and starts to pull me. I lock my legs in place.

'Don't touch me,' I tell him, a little louder than I'd intended.

He takes a half step towards me so that we're toe to toe. His hand is still gripping my shoulder.

'Are we going to have a problem here?' he asks, quietly, beyond the hearing of the other few people who are sitting waiting for their various appointments.

'I *said* don't touch me.' I knock his hand off my shoulder.

A few seconds later I'm outside. He remains standing at the door as I walk away, making sure that I follow his advice and sling my hook.

I spend the rest of the morning wandering from payphone to payphone trying Natalie's number. Every time it clicks straight into voicemail. I don't know what to do, so I do what I have always done when I've needed to remind myself that I'm not alone. I watch you, and I draw my comfort from your strength. For two millennia, I did this. I eased the loneliness of His disfavour by looking in on the lives of men. For so long I had nothing. Nothing but you.

One woman I see when I'm seated on a bench near some market stalls fills me with such intense emotion that I feel I might burst under the strain of it. She is there with a very old lady who is clearly her mother. The resemblance is unmistakable. The younger woman is already beginning to age in the same way – the stoop that has rounded the mother's back is already beginning in the daughter's shoulders; their hands, their eyes, all of it is the same. Their progress from stall to stall is slow because the mother must move cautiously, and even when they stop to look at something, the younger woman takes great care to make sure that nothing is rushed. She does not choose the fruit herself, which would be easier for her, but instead she reaches for an apple and gives it to her mother so that she might turn it over in her hands, or she selects a small piece of yellow-fleshed plum that the man has sliced up on a dish for people to try. The old woman chews it for a long time with her eyes closed, lost in the past, while her daughter waits patiently at her side.

It is these small acts of everyday love that sustain me as I listen each time to the empty ringing of Natalie's phone, and as I find myself surrounded by the lurid calling cards of prostitutes that are posted up in every phone box. The very paper itself seems soaked in squalor and abuse, but I know better than to risk being seen ripping them down, as I would like to. The kinds of men who put them there would be certain to hurt anyone who interfered with their business. And I am not sure I could cope with that. Not today.

It's just after midday when Natalie finally answers the phone.

'I'm so glad you're there,' I tell her, ecstatic at the sound of her voice. 'I've been trying you all morning. I've just been walking the streets calling your phone. I lost my phone when I was … Look, it doesn't matter now. The important thing is that I've managed to reach you now and …'

'Will, you need to slow down.'

She's right. I'm gabbling. I need to take my time.

'Sorry – I just really need to see you. I came to your work but –'

'Yes, I know. They told me.' There's a distance in her tone that I hadn't expected. The plan we made seems to be a thing of the past. Confirming this, she adds, 'That's my place of work, Will.'

It's an oddly formal phrasing. Once again, I feel the stab of concern that she may not be alone, that others are orchestrating this.

'Look, where can we meet?' I need to get her out of there. 'I don't think me coming back to your office is such a great idea after this morning.'

'I'm not sure meeting is such a great idea either, Will.' It's a little startling, the way she suddenly raises my name like a barrier between us. 'We can just talk on the phone.'

'What? No. That isn't going to work.'

I don't like how this conversation is going, how this whole day has gone. My Magpie never brushed me aside like this. I try hard to make myself sound reasonable, like how I was by the fire in Jersey – at rest.

'Look, there's clearly some kind of misunderstanding. I don't know what it is but all we need to do is sit down and figure it out. We just need to talk it through. If you want me to explain what all the figures mean, I'd be happy to –'

'I can't print any of what you sent me,' she says quickly, like she's been desperate to get it off her chest. 'I'm really sorry but there's just no way. I can't take a chance on material like that. I'm sure you understand, Will – especially not now, after Leveson. I've spoken to the lawyers about it – that's where I've been all morning, in meetings with them. They say there's just no way. Not unless you can prove to us that this data has not been obtained illegally and,' for the first time, she softens her tone a little, 'I think we both know you can't.'

'I …' My vision is going a bit grainy. 'I don't really understand what you're saying to me.' I have to half-bend over and lean my arm against the glass of the phone box to keep from buckling. 'The information is accurate. It's all true. What does it matter how I got it?'

'I know this is a shock,' she sounds pretty shaky herself, 'but there's nothing I can do about it. The legal team have the final say and they …' she trails off. 'There's no point in me repeating myself. Obviously, though, I'm not saying that there won't be a point in the future when we can revisit this. I'm not going to just leave it, Will. I want you to know that. I'm going to keep pressuring for comment –'

'Stop!' My head is reeling. 'Just … just hold on for a second. Please. I can make this right, I can …'

'No, Will. You can't. You're not getting it – this is a detrimental issue for the paper now, after you sent those mails. I have been told not to touch it.'

'But it's the truth! We both know it is. Isn't that all that matters these days?' I can hear the pleading in my voice, but so what? This *is* a plea. 'People publish all kinds of things, everyone leaks stuff. You can't just say you're not going to try.'

'You're being naïve. I'm not an activist, Will, I'm a journalist.'

'Exactly! And you sat there and you said to me … do you remember what you said? You said the paper couldn't run it as it was, that you needed some "hard evidence". Those were your exact words. Well, now you have it. That is precisely what I've given you.'

'I know what I said.' She sounds irritated with me, as if I'm the one who's making this unpleasant. 'I don't like this any more than you do.'

'Then do something about it.' I let that hang for a second or two. There's really nothing more to add. People can't just turn away from their responsibilities. But after a few seconds when the line is still silent, I find myself asking, 'Is this why you became a journalist? To have a bunch of lawyers tell you what you can and cannot write? That doesn't sound much like *Veritas vos liberabit*, or whatever grand motto you have printed on the front of your newspaper. It sounds like toeing the party line.'

'Oh grow up, would you? I have to live in the real world, Will. Okay?'

She sounds really upset. I am too. The receiver is shaking against my ear. Getting into a fight with her is the last thing I wanted. I tell her that.

'Me too,' she says. 'I'm so sorry. I wish that …'

'It's okay,' I just about manage to tell her before hanging up. But the thing is, it's not okay. It's about as far from okay as it's possible to get.

I stand there for a while just staring into space, trying to make sense of what I've just heard. I realise at some point that I'm staring at a postcard touting the number for an escort service. I swipe at it and catch the edge of my palm on something sharp. I watch the blood well out and drip on to the cement floor.

The sharp rapping of someone knocking on the glass snaps me to my senses. I step out on to the pavement, leaving a single bloody handprint on the door. Seeing this, the man who was in such a hurry to get in there thinks better of it and walks away without a word.

'Is this what You wanted?' I shout.

Thinking I'm talking to him, the man quickens his pace.

'Why do You thwart me?' I raise my face to the sky. 'Why do You hate me?' My words have deflated to almost nothing, just a low sob, barely audible even to me.

Overhead, the clouds continue to drift, dark-boned, unmoved by the dramas below.

11

The rest of the day is a blur. It only comes clear to me again when I find myself back where I started, outside the newspaper offices, trying to pick out a window where I might catch a glimpse of Natalie. It is dark now and getting on for rush hour, so I am able to stand here on the pavement without fear of being noticed and chased off by one of their henchmen.

Dumb instinct has led me full circle, to the only real foothold I have. There must be a way for me to persuade her. All I need is to see her, and for her to see me, and hear my words in person, not dying in the vacuum of a phone conversation. Spatial proximity: a core requirement for bonding. Any chemist will tell you that.

This is not her fault, I keep reminding myself. *She knows not what she does.*

I have to wait a long time before she appears. At one point shortly after dark, people were flowing out of the building in a more or less uninterrupted stream but by the time Natalie emerges it has reduced down to just dribs and drabs, sputtering out singly and in pairs. There are even some who are beginning to arrive, ready to start working the night shift.

As I cross the street towards her I am suddenly acutely aware of my dishevelled appearance. I pull the lapels of Will's jacket tight together to hide my rumpled shirt, I even reach up to pointlessly smooth down my clippered hair. It is not until I'm just a few steps behind her and am about to call her name that I realise the man she is walking next to is actually with her. They are deep in conversation. He is quite a bit older than her but is broad-shouldered and vigorous, a real straight arrow. Natalie seems small and girlish at his side. She is doing most of the talking. Once or twice he says a few words to her but mainly he just listens, strong-jawed, presidential in his bearing.

When I call out her name they both turn at the same time. I barely notice him anymore, though – my eyes are locked on her.

'Will! What are you doing here? I thought … What's *happened* to you? You look awful.'

She's right. I caught sight of myself earlier in the rear view mirror of the cab – the bruise on my nose now spread across to my eye, the black frosting of blood around my nostrils. And now my scabby hand, tightened to a half claw.

'It's just a couple of bumps and bruises – it looks worse than it is.' I try to give her one of those closed-mouth smiles that let people know there's nothing to fear – a wonderful relic of your animal past, if you don't mind me saying (*Look, no teeth!*).

But it clearly doesn't work. She looks afraid. Instinctively she puts her hand on her companion's arm and turns to him for help. I look at him too.

Oh no.

He's staring right into my eyes.

Oh please, no. It can't be.

'Christ alive, you *have* been in the wars,' he says, with such a depth of private, targeted nastiness that there can be no doubt.

It is. It's him. It's Abaddon – if that is in fact his real name. Only He knows what he's called or where he came from, the rest of us just know him by his blood-soaked track record and the various *noms de guerre* he's picked up along the way – Abaddon, Angel of the Lord, Malak, Apollyon, the list goes on. The point is he's the Big Man's thug, the one who gets sent in to do the Good Lord's wet work, which means if you're seeing him, you're not long for this world.

Like most people who find themselves faced with him, my first impulse is to bolt, to just turn on my heel and run as fast and as far as I can. But somehow I find the courage to stay.

His eyes are still boring into me.

Look at the state of you. He says this without moving his lips, without altering a single muscle in his face. *You're shaking like a schoolgirl. It's a disgrace. You, my son, are a disgrace.*

He may have chosen a shiny white corporate captain to jump in with but Abaddon is always Abaddon – he can never be fully disguised. It's the eyes. I've seen those eyes before, and once seen, never forgotten.

'Will, this is David Saint-Clair, head of our Legal Department. Will?'

I am only dimly aware of her voice. I cannot tear my gaze from Abaddon.

'Why don't you head back to the office,' he says to her with horrifying gentleness. And as he's speaking these words I realise that it was him on the phone this morning. Of course it was. He's had me pegged this whole time, letting me run around collecting up my evidence, knowing that all he had to do was wait downstream, mouth agape.

As she starts to go, I step sideways to try to grab her arm, to stop her from leaving me alone with my defeat, alone with him, but he manages to get between us and push me back with a sharp, deliberate nudge in the ribs, right between the fifth and sixth – where the lance went into my crucified body – taking his opportunity to remind me of that.

'Any physical act of aggression,' he informs me loudly enough for her to hear, 'will be construed as assault.' He keeps his face turned towards me so that she is unable to see his gloating expression. 'I must warn you of that,' he adds, with a little wink.

And so I am forced to watch her walk away, my only hope

disappearing into what, just a few short days ago, had seemed to me a luminous bastion of truth and integrity.

'Jesus Christ,' he says to me, 'get a grip on yourself. You look like you're about to cry.' He sounds positively delighted at the prospect.

'Stop calling me that,' I whisper, unable to look him in the eyes.

'Oh I'm sorry, painful memories?'

I have seen this happen so many times, people coming face to face with their torturers and finding themselves suddenly drained of the rage that sustains them. And now it's happening to me – his physical presence is simply too much to bear, too resonant of everything he did to me. I am paralysed by it – the dog that tires of barking and just wants to lick your hand. I hate myself but I cannot stop it.

Still I stare down at the ground.

Having a nose for weakness, he leans forward so his face is only inches from mine. 'Don't worry, pipsqueak, I'm not going to hurt you this time. Not like that, anyway.' He takes a step back and straightens up before me, his clothes perfectly creased, not a hair out of place. 'The game's changed – I'm going to shut you down a different way.'

'You'll have to kill me,' I find the strength to say.

He laughs at this. 'Aren't you just precious?' I feel his meaty palm pat my head. 'No, no, I'm afraid I won't be doing anything like that – more's the pity. It's been decades since I so much as set foot on the earth, let alone laid a finger on one of these ...' he doesn't deign to put a word on it, he just gestures in the direction of some passing people. 'Only a halfwit like you would think about jumping in during this day and age.' He chuckles at this thought, shaking his head.

I start to feel some of that fortifying hatred trickle back into me. 'Don't try to make out that He parachutes you in like you're some kind of consultant – we both know what you are. You're a two-bit killer, always were, always will be.'

Forgetting himself, he snatches me up by the throat and rams me against the wall. I look wildly about for someone to raise the alarm but the street is momentarily empty. Then he drops me just as suddenly as he grabbed me, and watches me crouching on the pavement, spluttering and coughing.

'Why would I kill a footnote like you?' He takes a second to light a cigarette and take a long, contemplative drag. 'Because that's what you are, son,' he blows smoke down into my face, 'a footnote, an irrelevance. Do you honestly think He gave a second's thought to casting you out?' He makes a kind of *pfff* sound. 'You are so deluded – it's tragic. No one's been looking at you and your pointless abominations. They've been watching the assets. They're always watching the assets. It just so happened that you managed to bungle your way close enough to something important for me to have to jump in and sort it out.'

Here he breaks off and looks around in disgust. 'Do you have any idea …' the coast is still clear, so he aims a quick, hard kick into my stomach, grunting the word *idea* as his shoe connects with my gut '… how much I hate …' again he swings in his foot, this time on *hate* '… jumping into this freak show?'

I can taste the rust of blood in my mouth along with the bile. My breathing is hectic and shallow. I can hear myself making a little noise as I struggle to get the air into my lungs. I sound like a rusty hinge.

He flicks his cigarette at me. 'Get up.'

When I don't respond he leans down and drags me to my feet. He then positions his body in such a way that anyone walking along the pavement behind us wouldn't properly see me. It would look like we're just standing off to one side, deep in conversation.

From inside the expensive folds of his coat a phone starts ringing.

'Saint-Clair,' he says, all businesslike.

I can hear Natalie's voice on the other end. He keeps his eyes fixed on mine as he instructs her to remain where she is, and tells her that no, there's no need for her to speak to me. He's loving this. He wants me to hear this commanding way he talks to her, he wants me to understand that he has power over her. It's his chance for a bit of payback after what happened last time, when he tried to chase off Maryam as she wailed at the foot of my cross. Even the other Roman soldiers thought he was out of line, in fact they were about to wade in and put a stop to it (because there are always lines that can't be crossed, even on days like that), but as it turned out, they didn't need to. She took care of it on her own. She clocked him a sweet sucker punch right in the throat (a little tradecraft from her bad old days, no doubt), and there was nothing he could do about it. Obviously, though, not something he's forgotten about.

'The way she fawns to authority,' he says to me as he flips shut the phone, 'it's pitiful.'

I feel deeply nauseous.

'You know,' he continues breezily, 'I've barely been off this thing all day.' He still has the phone in his hand. 'First of all there was my call to Ben Zetterling – you do know who that is, don't you?'

I can't think straight. 'I don't remember. Leave me alone.'

'Oh come now.'

'Please. Just leave me alone.'

'Yes, yes,' he says thoughtfully, 'I will be leaving you very much alone, but all in good time. First, though, I must tell you about my conversation with Ben: you see, he wasn't sure who you were either. But don't worry, I soon set him straight. I told him *all* about you. And he was frankly astonished at my tale, the way you had emailed all those highly confidential, extremely sensitive documents to us at the newspaper, and how you had used his email account to do it. That was the part, I think, that he found most extraordinary of all – I had to tell him twice.'

He reaches down and wrenches up my chin, which I had dropped down against my chest in a kind of a daze, just staring at the ground.

'Criminal, he called it. Unlawful. Unbelievable – yes, that was the word he used the most. *It's just unbelievable*, he kept saying to me. And yet,' he gives me a gentle, almost playful little slap, 'I felt bound to point out to him that it was all too believable, all too real. *A very grave matter*, I said to him. It would have been remiss of me to have done anything less. I even offered him my advice on what should be done next. *This*, I told him, *is a matter for the police*. And he couldn't have agreed more.' He lights another cigarette and waves it absently in the air between us. 'I imagine they are looking into it at this very moment.'

He makes the occasional little stabbing motion with his hand, darting the glowing tip of his cigarette towards my face. I can't help but flinch back from him. He seems satisfied with this reaction.

'Needless to say, Ben was mightily relieved when I told him that there was simply no way that a newspaper like ours would even for a second consider the use of such material. I was at pains to impress that on him. That, and the fact that our reporter had in no way, shape or form solicited it. And what do you think she had to say about that, the lovely Natalie? What do you think she said to me?'

He has allowed me to drop my head again. I'm not even going to try to respond, and nor am I expected to.

He just rolls right into it, 'Nothing. Not one solitary word. She just nodded her little head and went about her business.' He bends his knees so he's level with my cowering. 'It's this Leveson, he's got them all worked up about where their information's coming from. Doesn't matter what's true, all that matters is how you got it. It's the lawyers who are piping the tune now, son – you didn't really reckon on that, did you?'

I have no idea what he's talking about. I mean, yes, I remember the name from the television news, and I vaguely recall the man's bespectacled dome, microphones sprouting up to it like tendrils pulled towards the sun. But as to what he said, I couldn't even begin to tell you. It was the kind of voice that almost wills you not to listen.

'It's a shame,' he says, almost too quietly to hear. He seems to have forgotten I'm there. 'It's a shame we had to change everything. It used to be so straightforward ...' He grinds out the butt of his cigarette beneath his shoe '... just snuffing out the difficult characters.' He looks at me again, 'But I don't do that anymore. People don't want the blood and thunder anymore,' he tells me ruefully, 'at least not from us, anyway.' He gives me a strange, almost apologetic smile. 'It ruins it for everybody – takes the poetry out of it. It robs it of that ...' he twiddles his hand in the air '... that epic quality.'

He's contemplating me with something almost approaching warmth. 'You remember how it was – the good old days ...' He shakes his packet of cigarettes at me. 'Smoke?' I just stare at him. He takes one out for himself and pops it in his mouth. 'Yeah, the good old days,' he mutters as he lights it. 'When I think of the number I did on you – remember?' He grins at this shared nostalgia. 'Man, I really worked you over.'

'The ... number ...?' But I only manage to hiccup the words. To my immense irritation, I have begun to cry, and the more I try to stop, the more the tears keep coming, burbling up from a well-stocked source.

His grin broadens until he is positively beaming. 'It really suits you, this new life you've chosen,' he says.

I'm trying desperately to regain my composure but all I can think about is Abaddon, the way he was on that day – the day he did his 'number' on me. I hadn't even known it was him at first. At Gethsemane, at the Praetorium, he just hung back in the rank and file with the other soldiers. I remember noticing him, though, those eyes watching my every moment, and the murderous hunch of his shoulders, but it was only as the morning wore on and the journey to my crucifixion began that he started to reveal himself to me.

I am putting you back. Those were his first words to me, as he pushed that thorny tangle into my scalp. *You know who I am*, he said into my ear. Not a question, a statement. And the moment he said it, I understood what was happening to me. I understood that he would use every second of these final hours on earth to visit unspeakable pain on me. And if there is one thing that Abaddon knows, it is pain. The atrocities he committed at His behest were infamous among us. We all knew that he'd waded knee-deep in gore at the Assyrian camp. In that baptism he discovered the esoteric pleasures of violence. And from there he refined that understanding to an addiction. It became a passion. A holy passion for pain. And so by the time my day came around, he was a past master at it. He manipulated those soldiers with clinical precision, worming into the crawl-space of their minds, urging them towards greater cruelties. Under Abaddon's approving gaze, they tore my back to ribbons with their whips, they battered fractures into my arms and legs with wooden rods. I wasn't even carrying the beam of my cross when I finally collapsed, it wasn't about that – I just couldn't go on, I was hysterical, very near to death already at that point. And yet still he yapped and goaded like a hyena, and still they beat me.

Everyone was afraid of how he looked. That's what was written, how they remember it now, in all the churches and the pictures, making a festival of my beasting. *He did not even look human. Nobody would recognise him as a man.*

So by the time they were driving the nails through my feet, I was just babbling. Anything, anything to make them stop. But they wouldn't stop. Even as my heart surrendered its final beats to my flooded chest, he was still there, conducting the mocking and the jeering and the spitting. God's most decorated soldier, bullying me towards an unthinkable death.

'You're psychotic,' I croak, shuffling backwards in an attempt to get away from him but bumping into the wall.

He nods slowly, like he takes my point. 'And you? What is your part in all this? Tell me – I'm genuinely interested to know what you think you're achieving here, among the people.'

'I'm telling them the truth.'

'Oh, are you really? And why do you think they need to hear this truth?' He mimics my voice when he says *truth*, making me sound high-pitched and womanish.

'I promised them something they can never have, and I –'

'And you *what*?' He snaps, right back up close again, in the space where he likes to be, just inches away from me. 'There *is* no you,' he exhales the sourness of these words right into my face. This time, though, I force myself not to look away. 'None of this, none of anything, is about you.'

He desperately wants to hit me – he is almost quivering with the effort of restraint. I'm just hoping that passers-by might notice it too, the way he is standing over me like a wolf.

'The truth, you spectacularly misguided little renegade, is that it doesn't *matter* what you promised them. No one cares. No one cares what happens to them now, no one cares what happens to them when they die – it affects nothing. They're just weeds. They sprout up, they rot back down. And so *you*,' he grabs me by my shoulders and shakes me hard so my head whips back against the wall 'do not get to start meddling in it. It is not *your* story,' again he snaps my head back, 'to tell.' My ears begin to buzz, still he looms.

He's about to say more but finally someone, a man, has come to help me. He is standing behind Abaddon. He clears his throat.

'Is everything alright here?' the man asks.

I look with plaintive gratitude at him as he dances around through the shimmer of fresh tears.

'Go away,' Abaddon says to him without turning around.

'I'm sorry but I –'

'I *said*,' and this time he does turn around, 'Go. Away.'

The man hurries away.

'You need to learn some humility,' Abaddon continues, as if no one had interrupted him. 'You need to remember who made this universe and you need to let the people remember it too. It doesn't matter that they think they're going to flutter up to this little paradise you've promised them. Let them think it. In fact, the more they think it, the better – you actually did The Boss a favour with that nonsense. It's the perfect outcome – He didn't ask you to lie for Him, but you did, and now that you have … well, let's just say it doesn't hurt our numbers. As long as people still think there's something in it for them, then they still keep Him in mind, they still praise and honour Him for the life He has given them. And by the time they find out it's just a simple switch-off, well at that stage there's no turning back – and besides, they never do find out. The human brain is a well-wired bit of kit.' He pauses for a second, probably thinking about the brains he's seen, spilled out of cracked heads. 'But I wouldn't want to spoil the surprise,' he gives me an evil smirk, 'you'll be seeing it for yourself soon enough.'

'You're a liar.' He's right, my voice does sound small and pathetic. 'He cares, I know He does. Don't forget, I knew Him once too – better than you, better than any other – and I know that …' but the words peter out into nothing, because I don't actually know. I'm beginning to wonder if I ever knew. 'Just because you don't care about anything,' a last thought hisses out of me, 'don't assume the same is true of Him.'

'You, my friend, are adorable.' He pats my cheek lightly. 'Why don't you just go ahead and believe whatever you want?'

He turns to go, then thinks better of it – one more thing to say.

'Oh yeah – I didn't tell you, did I? I also had a chat to your employer, and to those good people at InviraCorp. I just felt it was important for them to know where their leak was coming from. You can imagine what they made of it all. But that wasn't even the best part. No, the best part was when I told our friends over at the Vatican – and, believe you me, we do have friends there. Good friends.' He shakes his head, smiling, '*Dio mio*, what a rumpus. They were *not* impressed – they were even talking about putting some of their *esperti* on it.' There's an almost reverential light in his eyes when he says this. 'Have you ever seen those guys work? So much more subtle than I ever was, and so careful too. You can always trust them to do a good, clean job.'

He holds the barrel of his finger to the side of his head and makes a silent *Pow!* with his lips.

'And fear not, they'll be sure to make it look like an accident,' he tells me as he begins to walk away. 'They always do.'

12

Everyone better just get out of my way. I can't *believe* that not one single person found the courage to step up and help me tackle that monster. Again!

'Where were you?' I scream at some people outside a restaurant.

'Where are they when I need them?' I growl to myself as I jog along the pavement.

Of course, the moment Abaddon was out of the picture and it was just me there, recovering myself, half collapsed against the cold bricks, I had no shortage of strangers coming to check on me, wanting to know if I was alright, if I needed any help.

Too little, as I told them all, and too late. I actually had to shove one woman out of the way as I struggled to my feet. Too persistent for her own good. *Let me help you,* she kept saying to me.

'You were not here when I needed you,' I hissed to her as she tottered backwards from my push, 'You never are.'

'Help!' she called out. The irony of it.

That was when I started to run, a run that has now slowed to an erratic, panting trot. It soon becomes clear that I will not be able to continue any further on foot. My head is throbbing with the strain. I touch my hair and find that once again my crown is wet with blood from Abaddon's beating.

I come to rest at a bus stop. Its destination is obscure to me, nor do I bother to look. I know only that its number, 38, is perfect for the occasion. As I stand there, I become aware of the others who are waiting, a lowing, mulish throng pressing around me, the miasma of their smells, the prattle of their talk.

Breathless from my exertions, I have to squat on my heels. Every few seconds I need to hawk up the bile that seems to be pooling in my lungs and gob it out into the road. Some of them shrink away from me, others barely seem to notice. Their chewing, speaking faces stare with the effort of menial tasks. They witter to each other about nothing, they gawp at their phones in a paralysis of fascination. Nowhere do I see the promise of meaningful exchange. Nowhere is there evidence of real inquiry. There is no penetrating gaze, except for my own.

Disgust makes my mouth begin to work, but silently, not giving voice to the words, just shaping them and aiming them at those who are watching me through the slanted sides of their vision.

You ruined me, I secretly say.

On the bus, I sit alone at the back. Occasionally I look out of the window. I have no idea where I am going. At some traffic lights I see a billboard next to a man selling newspapers. It says 'Father Behind Honour Killing'. As the bus sets off again the vendor looks up at my window.

I burrow back into my seat. I shut my eyes, I shut them so tightly it makes the muscles in my face tremble. Abaddon was right, I am a joke. All these people, it's not truth they need, it's comfort. They reach out their arms, slack-jawed with wonder, always trying to touch what they cannot have. And to think I tried to bring it closer to them, I tried to compass them, teach them a way to love Him and to love themselves. To live in love, that was my dream. And now look – the name of Christ snatched up like a trademark, bartered to a tribe of thugs and crooks.

What an imbecile I have been. To think I was ever moved by the sucking thirst of mankind – to think I actually sacrificed everything for it.

'Stop that.'

There is no one else left on the top deck of the bus except for me and this man.

'Stop that,' he says again. He is sitting a few rows away, turned round to face me.

He means my hands. They are drumming on the back of the empty seat in front of me. I can't seem to stop them.

'You deaf, mate?' He has stood up now, or halfway up – he cannot stand in this space. He is holding a can of lager. He has big square hands and a poorly reset nose.

'No,' I mumble. With great effort, I force my hands under control by gripping the metal rail I have been banging.

Still he stands in the aisle, trapping me like an animal. He is dark – jet black hair, coarse stubble – a *contadino* with murder on his mind. There is a bulge inside his jacket – it can only be a gun.

I prepare myself for death. Once again, I shut my eyes.

'You can't sleep here.'

This is the next voice I hear. A hand is shaking me, not roughly but briskly, part of someone's work.

It is the bus driver. We're parked, stopped for the night, and I am down on the floor wedged between the back seats. My back is twisted somehow. Hot needles of pain shoot down my leg and up my spine as I struggle to my feet. We are in the bus garage.

'I must have passed out,' I tell him. 'There was a …' I don't bother to finish my sentence. He's no longer there anyway, he's halfway down the stairs.

'You need to get off the bus,' he calls up to me.

As I hobble out into the street, still hounded by the pain in my back, I start to notice an arrhythmia in my heart that had not been there before. It occurs to me that the man on the bus must have injected me with some form of slow-acting poison. It happens all the time.

I double back into the garage in search of some private corner where I might perform an intimate appraisal of my body. I end up in an unlocked store cupboard, with standing room only among the mops and buckets and bottles of cleaning agent. I disrobe and by the light of the half-open door I spend thirty dismal minutes examining every inch of my body for signs of needle puncture, rubbing at each blemish, scratching at every fleck of skin, like a witch hunter searching for a mark.

The results, though, are disappointing. Inconclusive might be a better word since my other symptoms persist, are worsening even, despite the lack of any obvious puncture point. The pain in my back, for example, has now spread to my left leg. Each time I move it the sciatic nerve flashes down through my buttock and into the back of my knee. It takes a great deal of time for me to put my trousers back on. My shoelaces I have to leave undone, my socks lie discarded on the cement floor – bending to reach these things is now impossible. Wounded, limping away from there, I know that I must go to ground. I cannot stay out in the open like this.

When I reach Will's flat it is well past midnight. I ask the taxi driver to stay and watch while I unlock the door and go inside. But as soon as I am upstairs, shut away once again in the airless apartment, I realise that this is not the refuge I was looking for. I need to get further afield. There will be others like the man on the bus, and it won't be long before they come looking for me here. The hemmed-in geography of the city makes me feel like a laboratory rat, forced on through the plastic corridors of an experiment, ever nearer to death. What I need is a more natural space, with large, solid houses. A picture of just such a place flickers half-formed at the edge of my consciousness – a memory of Will's still snagged in this flesh – but it's enough. Enough to know that I need to find my way to his parents' house. It's an added complication – just talking to his mother on the phone was exhausting enough – but it's safer than this, waiting here in this cell.

I take something for the pain and I work deep into the fretful hours of the night gathering what I need. The first thing to find is Will's address book, a dog-eared little thing I have seen somewhere. I can visualise everything about it, except for where I saw it. I perform my search in total silence, creeping from room to room, my limp slowly ironing out as the pain killers kick in. Voltarol, this one was – a swart mythology to its name. A muscular, hammer-wielding name. I soon find it and, along with some clothes, other scattered papers, anything really that looks useful, it gets stuffed into a canvas bag.

Then comes a soft knock at the door. I listen, stock still, as this is followed by a gentle scraping in the lock. Someone is trying to pick it open. In a reflex of panic I start to shout at the top of my voice, yelling that I am calling the police. I collect pans from the kitchen and bang them together, advancing towards the closed door as I would towards a bear that has come sniffing around my camp. I stop only when I hear a different kind of knocking, the hammering of angry fists, and the sound of Alice Sherwin spitting my name. I know then that the intruder must have fled.

I remove myself to the bedroom. There, ears covered with a pillow, eyes sealed tight, I wait for the deliverance of morning.

13

As I step off the train a woman who can only be Will's mother waves to me from the far end of the platform. She had sounded relieved when I'd called her from a payphone in the station but that's not how she looks now as she walks towards me. The nearer she gets, the more her determination to look cheerful starts to waver, to the extent that when we actually meet and hug she finds it hard to let go. I can tell that she is crying into the folds of my coat, so I decide to let her stay there for a minute or two. Unlike the city dwellers I left behind in London, the people around us here are unashamedly curious. One lady in particular almost seems to be thinking about coming over.

Will's mother has noticed this too. 'Quick,' she says, sniffing and blinking up at me, 'before Mrs Evans sticks her nose in.'

She doesn't pry too much into what she calls my business as we drive away from the station into a nexus of overgrown lanes, but she does want me to see the doctor. I remember his name from our last conversation – Dr Bundt. She glances over at me to see how this request has gone down.

I nod but continue to stare straight ahead. I can feel her eyes on my battered face, as if she's trying to make it match up to my laconic explanation (*I was in an accident*).

'Oh Billy, you have got yourself into a pickle.' She sounds like she's going to cry again.

Back at the house, though, there's too much chaos for any of that maudlin feeling to last. As we were reaching the end of our journey, Will's mother had said to me that Izzy, Luc and the kids are staying – she'd wanted it to be a surprise, she said, but (again with the glances at my face) she'd decided I'd probably had enough surprises. I had no idea who any of these people were but, now that we're here, I can see quite clearly that Izzy must be Will's sister. Same forehead, same way of standing.

'Good grief,' is the first thing she says to me, 'you look dreadful.' But unlike Will's mother, who is clucking disapprovingly at my side, Izzy seems to find it vaguely amusing. 'Someone obviously doesn't share your unique sense of humour – or did you walk into a door?'

Before I get the chance to answer, Luc (I'm assuming) appears in the doorway flanked by a little girl and bearing in his arms a wriggling baby. '*Oh la vache!*' he says. 'What happened to you?'

I'm beginning to think it might be worth getting some kind of card printed up for me to give to people. 'I got hit by a car,' I tell him. 'It's a long story.'

Secure in the safety of her position behind Luc's legs (which she took up the moment she saw me), the girl announces, '*Je suis dans ta chambre.*'

'Ah yes, I meant to tell you about that,' Will's mother says a little sorrowfully, as if she might now be thinking that her son is the one in most urgent need of a proper bed. 'We're a bit short on space, so I'm afraid you're going to have to make do with the sofa.'

'He doesn't mind, Mum,' Izzy says, still the only one looking at all cheerful in this situation. 'Look at him. He looks like he's been sleeping in a skip – I'm sure the sofa will be a step up in the world.'

And with this she gives me the most natural and warmest embrace I think I've ever had. 'Honestly,' she murmurs, 'what *are* we going to do with you?'

Will's mother, still helpless by my side, turns her attention to the only practical task she can think of. She starts fussing around, brushing the sleeve of my jacket in quick little movements and frowning at the dirt on my shoes and trousers. 'Please tell me these are not your work clothes, Billy.'

She tuts and frowns a little more, then orders me to go and change out of them right away and begins to fret about which dry cleaners would possibly be able to sort out this mess in time for Monday. Clearly though, she's relieved to have found something she might actually be able to help with.

When I get back from the bathroom carrying my bundle of dirty clothes, they have all disappeared into the kitchen. I am back in a tracksuit again (the only thing I could think to pack during my panic at Will's flat) and a pair of trainers from his wardrobe with a trinity of black stripes at the side.

'Why don't you go and relax through there,' Will's mother suggests as she confiscates the dirty clothes from me. She means the room next door, where Luc and the children have also been shooed away to. We're not wanted here in the fug of roasting meat and vegetable steam.

Izzy, who was just on the phone (keeping it cradled between shoulder and ear while chopping vegetables), says, 'That was Dad. He's stuck up at the church. He says start without him and he'll get back as soon as he can.'

Will's mother rolls her eyes. 'He'll be up there all afternoon, in other words. I'll take him something cold after lunch or he won't eat anything at all.'

This conversation makes me realise that I am ravenous. It must be twenty-four hours since I last ate.

'When's it going to be ready?'

'As soon as you're out from under our feet – now get going.' She makes a little flapping motion with her hands.

I use the opportunity of being alone with Luc and the kids to fill in some gaps. I ask the little girl, whose name is Maia, various questions about where she goes to school now, what she likes to do and so on. She's fairly monosyllabic, also I'm not sure what level of French Will is supposed to have so it takes me longer than it normally would to get my questions sounding pidgin enough to be passable, but she does at least divulge that they live in Paris, and that *Papa* is always at work (to which Luc, who is feeding the baby, shrugs in that way the French do). But what she really wants to know is how I managed to disfigure my face.

'*C'est dégueulasse.*' She has climbed up on to the sofa next to me and is scrutinising my scabs and bruises. Her own nose is wrinkled in fascinated disgust.

'Maia!' Luc warns her, then to me, 'Sorry.'

She doesn't back down, though. She continues peering into my face. The self-assumed duty of carrying out this investigation has given a slightly pious set to her mouth. She looks like one of those pudgy cherubim you see buzzing about in Renaissance paintings which, for obvious reasons, I find particularly entertaining. Perhaps my amusement is showing because Luc seems to consider the task of policing her to be less urgent than it was a few seconds ago and has returned his attention to Paco, the baby.

She's asking me how it happened. I can tell that Luc is also listening for the answer, even though he's pretending not to. I wish I could think of something to say that might satisfy them both, but I can't, and nor do I trust myself to try. My mind feels skittish, the memory of Abaddon still prowling there, rattling at the windows like a nasty drunk.

'I should have been more careful,' I tell her. *Sage* is the word I use, wise more than careful. She sighs then slides off the sofa and disappears from the room.

And it's true, I should have been. I have done this all wrong. Every single step of the way has been dogged by mistakes, every action ruled by impulse, every outcome boxing me deeper into this corner.

Luc is hunched over Paco, rubbing the child's cheek, trying to get him to wake from his milky stupor and continue sucking. Every few seconds the tactic works and Paco resumes his gummy squeak then subsides again into sleep.

I stare at them – or not so much at them as at the whole of this irrelevant, nonsensical situation – and I understand that I have lost. This, right here, is what defeat looks like. After all those centuries of gnawing guilt, I have arrived right back at the same fate. Another violent death awaits me, sure as a falling axe, except this time my presence here will not have left the slightest mark. Not one single knot of my bird's nest tangle will have been loosened. Abaddon has made certain of that.

'It's funny.'

'What is?' Luc wants to know. I dismiss the question with a wave of my hand.

'In fact, no: it's hilarious. Hilarious is what it is.'

I'm standing. My back is lit up with the pain of it.

Luc is gathering Paco's stuff together, preparing to leave the room. The baby gurgles in his arms.

'You know what? It doesn't matter.' I try to smile but my face won't move, stolidly representing the part of me that knows that it does matter. A lot. 'It's not like it could have ended any other way.' I spread my arms and let them fall, the international sign of resignation. Broken wings. 'The house always wins,' I tell him.

He doesn't even try to reply to that, and to his palpable relief, whatever else I might have been about to add is cut short by the appearance of Izzy in the doorway.

'So,' she asks brightly, her face flushed from the heat of the kitchen, 'who's ready for some lunch?

The only position that does not hurt me is to perch, stiff-backed and formal, at the very edge of my seat. I am aware that it gives me a kind of priggish haughtiness – a Victorian gentleman dining vastly below his station – and the fact that I have chosen not to utter a single word since we began lunch won't have helped either. But what is there for me to say? I have no place at this table, I am a stranger in their midst. An identity thief.

'Strange,' I say aloud. They stop their conversation to look at me. '*Etrange*,' I tell the French speakers, '*estrange* in old French. It's from the Latin. *Extraneus, extranea, extraneum*,' I add, for a bit of fun.

'Billy, sweetheart, why don't you eat some of your meat?' Will's mother looks like she would give anything, her life even, to see me eat a forkful of beef. 'You haven't touched a thing.'

I had been wrong before – when the steaming plate was set down before me, I found that I wasn't hungry after all. In fact, I could think of nothing more repellent or ultimately futile than to begin shovelling this slop down into the fuel belly of my flesh suit. But now I find myself loading up my mouth with the cold, gravy-sodden beef simply because I cannot bear her to look at me like that anymore.

'Foreign is what it really means,' I inform them through the food, 'not peculiar or weird,' I make a bit of a face for that last word because I despise its mindless dismissal of what cannot be explained. 'Most formally, it means "from without" – again from the Latin, *extra*.' I force a swallow and immediately start loading the fork again so I can repack my mouth before my gullet sends everything back up and out on to the table. As I raise the dripping meat it reminds me: 'There's strange matter too. I bet you didn't know that.' I fill my face and start chewing again. 'It is only stable at very high pressure,' I try to say, but it gets lost in the chew. Only a small shower of gravy comes out.

When the table is being cleared, Maia, who has been told that she must finish what's on her plate before she can have any ice cream, points an accusing finger at me.

'But *he* didn't finish,' her voice is wobbling on the edge of justified tears. She has made the effort to say it in English, presumably so she can include her grandmother in the appeal. The way she says *finish* makes it sound like *fiendish* with the *d* filleted out.

'Yes but Billy isn't feeling very well today, my darling,' I hear Will's mother say from behind me, where she is loading things into the dishwasher.

Luc and Izzy exchange glances. Clearly none of this is in the least bit helpful. Luc tells his daughter in a rapid burst of French just to eat a couple of carrots. Izzy tuts and goes off to join her mother. It seems to me that they're focussing their energy on entirely the wrong things but I refrain from saying so.

Maia, still giving me the evils, nudges her carrots around the plate with the little tines of her fork. When Paco begins to grizzle in his carrycot and Luc's back is turned for a few seconds, I snap my hand across, snatch up two of the carrots and pop them in my mouth. A minute or two later when the opportunity presents itself again, I repeat my act of kindness. They're baby carrots – is that what they're called? The little ones, anyway – so they're easy to swallow quickly and discreetly. Maia, who has been in awe of me throughout this operation, is now looking over my shoulder, where, now I come to think of it, the sound of the two women clearing up seems to have stopped. I look round too (having to rotate my entire body like a robot because of my back). The garden door is open and I can see through the window that they are both outside, standing by the bin store, deep in conversation. Their body language seems conspiratorial, bent in too close together or something, it's hard to define, but more than once Izzy shoots a furtive glance at the house.

When they come back in I pretend not to have noticed their absence. Maia marches up to her mother and presents the carrot-less plate in triumph. I meanwhile try to extract some details from Luc about his work but, given that Will has presum- ably known him for a number of years, it's not easy to find the right questions. All I manage to discover is that he's a doctor or surgeon of some kind, although it's a shame that his specialty is not the kind I need. His words, not mine. As soon as he says it, the delighted commotion of Maia receiving her bowl of ice cream comes to an abrupt halt, no doubt because both women have stopped what they were doing to stare at him. Even Paco has fallen silent.

'No,' Luc splutters, 'I didn't mean ...' But he decides that's not going to be the best way of tackling it. 'What I *meant*,' he says instead, 'was I am not ...' then he fizzles out again. He's getting stressed, he can't find the English for it, he cranks his hand like he's dredging the word from some pit '... osteopath,' he finally says, glancing over my shoulder, presumably at his wife. He relaxes a little. 'You are in pain, no? With your back. I have noticed how you sit, it's all ...' he does quite a good impression of me, bolt upright and robotic-looking. 'But perhaps I can help – just a little. As I have said, it's not my specialty,' working that in again nicely, just to slam the door on any doubt that he might have voiced what everyone is clearly thinking, 'but I do have some knowledge of ...' again the hand, but this time no English arrives '... *les vertèbres*.'

Izzy thinks it's a great idea, Maia does too. My opinion is not really sought. A space is cleared on the sofa and I am laid out there. The mewling Paco is taken away by Izzy and, despite her protests that she'd rather stay to watch her father perform an *opération* on me, Maia is pressganged by her granny to help with the afternoon's errands, not least the task of finding someone to clean my suit.

I am left alone with Luc, who is sitting on the edge of the sofa, telling me what he thinks the problem is. He has already examined me from all angles. Before I lay down, he got me to strip to the waist and stand naturally, as he put it. He then probed various parts of my back and waist, occasionally pushing down on my shoulders, shaking them a little, as if to loosen them, telling me again to be natural. There is plenty I could have said to that, but I didn't.

Coincé, that's his verdict. It means jammed, locked tight, but also, more literally, cornered. How have I done it, he wants to know. How have I trapped this tension into a corner of my body?

'I think I might have slept in a strange position,' I tell him, my voice muffled by the sofa cushion.

He only grunts in reply. '*Ai, ai, ai,*' he says to himself as his fingers discover a particularly taut block of muscle. He kneads it lightly with his knuckles.

'That's it,' he announces, in English, his accent adding a certain authority to the diagnosis, I don't know why. 'Here,' he prods gingerly at my disc. I yelp. He moves on to the floor and, kneeling beside me, he raises my left leg a few inches. I yelp some more.

'Yes,' he says. 'There is no doubt, you have ruptured that disc.' He says *rupture* in the French way, making it sound like a silkier process than the harsh *rup* of the English would suggest, with its connotations of ripping, worse than ripping: a flesh-tear. 'It can happen from tension,' he is explaining, having now moved up level with my head. I have turned to look at him through one eye, the other half of my face still buried in the warm musk of upholstery. 'Sometimes the muscles can just ...' He demonstrates with his hands, meshing his fingers together and slowly squeezing.

'I can give you some tablets for the swelling, and you should put some ice or a warm bottle –'

'Hot-water bottle,' I correct him but he doesn't seem to hear me.

'If you like, I can make a small adjustment here,' he rests his hand lightly on my lower back. 'There is a very simple manipulation for this. To release some pressure.'

Whatever is *coincé* in there, he means.

'Yes,' I tell him, 'please. Release away.'

I allow myself to be delicately choreographed into a position where I am lying on my right side at the edge of the sofa. He is crouching beside me and has brought one of my knees up level with my hip and is holding it lightly in the crook of his left arm. With his right arm he is reaching across me and very gently rocking my body, his free hand resting on the injured disc. He is telling me to relax and to take deep breaths in and out. We continue like this for a few moments, then midway through one of my long exhalations, he forces my leg and hip sharply downwards in a swift, sudden movement. There is a deep crunch in the base of my back.

I make a noise I haven't heard myself make before, almost like a bark. It doesn't faze Luc though.

'Let's try one more,' he says. 'Breathe in,' he eases me back into the sofa cushions, making sure that my arms are right (my right limply at my side, my left wrapped across my shoulder in a loose embrace). He positions his weight in readiness over the top of my hip and starts to roll me back towards the edge again. 'And breathe out,' he sighs.

This time he waits until I am nearly at the end of my breath before pushing his body into the top of my leg and bringing another muffled crack from my spine. It sounds like someone biting down on an ice-cube. It is not as fundamental as the first time but the relief is still enormous. He keeps me in that finish position for a few seconds then slowly shifts me on to my back. I lie there looking up at the ceiling, not really seeing it, just allowing the white canvas of the plasterboard to settle over me, clean and pure as a shroud.

'I feel different,' I say to him at length.

But he has gone. He must have crept away, thinking perhaps that I needed to sleep.

I sit myself up. The movement is free and easy. I try standing, then tentatively rotating my hips, raising my leg – the pain has completely disappeared. It's extraordinary. Luc would want me to continue resting, I'm quite certain of that. He would want me to lie still for a while, because that is what people always want after some adjustment has been made to the way things are. Always the belief that stillness and silence will help the transition of change into permanence – but that is wrong, that is not the operation of the universe. And anyway, I have a reason for getting to my feet. There is something I want to look at. Luc's hands freed more than just my bones, it turns out – they also disturbed certain sensations, memories of a sort, that were hiding in the tissue of this body. And now more are following, all in a rush, like a structure suddenly giving way. Glimpses of the life I stole from Will are flooding into me and now I want to go over there, to the shelves on the other side of the room, and look at the photographs that are arranged among the ornaments and the books. I want to look at those too, or re-look, that's how it feels, at things that already belong to me. Things to which this body, in its own dumb, blind logic, also belongs. This is how lives are stored. Memory is not a data cloud, it is not a mystery abstracted from the self, it is an essence that inhabits us, suffusing the body and shaping us, until finally we take on the look of our life. Our age becomes a physical truth of ourselves – that which cannot be concealed. Even the shadow parts of us, those moments of our lives that we are unable to accept, cannot be kept boarded up. To believe they can is to court tragedy. The unwanted self is restless. It will either work inwards, creating disease, chasing out sleep, or else it will break loose, shocking the world with its strange and sudden appearance. Just as Will's life is breaking out in me now, leaping heroically between my synapses, forcing itself on my attention.

Again that word *rupture*, the French way, comes into my mind. *Cette lumineuse rupture*, such an elegant description of this process, the secret architecture of mind and memory split open like a pomegranate in the sun. I had a lot of time for the guy who wrote that, used to watch him all the time – bow tie, very clear eyes – although his name escapes me for the time being. The point is, I can't be in Will's body and not expect to take on the vestiges of his life. I was a fool to have believed I could.

The first of the pictures I pick up is of Will and Izzy holding hands in a garden, not here – it's the garden in St Lucia. I know that without even having to think about it. I know the house too, up on the brow of a hill – I can see the tatters of mist in the morning, I can hear the squabbling of the birds, I can the smell the flowers – that, more than anything: the rich scent of flowers thickening the air. And the heat. The lawn is a dense carpet of Bermuda grass edged with spiky bougainvillea and the small peeping blooms of crotons. In the far left of the picture the white boards of the house are only just visible behind clumps of coleus plants, their broad, lurid leaves spread like butterfly wings in the sun. The sky is a saturated, tropical blue. Will is just a child here, no more than four or five. He is holding some-thing in his hand, a stuffed monkey, worn and stringy from never being allowed out of his sight. *Chop-Chop* – that's its name. His sister is looking right into the camera, a head smaller than Will, the spitting image of Maia, her skin brown as a nut and her hair bleached white by sun and sea. But Will is looking slightly off to the side, as if someone is approaching, someone his sister and the photographer have yet to notice.

Luc, who must have heard me moving about, has come back in the room.

'You're up,' he says, his tone and expression both suggesting, as predicted, that he considers this to be unwise.

'I am,' I say, placing the picture carefully back where I found it. 'And Luc, I have to ask …' I turn to face him with my friendliest grin '… what *have* you done to me?'

He looks a little taken aback. 'Has it not helped?'

'No, no, no,' I tell him, 'I'm joking – I'm fine – better than fine. The pain has completely disappeared – you're a magician. I'm just saying that something else has happened too. What you did has loosened something, in my mind, I mean.' Again, I'm doing my best to make this sound like a positive thing but the expression on his face would suggest that the message isn't getting through; in fact, this would appear to be the worst news he has heard for quite some time.

'I think you should lie down,' he tells me.

'No really, I'm fine.'

The trouble with these situations (by which I mean those times when other people have come to view you, rightly or not, as slightly unhinged) is that whatever you say to them takes on the air of exactly the sort of thing a slightly unhinged person would say. Such as *No really, I'm fine.*

'I just want to look at the pictures,' I tell him, making it worse.

'I'll go and get Izzy,' he says.

When she comes I find it difficult not to think of her as a child, if that makes any sense. It's almost like we're both still children, the tiny, sun-kissed shoots from the picture. She stops halfway across the room to set down the tray she is carrying – she has brought tea and biscuits. I have a different picture in my hand now. It was taken in the Fifties by the look of it: a man in a suit standing in front of a black touring car. He's wearing a hat like they all did then, and he has a pipe in his mouth, clenched between his teeth. He's not smiling. It must be one of Will's grandparents, and yet I can't seem to place him – I know something about him, though, I just can't put my finger on what it is. It's too quick to grasp, flitting past me like a bat.

'Which one have you got there?' She has walked up behind me and is peering over my shoulder.

It gives me quite a start and I thrust the picture back on the shelf a little too quickly, making some of the knick-knacks fall over. A china toad dressed smartly in a top coat and tails has the delicate stem of his umbrella snapped out of his hand. I start fiddling around trying to get it to stand back in place but it won't balance properly without the umbrella.

'Don't worry,' she gently takes it away. 'My fault. I'm always doing it to Luc – he says I should tie a bell around my ankle or one day I'll give him a heart attack.'

There's such an easy way about her, I feel like I've known her all my life. Before Will even, back in the dark light. That's how I think of it now, my state before this: a dark light. It's nonsensical, I know, but it's the perfect description – I guess you'll just have to take my word for it.

She has picked up a different picture and has wormed in against the side of me, cuddling me with her spare arm, holding the photo up for me to see. It's Will in school uniform, not that much older than in the Caribbean pictures but in a different time, with less sun in him. Two teeth are missing from his smile.

'Billy the kid,' she gives me a little squeeze. 'Come on,' she says, putting it back, not where she found it, just shoved at random among the others. 'Our tea's getting cold.'

We sit happily together on the sofa. In fact, with the possible exception of Luc's medical attentions, which don't really count, it's the first time I've managed to properly relax in the company of another since I jumped into this mess. I ask her questions about life in Paris, about when she thinks she might start back at her work again. I find I know things about her – such as the

fact that she's a translator, an occasional writer of movie sub-
titles, a keen runner – and so my questions make a little more
sense now. That jarring note has gone. She tells me she doesn't
know anymore, that it's been so long since she had the time to
take on any proper jobs, as she calls them, that all her clients
have moved on. It would mean starting over.

'Maybe it's time to try your hand at something else?'

'Maybe. But what? Teaching?' she frowns like Maia frowned
at the mention of her carrots. 'No thanks.'

She lifts the saucer with the last remaining biscuit on it and
offers it to me.

'You can't let me eat the last one, Billy. Please – I'll have eaten
all of them if you don't at least have one.'

My stomach contracts just at the thought of it. That's one
thing that hasn't been loosened by my spine.

'Just because I'm not having it doesn't mean you have to.'

'Pah,' she says, shoving it into her mouth. 'You know nothing.'

We sit on in comfortable silence after that until the sound of
Paco crying in a nearby room brings the relaxed part of our
conversation to an end. She has other work to do besides this.

She takes my empty mug from me and puts it alongside her
own on the tray, then she gathers up my hands in hers and says,
'I'm going to give it to you straight, Billy. If you don't start dial-
ling down the loony stuff, you're going to find yourself back in
that place again. You don't want all that, do you? And presumably it's not ideal for work either?'

I shake my head.

'Well, in that case you need to start doing whatever it is you're
not doing. Do you have the right medication?'

I probably seem a little disheartened at the turn things are
taking. She says, 'I'm sorry to have to pry into your business but
Mum's serious about this. She spoke to me after lunch. She said
they're going to get Dr Whatsisname –'

'Bundt.' I remember him now, or parts of him – his office, his polo neck under his jacket, his habit of saying *Mm* when other people are talking.

'Bundt,' she repeats, 'that's him. Mum says they're going to get him to hospitalise you again, unless you can manage to get your act together. It's too much for them to cope with – you see that, don't you? It scares her, Billy. She'll convince herself that you're suicidal or something – you know what she's like. And Dad isn't going to get in the middle of it – you know what *he's* like.' All I know is the photos I've seen, and the certainty when looking at them that he loves me. Loves Will, I mean. 'She just needs to see that you're on top of things – that's all it is.'

She gives my hands a little shake. 'You can do it, I know you can. You just take things a bit too seriously sometimes – but you can get a handle on that. That's what the pills are there for. I know it's not brilliant taking them, I'm not saying that, but they're all there is at the moment, and it's better than letting yourself get really bad again. You have to help yourself, Billy.'

I smile feebly. 'I know.'

What can I say? Dozens of languages at my command, all of them teeming with words and images, and yet no way to explain myself. Not even to this willing ear.

'Tell you what,' she says, 'why don't we go out for a walk? Mum and Maia will be back soon, then Dad, and then we'll be into the kids' meal times and … Let's just say this might be the last chance we get to have a quiet chat, just the two of us. We could collect some things for church tomorrow, like when we were kids.'

I like the sound of that.

'I'll go and grab Paco – he can come with us in the push-chair.'

I like the sound of that too. I want to savour every moment in the bosom of this family. I don't have long, I'm guessing a day or two, before Abaddon's hounds catch my scent. I have no intention of running from them – what would be the point? They cannot be outrun. But just for now, just for today, I will allow myself to forget about all of that. I will crawl into the nest of this man's life and take every morsel of love that I'm being given, even if it is meant for another. This is my reward, scant as it is. Tomorrow I will slip away and face my fate.

Outside, a thick fog has descended. It has swallowed the lane that leads into the village. There is no sound from the unseen fields and the wood beyond them. We walk through the dripping silence as if through a dream – I make a comment along these lines but clearly it's the wrong thing to say.

'It isn't a dream, though, Billy. This is reality. You need to start focusing on what's real. Use that big brain of yours.'

'I know,' I say again. But it sounds a little weak this time, so I add, 'Your old men dream dreams, your young men see visions.' She's looking at me like it's just some more random nonsense. 'As it says in the bible,' I tell her, by way of explanation.

She has stopped pushing Paco. She reaches up and touches my cheek. Her face is strangely contorted, her neck flushed. She's crying.

'What are we going to do with you?' she says.

I give her a hug and tell her I'm sorry.

'I'm the one who should be sorry,' she weeps into my shoulder – the second person to do that today. 'I'm asking too much. You can't just turn it off – I know that really – I suppose I thought that ... I don't know what I thought.' She pulls back to look up at me. 'Maybe you do need a rest. Some time to get yourself right again.'

'Yes,' I tell her, because it makes no difference what either one of us says. 'I think I do.'

After that we pick up the pace a bit and go for what Izzy calls a proper walk – she needs to work off those biscuits, she says. The fog begins to lift and we notice that many of the hedge-rows we have been passing are thick with damsons or black-berries, perfect for the harvest festival display at the church. Paco shrieks and gurgles with excitement as we return from bending into the bushes with our handfuls of fruit, which we stow in the bottom of his pushchair. He is even allowed to try a blackberry. He mashes it up enthusiastically and lets it dribble down his chin and on to his coat. It gives him a sinister air, I think, like one of those bald devils in a Bosch painting that bites the heads off things. Izzy finds it hilarious, though, and she takes a picture with her phone. I notice she doesn't invite me to be in it but I can hardly say I blame her. The blood on my face is real.

Speaking of which, the cut on my hand is not healing as well as I'd hoped it would. It's not really healing at all, in fact, and now that it has been scratched and stung during our hedgerow harvesting it has started to properly hurt.

'You'd better get Luc to take a look at that too,' is Izzy's verdict when I show it to her. 'It looks infected.'

She has a few scrapes of her own across the backs of her hands and up her wrists, and like mine, her fingers are stained purple from the berries.

'Worth it, though,' she says, as we get moving again. 'It's one of the biggest dates in the calendar for Dad, believe it or not. It's still pretty rural around here.'

'Yes, except it's … funny … because it's … not even …' I'm getting out of breath trying to keep up with her. It's more of a jog than a walk. Paco loves it, though, his *Da-da-da* a ringing descant to the hiss of pushchair wheels on damp tarmac.

'Good God, Billy, when was the last time you did any exercise? You're like a wheezy old man.' But she does slow down a little, enough at least to allow me to get my words out.

'I was going to say, it's not even a religious holiday.'

'What do you mean? Of course it is.'

'No, Izzy, it's not – it quite clearly has nothing to do with Christianity.' An aggressive edge has crept into my voice, which I can hear but am unable to stop. 'It's just a pagan salute to the seasons. It's just typical of the church, taking the credit for whatever they can get their claws into. Like it has anything to do with them that crops thrive or fail. They should go back to their celestial spheres and their holy wars.'

I leave it there but she is already clearly shaken by my little outburst. She pretends not to be, though, and what she says next has that deliberately jovial quality you hear people using when they find themselves in the kinds of mildly threatening situations that make them feel silly for being scared. Confronted by a growling dog, say.

'Okay, smarty pants, *technically* speaking it's not a religious festival. I'm just saying it's still a major bums-on-seats event for Dad. Which is great, right? And it brings people flocking to the church,' she adds. 'No pun intended.'

'It's not a pun. It's just where the expression comes from. It's a metaphor.'

'Look,' she stops again, as seems to be her wont when there's something serious to say. Paco emits a mildly interrogative *Da?* from beneath the hood of the pushchair. 'Don't start getting hostile with me, okay? That's the one thing I won't put up with.'

We walk on in silence, the dusk gathering around us.

'You need to address some of these issues,' she says as we get close to the lights of home. 'It's not enough to just take your pills and go to work and … whatever else it is that you do. You need to confront some of this stuff that is plaguing you.'

'What stuff?'

'Oh come on, Billy, we both know what I'm talking about – the religion, the guilt. We both know that's what set all this off. You felt bad about ditching your religious studies. You felt bad for Dad and,' she makes an exasperated gesture at everything around us, 'for God, or whatever.'

We've arrived outside the house and she's unstrapping and hoisting on to her shoulder the sleeping Paco. 'He's going to be a nightmare at bedtime now,' she mutters, momentarily side-tracked.

Then back to me, 'You need to make your peace with it. That's all I'm saying. You didn't go into the church like Dad wanted – but so what?' She has lowered her voice, not because she doesn't want to wake Paco, which she's in fact actively trying to do, jigging him around in her arms, to his evident displeasure, but because she doesn't want to be overheard. 'It wasn't easy for me either, you know, growing up with all the religious stuff ringing in my ears the whole time. As you know,' she steals a glance at the windows of the house, like she did earlier when she was talking to Will's mother, 'I was no angel growing up. I have guilt of my own, by the sackful, but you can't let it ruin your life, Billy. Do you understand? You have to learn to let go of things.'

'I know.' And this time I really do. I know it better than anything I've ever known.

But she's no longer looking at me. Her face is turned towards a man walking down the lane towards us, the crisp white band of his collar floating in the gloom.

14

Dinner is a far more successful meal than lunch was, due in no small part to the wine that is brought out. Izzy practically has a whole bottle to herself. Even Will's father allows himself to be talked into trying a glass, despite there still being work to do on tomorrow's sermon.

'Cheers!' we all say, glasses raised like nothing is wrong.

'So what's it about?' I ask Will's father. 'Your sermon – what are you going to say to them tomorrow?'

It's an uneasy moment – clearly they all think we'd be in much safer waters if I hadn't broached the subject of religion. All, that is, except for Will's father, who has either not noticed or else simply doesn't care about the tension my question has caused. He seems to be the only one who isn't afraid of Will on some level, of what he might say.

'It's an opportunity to speak about inequality, I suppose,' he says, not seeming hugely enthused by the prospect. The down-lighting above the kitchen table has put deep shadows under his eyes. He looks worn out. What he needs, as Will's mum has pointed out several times, is an early night. But he finds the energy to rouse himself, and as the animation returns to his face I begin to see a resemblance to Will – same intensity in the eyes, same face, just older.

'Scripture has much to say about those who have and those who have not. The lessons of the past have not changed – there is still a great deal for us to learn.' He's beginning to sound as if he may be about to launch into a mini version of his sermon.

He straightens up in his chair and leans forward to better look at us all. Izzy pours herself another glass of wine.

'If Christ were alive today ...'

And that's where I let myself tune out. I simply can't bear to hear what the next part of that sentence might be. I let the unheeded drone of his words carry me along, a weightless spore borne by the river. I remember the professor's house in Jersey, lying cradled in darkness, wrapped in fresh linen, ready for sleep ...

The noise of his voice has stopped. They are all looking at me. Clearly the father, who is looking most intently of all, has just asked me a question.

'I'm sorry, what?'

Will's mum tries to put a stop to it there. 'Let's not spoil a perfectly lovely supper with any silliness.' She looks at her husband. 'Now is not the time,' she tells him. 'Please.'

But he pays no attention to her. 'I asked what you think the right message would be.' There's a challenge in his voice, nothing aggressive, just serious. These aren't topics to be treated lightly, and he can see that I feel the same.

'The right message – what, for harvest time?'

I know, I know – I shouldn't even be engaging with this stuff, it's a waste of my time – but I'd be lying if I said there wasn't a part of me that feels grateful that someone actually wants to hear what I think. It's tragic, really. Abaddon would love it.

'The first thing I'd say,' I tell him, 'is that it cuts deeper than just some rich/poor morality tale. I mean, share, feed, clothe ...' I raise my eyebrows in a *Really?* kind of way '... love enemies, hug neighbours – that's just the surface story. It's kids' stuff.' And since it was me who went round preaching it all in the first place, I feel justified in saying so – although, sadly, that's not really a point I feel I can make right now.

'So what am I missing?' His face is capable of a watchful, almost hawkish quality – the same look that has sometimes surprised me in my own reflection.

Will's mum shakes her head and starts clearing the plates. Luc mutters something about helping and slips away too. Only Izzy sticks it out with us, eyes down, hands in lap.

'You shouldn't be telling them that greed is ruining the world – they know that already. But what they *don't* know – and what you should be explaining to them – is where that greed comes from. You should be talking to them about gold.' He looks like he's going to interrupt but I talk over him. 'Think about it: what is it about gold that has always fascinated mankind? It's something more than just greed. Gold isn't about wealth, not really. It's a symbol, a seam of light in the dark, closed earth. We look up at the sky and we see how very far from our reach are the sun and the stars. And yet we long to be near them, to bring our beastly lives closer to their orbit.' I hear my chair scrape. I feel giddily high above him, on my feet, looking down from the vast height of my knowledge. 'The call of God: *that* is why men burrow into the ground – so they can chip out the golden light of heaven. They emerge from their holes with their gold, their rubble of diamonds, so they can …' I hunt for the words '… it's an attempt to be with Him. You see that don't you? It's a way of showing that we love Him.'

'Billy!' He's had to raise his voice to be heard. I've been shouting. Staring and shouting. I let go of the napkin I've been twisting and sit back down in my seat. All my energy has ebbed away. I slouch forward, elbows on knees. Izzy stands at my side, holding me against her, making a gentle shushing noise.

'Take a breath, Billy,' he says. 'It's okay.'

'No, Dad, it's not.' For so many reasons – because I have failed, because I am reduced to calling this stranger my father, because no one will ever care about the truths I carry – I just let it all go. My back, my shoulders, everything heaves with the force of my crying.

Many hands lead me from the room.

'Gold, Dad, you *must* tell them about gold.' My words are so urgent but they all act like they can't hear them. They look through me. 'Please.' It's Luc, that's his arm I'm gripping. 'Please, Luc.'

He too tells me that it is okay.

'Please,' I weep.

Maia is transferred, limp and mumbling, from Will's bed. It is the mother who undresses me. She cries a little too at the sight of my bruises and the skin drawn so tightly across my bones. The bed is warm and smells of the little girl. In the small circle of lamplight I can see the cover of her storybook, a picture of a rabbit in a swimming costume leaping along a strip of unnaturally yellow sand.

The mother leaves the room for a moment. There are voices in the corridor. I think about what the pages of the book might look like. It is called *Bérénice au Bord de la Mer*. I see colourful umbrellas and sea and rocks and gulls that wheel overhead.

Luc comes in and sits on the side of the bed. He gives me two blue tablets and a glass of water. I prop myself up on my elbow and swallow the pills without a word.

'It's okay,' he says again.

I roll over on my side. There is a small audience of stuffed toys arranged on the carpet, a couple of them have been knocked over, their wide-eyed grins now aimed at a blank strip of skirting board. I feel Luc's weight lift off the mattress.

'It's not gold – remember that. It's God.'

Will's mother is still here, in the background somewhere. She tells me to rest, to save my talking for the morning.

'Just an *L* between them ...' I slur '... the twelfth letter ... His twelve legions ...'

'Try to get some sleep,' is the last thing I hear as the light clicks off. Then the door is quietly closed, sealing me in with the darkness.

I am the first one to rise, awake even before Maia. I feel sick and muddled from the pills, and there's a bruised soreness where Luc did his manipulations. As I begin to move about, the ache radiates from my back into the pit of my gut. In the bathroom spots of light cavort in the air around me. I have to steady myself against the cold porcelain of the basin.

I dress myself quietly in the clothes I was given yesterday and I prepare myself, once again, to sneak away from a sleeping household. In the hallway downstairs a movement catches my eye – through the glass panel of the door I see Will's father at the far end of the garden, bundled up in a coat and hat against the chill of the dawn. He is among a copse of apple trees, gathering the fallen fruit. I try to ignore him but it's no good. I pull on some shoes and go to the garden door. I borrow an old wax jacket that's hanging there – one of his. It smells of damp earth and lawnmower fuel. As I walk towards him, I leave behind me a trail of footprints in the dew-sodden grass. My silvered approach. When I'm just a few feet away, he looks up at the sound of me. There is a curious blankness to his face – the slow, mechanical work of collecting the apples and laying them in the basket has taken him beyond himself.

'You're up early,' he says, finding his smile. It's the first time I've seen him smile. It's a beautiful thing, as natural as the bird-song that is now beginning to swell and repeat around us, pushing out far into the distance.

'I'm not much of a one for sleeping these days.'

'You never were.' He picks up the basket and moves across to the next tree, the last in his circuit. 'Me neither.'

I help him find the best of the windfalls, examining each one before adding it to the basket. If it has been chewed or is too badly bruised, then I follow his lead and toss it towards the longer grass where the boundary fence signals the beginning of the neighbouring farmland.

'The mice will have those,' he tells me.

When we're finished with the apples there are other jobs to be done, and we continue to work in an amiable silence broken only by his occasional remarks about this plant or that. But after a while the spell is lifted and he stops what he's doing to take a long look at me.

'What is it you're so afraid of, Billy?'

We've been tying back the wisteria where it has managed to pull itself free at the side of the house. I'm standing there holding a ball of twine.

'The same thing as you,' I tell him. 'I fear for mankind.'

'That's not what I mean. I mean you, Billy – what are *you* afraid of? In your own life. What is it that makes you keep returning to these same worries?'

Maybe he's right. Maybe we have been here a number of times before. It's the sense I get, from all the talk of doctors and the concern that seems to inhabit every look and remark. Will's is a life that has been scarred by the crash sites of emotional breakdowns. It has left everyone expecting to find disaster around the next corner. But that wasn't me. That was him.

I hold up the ball of twine. 'I want people to understand that this is the true shape of life. They have been led to believe otherwise but this is how it is: tightly wound, turned in on itself – nothing at the beginning, nothing at the end.'

It pains him to hear me say this. I can see he wants to reach out and hug me but he doesn't move. The feeling stays trapped in his body.

'But why do you feel the need to take this on your shoulders? People will believe what they're going to believe, Billy.' There's a hard-won wisdom of his own behind this statement. 'It's not your responsibility,' he tells me.

'But it is. That's *exactly* what it is. My fear for them is more personal than yours. It's in me, it never lets go.'

'No.' This time he does manage to bring himself closer to me. He takes the ball of twine from my hands and places it gently on the ground. 'It's not your battle to fight. You need to concentrate on getting yourself well before you start thinking about everyone else.'

He takes my right hand in his. This loosens another of those memories from Will's body – climbing across some rocks on the beach, his father reaching down to pull him up. *Give me your hand.*

He searches my eyes but doesn't see whatever it was he was hoping to find. 'You're not hearing me, are you?'

'I hear you, but you have to understand that I know things you cannot possibly know. You believe that your church can save people, but I *know* that it cannot. It's not your fault – I'm not blaming you. Far from it – I blame myself. But people need to understand that they have been misled. If they don't, then I'm afraid they will always believe in magic.'

'But Billy, there is a mystery to life. This is God's way. You cannot force people to believe one thing and not the other. They either choose to let the truth into their hearts or they do not. There is nothing that you can do to change that. God gave us all free will for a reason. So that we can choose Him, Billy. That's what faith is.'

I can feel that same pressure from last night starting to build in me again. I have no clue how to release it. I need to make myself clearer. Plainer speech. That was something else I got wrong last time, with Jesus – all those parables, too much aphorism and metaphor. It was too baggy in the end, left too much room for others to stuff their own meanings into it.

'You're right,' I tell him, because it's always the best way to start when you want to show someone how hopelessly and profoundly wrong they are. 'The mystery of God is real – and not just to those of us who have Him in our hearts …' I try to ignore the icy vacuum of His absence at the centre of my own self '… but also for those who deny His hand in the universe. To them, the mystery is just given another name – the unexplained dark matter that ignited the big bang, the elusive mathematics of coincidence and chance … it doesn't matter what you call it. The point is, whether you accept Him or not, it is still a mystery. And I have no argument with that. It is enough simply to recognise that there is a larger hand at work. But what I *do* object to is the storybook of the church – the codices, the bible verses, the liturgies, the promises of more, the fixation with perfection. This is wrong. I'm sorry to say it, and I mean no disrespect by it – but these are all lies, which you have in turn been teaching. And they are corrosive lies. They nourish a belief in magic and miracles, which power the larger machines of misery and conflict.'

He has been watching me with a mounting look of impotent sorrow. To him, I am the man trapped beneath the ice – there in plain view, suffering, drowning, and yet completely cut off. Not even words can carry between us. Despite this, or perhaps because of it, I press harder. I tell him that it is cruel to teach people that the life we have now is flawed, that it is just something to be endured until the final prize arrives. I explain to him how it stops us from loving one another, from loving our world. And when still he says nothing, and all there is to look at is the lonely end of string trailing away from the ball at our feet, I find my words continue to spill out. Because the idea that this is my legacy, that this mess is my doing and will never be put right, is too much to bear in silence.

'I wanted to put a stop to it,' I say, although I am no longer talking to him. I am reminding myself. I am overwriting the sourness of Abaddon and the coldness of His disownment of me. Or at least I am trying to. 'It was going to be my one true gift to the world. It came to me in the firing of that single second, as I watched Will poised to take his own life, and I realised that I could save this boy and that maybe, just maybe, I could use this second chance to achieve something amazing. To end the lies that I began so long ago. When you think about it,' I smile bitterly, 'it's what everyone would expect from me – the alpha and the omega. What begins with me, ends with me.'

But he doesn't smile back. In fact, he doesn't move a single muscle, not in his face, not anywhere in his body. He is frozen with the effort of what he is about to say.

'Billy, do you …'

But he sort of folds in on himself and falls quiet again. It takes a few moments for him to try again.

'Do you think that you're Jesus Christ?' he seems barely able to believe he's actually uttered those words. 'Is that what you are saying to me?'

What would be the point in trying to make him understand? An apparition of this kind is just not compatible with modern faith. The angels and prophets belong to the heat and the robes and the wild eyes of the bible. There is no place for God to move openly among you now. Abaddon was right about that at least. Besides, I can see that Will's father has already turned his thoughts to medicine, and the promise of a more contemporary kind of miracle.

Sure enough, he asks me, 'Will you see Dr Bundt with us? I will be there with you, Bill,' he puts both hands on my shoulders, 'there at your side. I will always stand by you.'

'*Abba*,' I say to him. 'Father. I am so sorry I let you down.'

When the others go to the church service, it is agreed that I should wait for them at home. It is also agreed, in a separate conversation, that Luc should wait here with me. No one actually says this but it is obvious that he has been appointed as the one who stays behind to keep an eye on me.

I find him sitting at the kitchen table with his laptop open. Paco is on a blanket on the floor, gurgling at some blocks.

'Hey,' he says when he sees me. 'I expect you want some coffee.'

Without waiting for an answer, he gets up and busies himself with filling the kettle, rinsing out the coffee pot and so on.

'Are the others up at church already?'

'Yes, but this one was feeling a little grumpy so ...' we both look at Paco burbling contentedly on his blanket.

'Right.' I take a seat at the table.

When Luc comes over with my coffee he turns his laptop towards me so I can see the screen. 'I wanted to ask your advice about this,' he says.

It's the perfect prop, saving us from having to discuss any of the real issues at hand. That conversation will have been scheduled for after the church service – with a different doctor, the kind I need.

'I'm uploading some *témoignages de client*.' He looks at me to check that I've understood.

'Client testimonials.'

'Exactly. For our new medical centre – I don't know if Isobel has told you but I have made a collective with many partners, in the *quatrième*. All kinds of practices take place there and ... What?'

It made me smile, the way he said that last part. Like they've partnered up with witches and palmists and whatnot. Talking with him like this is having a pleasantly relaxing effect after the morning's events. I'm afraid I ended up in what Will's mother termed *a bit of a state* again after my encounter with his father, and it has taken a good couple of hours for me to get myself back on an even keel. It's funny, I've observed it many times before, this vacillation between fear and acceptance, but this is the first time I've actually experienced what it feels like. Mostly I've seen it in people who are terminally ill or who, like me, have experienced the scourge of loss or defeat. Until now, the closest thing in my own experience had been the dread and anxiety that poisoned my final few days with Christ, but even that at its very height lacked the weight of the feeling I have now. It lacked the force of permanence. I guess it's something I'm just going to have to get used to, for what little time there is left.

'Nothing,' I say. 'Just a funny turn of phrase. Carry on.'

He tells me that more and more medical professionals are operating like this, *en collectivité*. They want to market the business themselves, he says, using social media. He's been reading up about it: what, he wants to know, should he be doing to improve his Klout score? Whatever that might be.

'But perhaps this is not what you do,' he says after I've been silent for a while.

'No, no it is – sort of – but really you need a specialist to help you with this kind of detail. Digital isn't my area.'

'I understand – a bit like with me and your back?'

'A bit – except you did manage to help me there.'

'And how is it now, your back?'

'It's sore, but nothing like before, not going down my leg or anything. It's more like an ache – a strong ache.'

'That's normal. It will be calmer in a couple of days.'

A distinct agricultural smell has begun to drift up from the vicinity of Paco, who is sounding a little less content than he was.

Luc gathers him up. 'Time to change I think.'

While he's off doing that I find myself looking at what he'd been about to show me on his computer. It's the YouTube channel for this collective of his, and he's right, there are a lot of different disciplines under one roof, a dozen at least, each of them uploading their own video blog (vlog, I think I heard him call it, although I may have imagined that). I'm surprised to see that there are already several hundred subscribers. He made it sound like they were just getting up and running.

'This is impressive,' I tell him when he comes back in. 'I hadn't realised you already had such a following.'

'It just takes a little effort,' he says, 'but it's possible. You don't have to be an expert …' he looks at me apologetically '… for this stuff, I mean – for the simple stuff. It's so easy to talk to people these days, *en directe*. Everyone is online.'

'Wait!' I touch his hand, which is poised over the mouse pad, about to move us on from this discussion. 'What did you say just then? Say that last part again.'

'I … Which part?'

'You said something about talking to people directly.'

'Just that, you know, you can communicate so much more effectively with people through all of this.' He tilts his head towards the computer. The deep ocean of life into which each of these little machines ultimately flows. The millions of people, watching, waiting, connected by a living plexus of tributaries and streams to the lambent pool of this screen. That is what he means.

'Luc!' I say, too suddenly. It gives Paco a fright. 'Luc!' I know I'm still raising my voice, and I'm sorry for that, I really am, but I simply can't believe that I … 'How? *How* did I not see this before?'

Luc is clutching the child to his chest, saying something to me, something I can't hear. I can barely hear my own voice. A torrent of blood is thundering through my head.

'It's so simple,' I'm telling us both, I think I am anyway, from way down beneath the noise of the blood and the baby and the choking tightness in my throat. 'It's so perfectly simple.'

I grab his arm. 'Don't you see? I need to talk to people, Luc – *en directe*, just like you said.'

'Get off me.' He stands up. 'You're scaring Paco.'

He looks scared too but I don't have time for any of that now. No time for smoothing feathers, no time to be here in this room even, let alone hidden away in this house, watching the days drip out of me until some doctor nets me or Abaddon's lot find me and shut me down forever. I need to get my message out there – me – *I* need to do it – from me to them. What a fool I was to think that Natalie could do my talking for me, when all the time the tools I needed were right there under my nose. Luc is right, it's easy. It couldn't be simpler, in fact. What I have to say is so virulent, so deeply contagious that all I need to do is inject it into the network and let the people do the rest. They will spread it for me. Not even Abaddon can contain the rampant circuitry of the internet.

'All I have to do is get myself noticed.' I say this in a quieter voice. I stop my pacing – I've been unable to stand still during all of this. Even now I am fidgeting, my feet scraping restlessly on the lino. Paco is no longer screaming and is now hiccupping into Luc's shoulder. 'I just need to find my miracle.'

It's just an expression – I don't mean an old-school *ta-daaa* kind of miracle. There's no room for those moves anymore, that ship sailed long ago. It's no longer a requirement of modern life to be able to explain what you see. No, what I'm talking about is a statement, a gesture really – one powerful gesture that cuts to the heart of the matter. That's all it takes. It's all it took the last time, too – my so-called miracle in Capernaum, the one that got the whole show started, that was nothing but a piece of opportunistic grandstanding. It certainly wasn't planned, and it certainly wasn't a miracle per se (not like my later stunts, anyway). Capernaum was just supposed to be a quiet backwater for me, somewhere I could take my time and get a feel for things fresh off the jump-in. It was the last place you'd expect it to kick off. I really loved it there, the cleansing blue of the Sea of Galilee working through the dust, and the fetid heaviness of the marshes behind it, deepening the air even up in the streets away from the shore. It was my first taste of earth, and it was beautiful. My plan was to take it slow, to get acclimatised, but I quickly discovered that life has a habit of getting in the way of such plans. I'd only been there a day or two and I was working a small crowd in the temple, just getting my eye in really with some light preaching in what I'd thought was a pretty inconspicuous corner, when some frothing lunatic decided to start shouting at us. I mentioned before how crazies are always first to get the whiff of us, and this one got himself properly worked up, ranting away about how I'd come to destroy them all. It was really distracting, and my little flock, try as they might, were finding it hard to block it out. Some of them were even starting to give me sceptical looks. I had to do something – if you don't snuff out these hecklers immediately it just emboldens them – so I stopped what I was saying and put the stare on him, one right from me, from behind the eyes if you see what I mean. It stilled him like a child, he just stood there gawping at me, then I barked at him: *Poq!* Get out! It just came to me on the spot – pure grandstanding, of course. Aramaic is the perfect language for that sort of thing, the word bursting from my lips and bouncing off the stone walls. The effect was instantaneous. He set about himself in a seizure, pulling at handfuls of his hair and gnashing and howling; then he was quiet as a lamb. That's what I called him when I went to crouch by him (as soon as I was sure it was safe): my lamb.

I'll be honest – I was amazed at how it went over with the others. They were so impressed they were practically wetting themselves. And that was when it hit me – they were ready. I mean they were *ready* – they were crying out for a messiah, the real deal, not just another shouty prophet. It was my moment – right time, right place. You could just feel it in the room: this thing was going to be massive. All I had to do was rise to my feet looking all drained and exhausted from my saintly exertions, mumble a couple of words about unclean spirits then make my way slowly towards the exit. For the briefest moment I stood framed in the doorway. My robes, I dare say, billowed about me in the blazing sunlight like golden raiments.

And there it was: job done. After that there was no turning back.

I take one last look at Luc. 'Thank you,' and I really do mean it. 'Thank you for this. You've made it all so clear: I just need to find my day in the temple,' I tell him, 'my way of making myself heard above all the …' I look at his laptop '… all the chatter. A modern miracle, Luc – that's what I need. I need to find a modern miracle.'

As I climb the stairs I see that it has started to rain. Thick sheets of water run across the panes of the window making the daylight tremble as it enters the house. I look everywhere for my work clothes. I'm not exactly sure yet what needs to be done but I do know that, whatever it is, it will require me to look the part. I eventually find my suit in its dry cleaner's cellophane hanging on the door of Will's parents' bedroom. There are socks in the drawer and a blue and white checked shirt hanging in the wardrobe. His father's shoes are a little too tight but I take those anyway – my own are nowhere in sight. At one point I hear a phone ringing and I follow the sound to the room at the top of the house where Izzy and Luc are staying, now with both of their children also squeezed into the small space. Izzy's phone is there, charging. Luc is trying to call her. I unplug the phone and slip it into my jacket pocket. Sorry, Izzy, but my need is greater than yours.

Downstairs I ignore everything that Luc says to me as I hunt around for the keys to one of the cars parked in the driveway.

I empty the contents of a china bowl on to the floor. There – I pick up the key and aim it through the window and press. The white Ford blinks its lights in reply. I was brought here in the other car, this one must be his father's.

'Is there anything I can say to stop you?' Paco is asleep on his shoulder, his fat little lips parted in oblivion.

I shake my head. 'Just tell Dad I'm sorry about borrowing the car.'

'Maybe you should tell him yourself.' He is looking past me, through the window. At the end of the lane is the bedraggled outline of Will's family, the adults huddling in the shelter of a single umbrella, Maia skipping ahead.

I run outside and dive into the car. I check my pockets. I have Will's wallet but the keys to his flat must still be somewhere inside. It doesn't matter, I won't be going back there anyway. I turn the key in the ignition. Above the sound of the engine I hear my name being called but I do not look. I rest back into Will's body and let his memory do what needs to be done. His foot presses down on the clutch, his hand slips the car into gear and slowly, smoothly he steers us out on to the lane, turning away from where his sister is running through the rain towards the car, waving her arms, and where his parents are standing, further back in the greyness, holding tightly on to their grand-child as they watch me slip away.

15

Driving is a lot easier than I thought it was going to be – the secret is not to concentrate too hard. If I just let myself zone out and let Will do the work, everything goes smoothly. The only problems occur when I try to focus my own attention on the task – that's when the foot on the accelerator becomes uncertain and the car begins to lurch or when the hands that are steering start to drift and send the wheels rattling across the hard shoulder. But by and large, the journey unfolds without a hitch. I decide to leave behind the train station and the village and the fields and allow myself instead to be pulled into the broad artery of motorway that runs to the heart of London. Signs tell me that there are less than a hundred miles left to travel. Trucks and cars hiss past me sending their spray across my windows. The wipers swish peevishly, never a second's rest from it. The sound is hypnotic, *creak-creak, creak-creak, creak-creak* …

The sky above me is blue and cloudless, the sunlight is on my face, the rigging of Peter's boat creaks with the rise of each wave …

The blare of a horn brings me kaleidoscoping back. My eyes snap open, my hands wrench the car back into line. My heart pounds, and what little is in my stomach threatens to rise. Up ahead I see the lights of a service station. With trembling hands I guide myself off the road and to a juddering stop in one of the parking bays. I rest my head on the steering wheel.

Izzy's phone, which has rung several times already, is ringing again now. I take it out of my pocket, the name *Mum & Dad* is on the screen. When it rings off I scroll through the other missed calls – all the same number. I would have answered if I could have been sure it was Izzy, I want to speak to her, tell her not to worry, that it's for the best like this. Something tells me she would understand. But I can't risk a conversation with one of Will's parents. There's no knowing where that would end. They would almost certainly get the police involved, if they haven't already, and that would be unnecessary interference with … whatever this is that I'm doing.

I decide the best thing to do is to send Izzy a quick email. In the end, though, there's nothing quick about it. It's not the logging in to Will's account that slows things down (those details, like so many others from his life, just seem to be there in my mind now), it's the fact that I keep losing the thread of what I want to say. Sitting in the cramped, cold seat of a car with rain thudding down on the roof is not the perfect setting for composing a farewell letter to someone you barely know and yet for whom you feel a deep stirring of love and loyalty. Also, it doesn't help that there is a whole host of unread emails to distract me. Chief among these is a burst of three messages sent last night and earlier today from Natalie, urging me to call her as soon as I can. At first I'm reluctant – part of me sees Abaddon behind it, perhaps wanting to get a fix on my location somehow – but curiosity soon gets the better of me. Besides, I seriously doubt Abaddon is still wasting his time with Natalie. For him, that loose end will be well and truly tied off.

I squint out into the murk. It's only three o'clock but already the dusk is preparing to come. Except for my car and a few other empty vehicles, the place seems deserted.

I dial Natalie's number. When she answers I ask her right away if she is alone. It's an odd question but it's the first thing that comes into my mind.

'Will? Is that you?'

'Yes.'

'Where are you calling from?'

I don't like the sound of that. 'Why? Why do you want to know?'

'I don't know.' She sounds tired. 'I just didn't recognise the number. And I've been trying to call you.'

'I lost my phone – remember?'

She's breathing heavily. 'Well, thanks for calling. I just wanted to talk to you. I thought perhaps we could meet up and –'

'No. I mean, thanks but I won't be able to do that, Natalie. I'm sorry. I need to try to keep a low profile for a while.'

'I understand.' There's a long pause. 'I can't tell you how awful I feel. I just didn't want to leave it like …'

Is she crying?

'Are you crying?'

'No.'

Er yes, yes she is.

'Look, Will, I need to tell you something. David is really going after you, he's contacted your boss and they're going to try to –'

'Hang on a second. Who?'

'David. Our head of legal, David Saint-Clair.'

Oh, you mean Abaddon. 'Okay,' I tell her, 'with you now. Sorry – carry on.'

'He's really got the bit between his teeth,' she says, and the way she says it tells me all I need to know about how he will have chewed her up and spat her aside. 'He's going after you, Will, and there's nothing I can do about it. I'm really so sorry.'

This time there's no pretence about the not crying.

'It's okay. Listen, I mean it – it's not your fault.'

'It's nice of you to say that but it is my fault, Will. You were my source and I've let you down.'

'No you haven't. I knew what I was getting myself into.' A lie, but then even if I had known, would I have done it any differently? Of course not. I've always been heading here, to this moment. 'Look Natalie,' I tell her, suddenly invigorated. 'He's just a nasty piece of work. Forget about him. I can take care of myself.'

This seems to decide her on something.

'Listen,' she tells me, quickly and quietly, which makes me wonder again if she may not be alone. She never answered my question. 'Don't ask me how I know this but he's meeting the people from your work tomorrow morning, he's going to hang you out to dry. But maybe if you got in there first, maybe if you came clean with them and explained your reasons, perhaps you'd still have a chance at … I don't know, a chance anyway.'

The final lines are being drawn, right before my eyes. What was just a compulsion, to run, to act, is now taking its shape. She is giving me my chance to make a miracle.

'When?'

'Eight o'clock.'

'Do you know where?'

'Some hotel in Marylebone, The Drum I think it's called.'

Again, I push from my mind the thought that she may not be alone, that this may be some kind of trap. Paranoia is a rot, I remind myself. You must cut it out before it spreads. I trust her. I choose to trust her. 'Thank you, Natalie. You have no idea how much this helps me.'

Even so, the moment the conversation is over I dismantle Izzy's phone and I walk through the rain scattering its parts in the sodden bushes. The wafer of the SIM card I place on my tongue. Drops of rain fall from heaven into my mouth.

'This is my body now.' I swallow it down into my gut, where it will be scoured of all memory.

Everything must be left behind me. They'll be looking for the car too.

At the lorry park on the other side of the service station a man is walking back towards his truck.

'Excuse me, mate.'

He looks at me once and carries on walking.

'Please,' I call after him. 'I've been on my stag do.'

He stops and halfway turns back.

'They drove off without me. I haven't got a phone, car, nothing. It isn't funny.'

Not that he's laughing, or even smiling, but I can see a little chink there. He's thinking about it.

'Where are you headed?'

'London,' I tell him.

'My depot's in Canning Town.'

'That'd be great.'

'Come on then if you're coming.'

As I climb up into the passenger side of his cab, he asks me, 'You're not going to puke in here are you?'

'No, I'm fine.'

'You don't look fine.'

'Trust me,' I tell him. 'I'm a whole lot better than I was.'

However much it hurts. That's what I wrote to Will's sister in the email I sent. I told her, however much it hurts, I will cut the cord that binds us to the false promises I gave humanity two thousand years ago. It was pretty grandiose stuff when I think of it now, and obscure too – *the impossible beanstalk*, I remember using that phrase at one point. But what can you do? These things come out how they come out. I wasn't thinking straight. What I *should* have said is we're all God's children. That would have made more sense to her, instead of my prattle about the wrongful elevation of Man. I should have just said that every-thing, every living thing, on the ground, in the sky, hiding on the ocean floor, invisible on the head of a pin – all of it is God's work. Not better, not worse, none more or less valued than the next: it just is. That's how He sees it – it's how they all see it. Habitat, consumption, decay – reload, release, repeat. There's no ace in the hole, no *deus* in the *machina*. There's nothing more to know.

But I didn't say that. I just waffled on. Which is precisely why, from this moment forth, I need to keep my big flapping trap shut. *I am afraid of the foolishness I have spoken*, as a great poet once said, *I must diet on silence; strengthen myself with quiet.* So that when the truth does come, it will not be from me. It will jump, quick and ugly as a toad, from the mouth of another. My only task will be to capture that moment, that miracle, and show it to the waiting world. I will transfuse it into the internet, this web that has become so much a part of you, that supports you, natural as the spider's silk – you must stop regarding it with such suspicion. You need to rid yourselves of this fear of technology – machines do not threaten you, they *are* you. Trust me, I saw how it started. It was no different then. I watched the dream of the ape slowly take shape, get pushed ashore by systems that were creating a network of unknowable life, just as you are now – bacteria, energy invisibly budding, blind life congealing to the first spasms of tissue. Not Christ's way, not science either, not humanity, whatever that is, or progress, not any of the vainglorious markers you care to put down, just life. Just God's work. And so it will continue, with or without your consent. So just please, for the love of God, make your peace with that. Let me help you to make your peace with that. Let me show you how to let go.

'You don't know what robotics or nanotech or genetics or any of that stuff will bring, any more than the furiously multiplying microbes knew what would crawl from the primordial sea.'

Boom! So much for keeping my mouth shut. I mean, I will keep it shut, when it counts, but I just couldn't hold that one in.

We've been driving for well over an hour and I've not said a single word. It's been building up. We're nearly there now, in fact – through the Blackwall Tunnel and into London proper.

'Are you talking to me?'

We are the only two people in the cab of his truck, of course, but you can see where he's coming from.

I want to tell him that no, I'm not really, I'm talking to all of mankind. But as discussed, I need to be holstering up that kind of rhetoric.

'Sorry, it just popped out. I don't even know what I said.'

'You just told me to fuck off, mate, the fancy way – go forth and multiply. That's what I heard.'

'No, no, no,' I reassure him jovially, 'A simple misunder-standing.' I wriggle up from my slump – ow, ow, ow, my back. I'm beginning to wonder if I should have been quite so grateful to Luc for whatever it is he did there. 'That's not what I was saying at all.'

'I thought you didn't know what you said.'

'Yes, that's true. Sorry – let's start again: I apologise for what-ever I said. No offence, okay?'

'What happened to your hand?'

I'm holding up my hand, the cut one.

'I lashed out at a prostitute's business card and cut myself on a nail.' I can't be bothered to lie anymore, about anything. 'It's an ironic stigmata,' I add to that end, 'probably put there by those who are able to influence such things, as a pointed reminder of my inept piloting of Jesus Christ towards doom and futility.'

'Right, that's it,' he says, and stops his truck with an almighty hiss of the brakes.

We're at the side of the road in a part of London I don't know. He opens the glove compartment and produces a wooden club shaped like a fat exclamation mark. It's about a foot long and looks like it always has and always will belong there in his fist. Cars are already hooting behind us. The truck is too big to go around.

'Get out.' He's admirably succinct in word and gesture.

As the truck pulls away and the queue of cars behind it is once again free to get going, one of the drivers is so angry at having been made to wait that he bothers to wind down his window and say the word *wanker* to me as he drives past.

It's a bit of a rude awakening. I resent being outside and noticed again, in the drizzle and the dark. I liked it in the bubble of his truck, lulled by the radio and the occasional sound of his unanswered questions as I watched out of the window. All those vehicles, going this way and that. But now I feel raw again, on my toes so to speak. Aware of the threats. Not for the first time, I find myself thinking about Caravaggio – I watched him closely during those final few weeks of his life – and I do *not* want to get sucked into the mistakes he made. He was so paranoid about who may or may not have been about to emerge from the shadows and stab him that in the end he was completely incapacitated. He went into defensive lockdown. He'd take a swing at anything and everything. Production ground to a halt. But not me. I am most definitely not going down that road. I've got too much left to do.

'Man up!' I tell myself in no uncertain terms. 'Man up and grow a pair.'

These are just expressions you overhear, of course. They always sound so much better coming from someone else. That truck driver, for instance. He'd be able to pull off a very convincing *Man up*, I reckon. But you work with what you've got. I'm a lover not a fighter (as I made a point of telling people the last time around; I even said it to one of the soldiers who was banging a spike through my feet – come to think of it, I bet he'd have been able to muster a solid *Man up* as well).

'Wait!' And I do, as I say it. I stop on the pavement, in the dark drizzle. 'This is actually a very important point.' I can talk to myself out loud like this because there's no one else in sight. It helps to focus the mind, I find, if you actually say the words. 'I'm going to need to get a lot tougher if this next part is going to work.' I wince at the memory of my performance last time I saw Abaddon. 'A *lot* tougher.'

'This is the time to be brave,' I remind myself as a bus, lit up and empty, comes swaying past.

'I am going to need a gun.' These words are more of a surprise, popping up on me out of nowhere, but no less true for it. Because I mean, let's face it, of *course* I'm going to need a gun. Look at me. How am I going to take charge of anything in this state? I will need an instrument of persuasion if I am to be taken seriously. A nine, a piece, a strap … it seems like only yesterday you were calling them barkers and persuaders. I find it very charming, this habit of euphemism. It's a crucial part of the deception. If you don't quite say it, have you quite done it? Anyway, call it what you will, I need one – and the sooner the better. It'll be morning before I know it. There's no more time for pussy-footing around. I need to start attacking this situation.

The question is, where to find one. I'm certain that Will doesn't own one. If his flat was messy when I first saw it, it's nothing compared to the condition I left it in after my various ransacking searches, and I certainly didn't see any guns. But not to worry: after all, this is London, one of the world's great stews of urban life. Iniquity cannot be far away.

I look around. Nope, it can't be far away at all.

16

It was in fact a little farther than I'd thought (nearly three hours of continuous walking, to be exact), but enough griping. I'm here now.

By *here* I mean a place called Medway Bounds, a dilapidated housing estate off Mile End Road. It sits louring among streets of squat, dirty houses, the tall pillars of its high-rises punctuated with hard little squares of light. Loveless, soulless, hopeless – it must be well stocked with firearms. Trouble is, it's not really the kind of place you can just stroll into without first getting the lie of the land, which is why I've spent the last hour shivering in a hidden corner, keeping an eye on the few comings and goings that are still to be seen at eleven o'clock on a rainy Sunday night.

I think I've more or less got the gist of it, though. I have a decent view of what's what from my hidey hole (a dark and filthy corner at the entrance to a raised walkway between the two main blocks). At first the place seemed devoid of life, but after a while I started to notice a few little whistles and noises from the balconies above. These, I realised, coincided with the times when a car would drive up to the interior courtyard, just below me. Whenever one of these cars pulls up, a guy comes loping, hood up, head down, from the graffitied porch and across the rectangle of patchy grass. After a short conversation at the car window, he then gestures to another and the car drives off around the back, to a part of the building I can't see, where presumably the transaction is made. I'll be honest: the details of exactly how it works are a little unclear to me, but it's really not the point – after all, I'm not here to buy drugs. What is important is the scout who shuttles round on his bike. Him I have watched like a hawk. He whips round the perimeter, pedalling like fury on his little bike with its pushed-down seat. Each circuit takes him about ten minutes by my reckoning, after which he reports back to the guys at the porch, then sets off again. It's quick work as there's very little for him to see, just the sheer boundaries of buildings and concrete overpasses, every door shut fast. I'm the only one stupid enough to be out, and he most certainly hasn't noticed me, even though his journey takes him within about two feet of where I'm sat.

The next time he comes past – that's what I told myself last time he flashed by me. And now here he comes. It's time. Just as he's about to draw level with me I pounce. I charge out soundlessly and at speed, shoulder first, and bang straight into the side of him. It sends him clean off the bike and into the wall. When he looks up at me I see he's bleeding from the mouth. He can't be more than twelve years old.

'I ain't got no gear on me, blud,' is the first thing he says.

'I'm not interested in that,' I tell him.

This is worrying and confusing news, and both of these emotions are more than apparent in the look he's giving me. What he's most focussed on, though, is the syringe. Did I mention the syringe? I found it (that's to say, I nearly spiked myself on it) when I first settled into my dirty corner, and I've been hanging on to it ever since. I thought it had potential as a makeshift weapon but, looking at this child before me, I feel suddenly ashamed of that thought. I let it drop to the ground.

The boy, who has been watching my face during this thought process, looks about ready to cry.

'I'm not going to hurt you,' I tell him. 'If you do what I say,' I feel compelled to add. After all, I am supposed to be threatening him. It requires considerable effort for me to manufacture the air of menace that comes so naturally to Abaddon and others like him. But the boy doesn't seem to notice. He still looks terrified. My appearance, together with the fact that I have just knocked him off his bike, are reason enough.

I drag him to his feet and march him back the way I came when I first got here. We leave his bike where it is, but my abandoned syringe I kick off into the shadows where it belongs. I tell him not to worry, that he is not in any danger, but he doesn't seem to hear. He keeps daubing at his mouth with the sleeve of his sweatshirt.

When we get back to the front of the estate, I have a quick look for convenient rat runs into which we might safely disappear. A nearby stairwell suggests itself. Without me even telling him to, the boy enters the code to get us in. I tell him to be quick. We run up all the flights of stairs. The door to the roof is broken and therefore permanently ajar. Just another few steps take us to the very top of the building.

None of the lights work up here, which leaves us in a twilight of litter and broken glass. A few shouts and calls from the courtyard below suggest that the boy's absence has already been noticed. I hold a warning finger to my lips. I have a quick peek over the chest-high wall at the edge of the roof. I can't see where any of the noises are coming from, but then you never can – that's the point.

I tell him to empty his pockets on to an old mattress that has been shoved into the corner by the wall – I shudder to think why. He has a cheap, disposable mobile phone, which I discard, a pack of gum, which I let him keep, but no knife or other kind of weapon. Good to know. It would be so sad to get stabbed by a child.

I ask him his name. It's Joel.

'Well, Joel,' I say thoughtfully, 'you and I are going to have a little talk, and when we do, you are going to tell me what I want to know. If you hide anything from me, or try to lie to me, I will know. And I will not be happy.'

He nods quickly.

'I need a gun,' I tell him, plain and simple. 'And I know that at least one of that lot down there will have one stashed away somewhere. So you, Joel, are going to tell me where that somewhere is. And then you're going to take me there, via a route that won't get us seen, by anyone.' I leave a meaningful pause. 'I don't want to hurt you, Joel.' Which, of course, is true, but I say it in a way that makes it sound like I definitely would if I had to.

It does the trick. He just comes straight out with it. 'Devan got a strap, innit.'

'Okay. So where do I find this Devan?'

'He don't keep it on him,' he glances at the wall beside us, leaving me to assume that Devan is currently out and about, conducting his business. 'One of the youngers holds it for him. In de yard we jus by.'

'What number?'

'I don't know no number, man. Jus know the one it is.'

I'm probably looking sceptical or homicidal or something because he quickly tells me everything else he knows in a bit of a rush. The boy's name is Blair. And Devan, apparently, is something of a 'bad man'.

'Sounds perfect,' I tell him.

He shakes his head.

'Dis butters,' he mumbles. 'Gonna get plain ugly.'

Suddenly, his mobile phone starts ringing. It sounds incredibly loud in this remote little corner, so I snatch it up as quickly as I can and shove it underneath the mattress. It continues for a few more muffled rings then stops.

Joel is shifting around from foot to foot. I've put him in a horrible situation, I can see that, but there's no other way to get this done. And anyway, I have an idea how I'm going to make things right for him. But first things first.

'Don't worry,' I tell him with a steering hand in his back, getting us started towards the stairs, 'you're doing really well.

You're just going to have to trust me. I know that's not easy but it's the only choice you have.'

We take a long way round. Whenever we get to a potentially tricky point in our journey Joel scouts ahead then motions me forward with militaristic hand gestures. All that sitting around playing *Call of Duty* is suddenly paying off for him.

Blair's flat is on an internal corridor, as opposed to one of the balcony 'walks' as Joel calls them. The strip lights above us must have got wet or shaken loose a wire because they are guttering like candle stumps, plunging us in and out of darkness. Joel is not keen on the effect, it's playing on his nerves. By the time we arrive at our destination it's all he can do to stand there and stare at the door.

'This it?'

'Yeah.'

'What's waiting for me in there, Joel?'

'Jus Blair, innit. And his sister.'

'And the parents? Where are they? It's the middle of the night.'

'His mum's working.'

When I ask about the father, all he says is 'in the pen', whatever that's supposed to mean. Prison, presumably.

'Okay, go on then,' I wave him on, 'ring the bell.'

It's a teenage girl who comes to the door. She's wearing a towelling dressing gown. Her hair is flattened and bunched up on one side. We've clearly woken her.

'Sorry,' I tell her, 'but we're coming in.'

I shove Joel in front of me and follow him inside, shutting the door quickly behind us. Understandably she kicks up a bit of a fuss. As she's demanding to know what the hell's going on, I'm readying myself for the sudden appearance of her brother, maybe even brandishing the gun in alarm. But no one comes.

'Where's Blair?' I ask her.

She stops her protest immediately. The mere mention of his name is enough to explain why a stranger has come barging into her home at this hour.

'He's not here.' She looks at me, or rather, she looks at my suit. 'You police?'

I'm not sure what kind of policeman would be muscling into someone's house looking like I do but I don't deny it. There's a certain primness to her that tells me she's used to picking up the broken pieces her brother leaves behind him, and if I can keep her believing I have the law on my side, I might just be able to get what I need without having to resort to scaring or threatening her. To be perfectly frank, looking at her studious, care-worn face, I sincerely doubt if I could so much as raise my voice at her. But like I say, hopefully I won't have to. Joel, on the other hand, I'm not so sure about. This is all making him a bit fidgety.

'Is there somewhere quiet we can talk?'

She turns and leads us into the kitchen. The washing up is all done and her schoolbooks are neatly stacked on the table ready for the morning. She gestures for me to sit down and takes the seat opposite me. Joel remains standing. I can feel him studying my every move.

'I need to speak to your brother ... Sorry, what's your name?'

'Alicia.'

'Alicia, I need to speak with Blair as soon as possible. Tonight. Do you have any idea where he might be?'

She shoots a glance at Joel before deciding whether to answer. She seems to weigh it up for a second or two, then says, 'He's at the farm.'

'Fuck you say that for?' Joel snaps at her. 'Gonna get us both shanked.'

He's scared. Some of the swagger that I noticed when I was first watching him cycling back and forth and dealing with the older guys in the courtyard had a moment ago been creeping back into his movements, his confidence and bluster beginning to build again. But now he's gone straight back to looking small and upset. It's easy to forget he's just a child. I would like to find a way to make him relax and stop fronting, as he would call it, but sympathy never works in situations like this. What he needs is to be treated like a man, for me to level with him.

'I'm not interested in the farm,' I tell him flatly. 'If I was, that's where we would be now.' I'm assuming it's some kind of marijuana plantation squirrelled away in the bowels of this block. Another of Devan's enterprises, perhaps. Then, turning back to her, I add, 'I'm here for the gun. The gun that Blair is hiding in one of these rooms.'

She is looking down at the pattern of the plastic table cover, as if its latticework of swirls and shades might contain an answer to why this is happening.

'You ain't no fed.' Joel is no longer slouching against the kitchen counter. He has straightened himself up. His chest is pushed out in cubbish confrontation.

'You're right,' I stand up, towering over him, 'I'm not a policeman. But trust me, the less you know about my people, the better. So just try to relax and let me get on with what I need to do. Okay?'

He seems convinced.

Alicia hasn't moved, she's still staring down in front of her with that same look of wanting to wake up from all this. On the wall behind her some photographs are pinned to a cork noticeboard.

'That your mother?' I ask.

She follows the direction of my gaze and nods.

'Where is she?'

'At the hospital. She works nights.'

'She's a nurse?'

Alicia shakes her head. 'Cleaner.'

Keeping things clean, a thankless task. And now this problem with Blair, yet more untidiness to manage – a mess that Alicia has failed to contain. Her mother trusted her to keep things in order and now she will need to be told just how bad it really is. Alicia will have to give her the news when she gets home, bleary eyed, already run ragged from a long night of slops and spills.

'I can see the position you're in,' is all I say.

It's enough to make her look at me.

'This isn't your fault.' I lock on to her eyes, not allowing her to look away. 'I know how things get – it's too much for you. A young man like that, without his father …'

It's true – men become unreachable too early. After a certain point there's no helping it. As if in deference to this truth, Joel begins to mutter to himself. He's on the brink of acting out again.

'I can help you with this,' I tell her. 'This doesn't have to end badly.'

Also on the wall is a cross. It's the kind I mind the least – not one of the ones with a little statue of me attached to it, bent-kneed, slump-shouldered, but a simple crux of wood. What I think of as a peasant's cross, although that's probably not something you can say these days. It has a naivety I find difficult to resent.

'Did you make that?'

She smiles. 'No, Blair did.' But saying that kills her smile. 'In Sunday school,' she adds with even less hope.

There was a time, a very long time, when I used to look at settings like this and be able to think to myself, *You know what? Maybe it's not so bad after all. What harm can it really do?* I would see people living in this way, clinging to my cross and its promise of some sense to their suffering, and I would be okay with it. Not properly okay, not at heart, not persuaded, but making do with a bad lot. That kind of okay. It's intoxicating – no, actually it's anaesthetising – to find yourself the magnet for such intimacy. *Drop Thy still dews of quietness, till all our striv-*

ings cease – that whole side to it all. It's so tender, so tired in its invocations. *Just let me rest, Prince of Peace – take me home.* It's hard to say no to. But after a while – and, as I say, it was a long, long while – the anaesthetic wore off and I was forced to admit that actually it's not okay. Because it's not just about comfort – it doesn't end there. It's not just about my lighted lamp in the benighted slums and the darkest hours. It's about wars, too, and persecution, and manipulation, and greed, and power.

I rise up from my seat and I take the cross down from the wall. She watches me do this without moving. Her expression has changed. Joel isn't sure what to make of it either.

'It's okay,' I tell her.

I hand it to her, the cross, to show her that nothing has changed. I just want her to look at it, to have it in her hands while I tell her something. I look at the boy too. He's pretending not to be watching.

I have had many conversations like this in the past, when I have tried to kindle hope in the hearts of those who need it most. And each time I resorted to pity, pity for that same helplessness that I see in her now. It moved me to conjure up a solution where none existed, and in the intervening centuries I have repented at my leisure, watching the slow metastasis of that mistake.

Not this time.

'That object in your hands,' I tell her, 'it reminds us that there are such things as courage and dignity.' Yet again I find myself having to push away the image of Abaddon, his eyes pressing into me. 'But it cannot live your life for you,' I use the words to move us forwards, away from the past. 'Only you can do that. Nor can it give you something more, some other chance to do it better. There is no more than this, so you need to make *this* count.'

I reach out to my side and I pull Joel towards me, so he's standing right next to the table. He squirms a little but I tighten my grip. Still she just watches me.

'Get off me, man,' he says.

'If you feel bad,' I tell her, 'it is because you need to make changes. If you feel guilt, it is unrelated to God. Its cause is rooted here in this earth. It is because you know that you have allowed yourself to become helpless while your brother – another boy, like this one,' I shake Joel's arm, again he tells me to get off him, 'loses his way.'

It is good that her eyes are brimming with tears. I am drawing the pain out of her, into this room, where I can chase it away.

'It is not too late,' I have to raise my voice a little, to keep her with me. 'Look at me. It is not too late. You can still change it. You just need courage. Take that courage not from what is in your hands, but from what is in your heart.'

We both look at the cross. She places it slowly on to the table.

'And you,' I squeeze my hand, his little arm so fragile beneath the folds of his sweatshirt, 'you have chosen the wrong family – those people down there care nothing for you – all they want is to …'

He wriggles away from me. 'You're mental, man.'

He tries to make a break for the hallway but I catch hold of him again. The effort of it pulls me off my chair, though, and we both fall to the floor, me on top of him. Wasted as my body is, it is still heavy to a child and the impact knocks the wind right out of him. I kneel up beside him and give him a little room to recover. He's gulping like a fish.

'Just tell me where it is,' I say to her. 'Tell me where it is and I will remove this weight from your shoulders. Come on, Alicia, let me do this for you. Let me start a change.'

She doesn't move. We stay like that, in silence, punctuated by the sound of Joel's breath beginning to return in patchy gasps.

Once Joel has managed to sit up on the floor, I start talking again. I tell them that I'm not stupid, that I know how this works. 'If I take this gun,' I say, 'then everyone suffers. I understand that. I know how men like Devan operate.'

Neither one of them speaks, although Joel seems to sag a little at the mention of that name.

'I know that if someone takes what's his,' I'm standing now, above them both, 'there will need to be some payback. Someone will need to be punished.'

Alicia's tears are back. The boy doesn't look far off it either.

'But I'm going to take the weight for this – you need to understand that, both of you. I am not going to let this come back on either of you, or your brother, Alicia.'

'Why?' She's wiping her cheeks. 'Why do you care what happens when you leave here?'

'Because believe it or not, I want to help you. Yes, I need this gun, but I want to help you too. I want to help everyone,' I add, getting slightly off track. 'Look, don't worry about why. Put it this way, I know you know where it is – a flat this size, with him coming and going at all hours, there's no way of keeping anything secret from you. I've watched you, you notice everything. But do you see me beating it out of you? Do you see me screaming and shouting? Turning the place upside down? No, because you're as much a victim as I am – you both are. I have no quarrel with you.'

She's almost there. She wants to trust me, I just need to give her the right permission to do it. 'If this is done right,' I say, squatting down beside her, eye to eye, 'your brother gets a second chance out of this – a turning point, where no one gets hurt. Because, Alicia, you know as well as I do that the next time someone comes crashing through this door in the middle of the night, it's not going to be a guy like me. It's going to be someone who will be bringing consequences in their wake – jail time, violence – you don't need me to spell it out.'

'Keep your mouth shut,' Joel says from behind me.

She glares at him. 'You're the one who brought him here. You and all of them, always dragging Blair into your mess. We've already lost one from this family, in case you haven't noticed.'

This silences him. Turning to me again, she asks, 'How?'

'We make it look realistic. Joel, look at me. What would Devan do to you if he knew you'd led me here?'

He doesn't look at me. He keeps staring at the floor.

'What would he do, Joel?'

'What do you think? He'd hurt him.' She's sounds a little cross. She thinks I'm bullying him, and she clearly can't abide that, even with this boy. I expect he reminds her all too much of her brother.

'I'm not trying to be nasty,' I explain, for her benefit as much as his, 'I'm just trying to illustrate to you the position we're in. There are only two things that will stop Devan from hurting either of you or Blair. One, if he can tell that this was done by force. And two, if he knows who did it.'

Now he is looking at me. He has his same expression from when I first jumped out at him.

'A cut lip and a few bruises aren't going to convince a guy like Devan. He needs to know that I forced you here, Joel, with a knife at your throat, and that you did something more than just let me do it. He needs to be convinced that you tried to fight me. And I'm afraid that means I'm going to have to cut you.'

I was expecting this news to be greeted with a degree of panic, or at the very least protest, but if anything it seems to come as a relief.

All he says is, 'Cut ain't nothing. Jus don't shank me.'

Like I said, all he needs is to be treated like a man.

'And then there's this,' I tell them, tossing Will's wallet on to the table. 'I dropped it in the struggle – that's what you tell Devan when he comes. There's ID in there.'

'There's money too.' I open it up and take out a tenner. 'You can keep the rest of it,' I tell her. 'I'm going to need to break a few things.'

She nods and scoops it into the pocket of her dressing gown.

'Now – Alicia, will you please tell me where that gun is?'

She shows me instead. It's buried at the bottom of a fish tank, in Blair's room. From beneath the loose shale of coloured stones I pull a dripping package. I cut through the tape with my teeth and one by one I remove layers of clear plastic bags until I am left with a black pistol in my hand. The word *Glock* is stamped into the smooth rectangle of its barrel. It feels alien, like something I have been asked to hold.

Back in the kitchen, Joel says, 'I want her to do it.'

She says she won't but I talk to her in the hallway. I tell her it will be easy, quick and easy. I explain where the arteries are. I tell her the hand is best, that it's the safest place, and a believable injury.

When she's ready, he sits on a chair in the kitchen, puts his hand out and looks away. I say to him, 'This will remind you that we pay for our choices.' He's staring at me hard, waiting for the contact of the blade. 'Make better choices, Joel. From this moment on.'

He cries out but he doesn't cry. After a few seconds, he starts to look faint. I show him my own hand. 'I know how you feel,' I tell him.

'Fuck you do,' he manages to say, and to my surprise he's trying to smile. 'That jus a scratch.'

I laugh and head out into the hallway where I sweep a couple of pictures off the wall and shout loud enough for the neighbours to hear. In Blair's room I empty out drawers, toss the mattress and generally ransack the place.

When I'm back in the kitchen I tell her, 'Before that dries he's going to need to put a couple of hand marks on the wall out there. But wait till he's feeling a bit steadier on his feet. You'll also need to take him to the hospital – it's going to need stitches.' I put a hand on her shoulder. 'Maybe you can talk to your mother while you're there.'

'He will come after you – you know that.' She has wrapped Joel's hand in a tea towel and is holding it up above the level of his heart, like I told her to.

'That's the least of my worries. Very soon you'll be seeing my face in the news, and so will he.'

Joel looks away from the bloody swaddle for a moment. 'You some kind of terrorist?'

'More of an activist, I'd say. Now you make sure you drink plenty of fluids and –'

'You need to go.' She doesn't say it angrily, just abruptly. She has a lot to do, and there's been more than enough talk already.

I leave by the staircase at the back of the building. My departure is not unnoticed but those who do see me pass – and I know they do, I can feel their look – take the warning of my gun seriously. At one point, I hear sirens in the distance. I stop for a second and wait but they do not come any closer. No one, it would seem, is rushing towards this particular emergency.

I keep my head down as I hurry north through the blank residential streets. When I see a bus up ahead I channel the last of my energy into a sprint. The doors close behind me with an encapsulating sigh and we pull out on to the empty road. As I sit down, the presence of the gun announces itself at the back of my waistband, angular and awkward against my injured disc.

'Just you and me,' I say to the driver as he takes us west through ancient streets overwritten with steel and glass. So much has been torn down and swallowed up. Even the rivers have been driven underground.

As we pass through, the city lets out its fitful shouts and screeches. I rest my head against the window, the cold of the glass feels good. The mist of my breath fuzzes out the view so all I can see are shapes and colours, but always moving, reforming, vanishing again. Never still, never silent. Like me, London is a light sleeper.

17

Standing here on Waterloo Bridge, I watch the wide reach of the Thames come to life beneath me. Its waterway, its embankments, the dome of St Paul's and the giant prisms of the city, all alight from the rising sun. The chroma of fire. Brick, branch, every detail of what we know, coloured by God. This air in my lungs, this light in my eyes … never have I understood His design more clearly – and never have I felt more alone. Like the renegades before me, I have leapt into an exquisite state, without country, neither man nor Godsent. But how else can a meteor make itself known on earth, if not by detaching from heaven? It can only be this way. Burn bright, burn up.

Even at this early hour people are passing me every few seconds, in traffic, on foot, ready to begin their day. Their energy makes me realise how tired I am, from last night, from the days and the nights before that. But it's invigorating too. I turn away from the river, to try to draw something from them instead.

It's not long before I'm ready to join the march myself. I walk to the northern shore and turn west past the pitted obelisk of Cleopatra's Needle. In Embankment Gardens, secluded from the path by a dense and musty camellia, I squat down on my haunches and take out the gun. I release its magazine into my hand, and one by one I squeeze out the bullets with my thumb. They fall like a drill of seeds at my feet. I brush over them with twigs and dirt, then carefully I slide the gun back into the waistband of my trousers. It feels lighter as I straighten up, as if I've removed the part of it that was pressing into me.

It is no more than a baton now, I tell myself as I continue my journey to the tube station. *A tool with which I shall conduct proceedings.*

I join the queue for tickets and find myself waiting behind a man who is talking unnecessarily loudly into his mobile phone. His conversation seems work related, although I am trying not to listen to it. It's making my head rattle. I ask him to speak more quietly, but he doesn't. There are two others in front of us in the queue. They too are bristling at the sound of his braying voice.

Again I ask him to please let us have some peace. I remind him that we are sharing this space. He pauses his conversation to give me a certain kind of look, as if he's peering at me over the top of spectacles, which he's not. He then resumes, at the same volume, with an apologetic, *No nothing, just some weirdo.*

Before I realise I am doing it, I have removed the device from his hand and cancelled the call.

'There,' I say to him, handing it back. 'All sorted.'

He looks at me for a second then lowers his gaze. 'Thanks,' is all he says. He goes to join another queue.

A few moments later the woman in front of me turns around, just as she's about to go and buy her ticket, and quickly smiles at me. It's not even a smile really, more a softening of the eyes, but it's enough for me to know that I am right. People should not have to endure the tyranny of bullies. Today, I shall make that clear. I glance at the clock – seven thirty. In half an hour I shall begin to tell this to the world.

On the train I make a mistake – I misjudge my audience. It's easily done, particularly when the sap of enthusiasm is rising through you, but in a setting like this it's hard to come back from, and very quickly I'm finding that things are beginning to run away from me.

The tube carriage is rammed, everyone alone together in that rush hour way with their downcast eyes and their headphones and their branded coffee cups, but I don't feel like that at all. Or at least I didn't, when I first got on. I had been supercharged with purpose, excited to share it. But since I tried to speak about this a few minutes ago, my enthusiasm has been replaced by a less glorious kind of energy. I am suddenly aware of the confinement of this space, the way my words are festering in here, malformed, rotting among us. There is no dry wind to catch them, as there had been when my most memorable utterances took flight from Christ – on the Mount, that crowd waiting for me there at the foot of the hill, not only wanting but willing me to speak. It was the right time – people could be told in person then. They wanted to feel it, they wanted to bite the truth between their teeth and test it. But that was then.

I feel like I need to correct my foolishness – first though, I need to calm myself. I have begun to sweat, my hands are damp and trembling. The moment a seat is available I pounce on it. I lean forward and try to force some oxygen into my blood through long, smooth breaths, but it's hard to find a rhythm to it with the train stopping and starting beneath me the whole time. There is an unsettling pattern to its progress. For the past minute or so we appear to have simply stopped. No one other than me seems to care – perhaps it's normal to grind to a halt like this in the dark tunnel, but I don't like it.

'I want to explain ...' I begin, in an effort to recover myself, but it is said a little too forcefully. The couple standing in front of me move briskly away.

'I want to explain ...' I resume, more confidentially this time, in the direction of the man sat to my left, who tells me that he doesn't want any trouble.

'Trouble is something you have come to expect ...' I tell him, and the others, widening it out gently to those standing near us '... from someone who suddenly starts to speak when custom dictates that they should not. You assume that they are mad, or that what they have to say must be rash or impulsive or ill thought-through. But consider how often you are willing to listen to perfect strangers in other contexts – television, internet … all of these things bring to you the views of people whose motivations you cannot possibly fathom. But it is a conventional source, it is the correct …' I use my hands for this next phrase – quote-unquote '… means of delivery.'

I am the only one in the entire carriage who is speaking.

'The disembodied words that we so readily absorb online – ghosted for the most part, generated by an unseen hand. The source is obscure.'

Further down, a few seats away, someone tells me to be quiet. I don't see who, it's a man's voice. There are others, too, who seem irritated at this violation of their right to silence. Most, though, just look away or else fix their eyes more determinedly on what is in front of them – books, electronic devices, newspapers.

'I have more to say,' I tell them, 'but I will spare you. I see that this has not worked. Delivering the truth in person is a thing of the past.'

Learn from this! I tell myself. *You have let your enthusiasm get the better of you. It must not happen again. There can be no victory without control.*

The silence that returns to the carriage is a deeper, more lasting kind than before. Even the screeching of the train as it arrives at its stations and the inflow/outflow of people do little to reset it. You can see in the faces of the new arrivals that they sense an atmosphere. I can feel myself the object of everyone's attention, and somewhere in here too there is a palpable aggression, turned towards me. I cannot tell where it's coming from, and as my unease turns to something more like fear, I stop looking and stare instead at the shiny tops of Will's father's shoes. The lightness of the gun at my back suddenly feels like a bad thing. Abaddon's wolves are circling – it has been a bad mistake to draw such attention to myself, out in the open like this.

The train is slowing down, starting to squeal in its braking. The recording in the carriage tells us that we are arriving at Marylebone. I bundle out with the other passengers, all of whom pretend not to notice me and try not to touch me.

I don't like the platform. There are too many people moving past me. I am frantically searching for the exit when a young man pulls into focus just steps away, olive skinned, elegant, the glint of a knife in his hand. I lurch backwards, perilously close to the line, windmilling my arms to recover my balance. One of the platform attendants rushes to help me. The man fades back into the crowd. I shrug off the questions from the attendant and look past him at the blistering of faces and movement – a painting dissolving in a fire. Further danger immediately appears, this time in the form of a woman, her hideous bulb of a nose, her thick black eyebrows, coming for me. A hag from the woods, muttering spells.

I throw up my arms and shout. It clears a space. The woman turns and recirculates with the others, biding her time for another pass.

'Get back!' There's a yellow line at my feet, a breadcrumb trail. I begin to trot, then run, looking down, staying on the line.

I hate these tunnels.

Courage is a bubble, courage is a bubble, I repeat to myself in time with my steps.

Courage is a bubble that rises.

People get out of my way.

From the deepest floor of the ocean, the bubble begins.

I am on the escalator, still running, clearing a path. I am taking too many breaths. I want to breathe more slowly. I think of the air outside.

It journeys up from the unseen bed, up and up, toward the vast embrace of the sky.

18

I caught sight of myself just now. It wasn't pretty. What I saw there, in the lobby mirror of The Drum hotel, was not the face of a calm, persuasive man. But now, shut away in the confines of a toilet stall, with Will's body in the same cramped attitude of prayer as the day I entered it, the strength that so quickly drained out of me in those hideous tunnels is beginning to return.

This position, knees to the ground, elbows resting on the black plastic of the toilet seat, was one that I adopted instinctively, a recovery position, but now that I am like this I realise that I must speak to Him one last time. I was wrong back there on that train, giving in to my urge to speak, and perhaps I am wrong now too, but this cannot be reasoned away. It is a compulsion as strong as any I have known. Whatever is left of me, what part of me that still survives in this human shell, must be heard. I refuse to believe what Abaddon said, that He has taken against me because I have chosen to defy Him. I know in my heart that it cannot be true, but it is not enough simply to know it. I must say it to Him, so that whatever is ahead of me can be faced, if not with His blessing then with the soundness of spirit that comes from knowing you have told your all and left nothing to ambiguity or chance.

I am surprised by what comes out. It is neither confession nor anger. I do not inveigh against Him as I thought I would. I do not beg for His forgiveness. I simply speak. I open my heart to Him, and I say the words that only a child can say to a parent – an innocent and unvarnished declaration of love, even as I stand on the precipice of treachery. For I am His child. That is one of the things I say – *I am Your child, Your son. Son of perdition* I do not say, but I think it.

As before, others overhear my prayer, and it is their interruptions that bring it to a close.

'You okay in there?' a man asks.

Without thinking, I reply in the tongue of prayer. This prompts a further question.

'Are you being sick?' asks another. 'Do you want me to call someone?'

'No,' I say, getting a hold of myself. 'I don't need anyone.' And it's the truth. That prayer has done what needed to be done. I feel right again.

When I come out I see that there are two men there, Will's kind of age. They're both looking at my cuts and bruises.

'It's nothing,' I say to them. 'I got into a fight this morning. I'm not much of a fighter.'

'You should probably get that looked at,' one of them says. The other one agrees. They seem like nice people.

'Oh don't worry, I'm going to sort it out right now.'

Before, when I rushed through the lobby and into the ground-floor toilets, I attracted a few looks, so now that I'm back out here, I'm trying to blend in a bit more. There are a few people at reception, checking in, checking out – I wait my turn, quietly and respectfully. I sit down in an armchair and leaf through one of the hotel's brochures. The Drum is a *louche bolthole for the twenty-first century libertine*, it says, somewhere to *attack life and work in a symbiotic hub of business and pleasure.* Reading on, I discover that these were once five large townhouses that have now been joined together and decorated with bespoke wallpaper and expensive chalk-based paints. And all around are faux Victorian portraits of cheeky guttersnipes and roguish villains with stovepipe hats and halfway smiles that let you know they're not all bad. In reality, of course (and let's not forget, I actually *know* what it was like back then), it was a slum of violent chancers, pimps, rapists and child molesters. But this has been airbrushed into marketing oblivion. Same thing with the Blinding Bar: it offers London's largest range of absinthes. I think I've read enough. I think I'm about ready to talk to someone.

The young woman at the reception desk is now free. She is wearing a dress that resembles a scientist's tunic and her hair appears to have been cut by someone either very young or very old.

I saunter across to where she's standing. 'I'm early for my meeting,' I inform her.

Like everyone I speak to, she needs the first few seconds to sort out how she feels about my face and my general demeanour. To help her in the right direction, I adapt what I said to the guys in the toilet, making it sound a little less brawling and a bit more fashionable.

'Things got a bit out of hand at boxing,' I tell her in my most bored voice.

She likes that explanation. 'Cool,' she purrs at me. 'Where do you go?'

The name Sparta comes to mind but I can't bring myself to say it. Those guys were properly hard – you have to respect history, even in a place like this. I go for Warriors instead. I also throw in the location: 'In Hoxton,' I say.

That seals it. My credentials are complete. Things are starting to move in the right direction again. Each second falls neatly into place.

'Got to do something to stave off the executive burnout,' I explain with a wink that draws the skin around my eye painfully tight. I wince a little, we both laugh.

'You said you were here for a meeting?'

'Yes, with Abaddon.'

She has a look on her laptop. 'Perhaps I'm not spelling that right but I don't think we have …'

Get it together. 'Sorry – work jargon. I'm here for the Abel-wood meeting.' Still no recognition. 'With David Saint-Clair?'

That name she recognises. 'I think they've already started.'

I glance at the clock behind her. It's quarter past eight. 'Yeah, I'm running late. Listen,' I lean in a fraction, 'maybe you could save me from getting even further into anyone's bad books.'

She smiles encouragingly. She likes me.

'I'm going to need to mail out some AV during the meeting – might be a pretty hefty file. I should've checked all this with you guys beforehand …' I raise my eyebrows, because of course I didn't, because I'm the loveable rogue.

'No problem at all. We have superfast broadband in all the meeting rooms,' she informs me proudly. 'We had fibre optic installed earlier this year. It's as quick as it gets.'

'Perfect.' I glance again at the clock. 'I guess I should prob-ably get moving. Which room are they in?'

A thin, handsome young man with an insultingly uninter-ested expression has appeared at my side. He is not wearing a uniform but he is without doubt a member of staff.

'Gregory will show you,' she tells me, confirming this. 'And if you need anything else, you know where I am.'

Gregory wanders off across the lobby and into the lift, then down a few corridors on the second floor, during which time he barely even bothers to check that I'm following him. He just drones out a scripted monotone about the week's activities (except here they are called 'happenings'). Needless to say I tune out almost immediately and so we both amble along together in perfect isolation. I am, if truth be told, starting to feel the nerves a bit. This is my moment.

'Sorry, what did you just say?'

Gregory stops his tired happenings summary and looks at me disdainfully.

'Filming,' I prompt him. 'You just said something about filming.'

'I – we,' he concedes generously, 'are making an online short about the hotel – webcasting some *tranches de vie* from the public areas.'

He is evidently slightly bemused that I hadn't been quietly marvelling at this project but there is no time for him to say more – not that he really looks like he could bothered to anyway – because we have reached a pair of double doors at the end of the corridor. The meeting room has a tastefully subdued sign on it: The Workhouse.

'Here you go,' he says and turns to leave, signalling the end of our acquaintance, but I can't let him get away now. This is far too good a chance to waste.

'Hang on a sec,' I tell him. 'I don't suppose you'd like to earn a little extra cash?'

I'm listening. He doesn't actually say this but every inch of his body language says it for him.

'I've messed up.' I'm talking quietly because I don't want the people in the meeting room to hear us – the element of surprise is going to be an important part of my entrance – but also because it adds to the sense that we're sharing a secret, a secret with which I need his help. 'We've got a bit of filming to do in this meeting and I was supposed to bring a cameraman but … well, like I say, I messed up. But if you could maybe help me out in there, for half an hour, tops … well, let's just say I'll make sure that a hundred pounds from petty cash finds its way to you. What do you think?'

'No problem at all, sir.'

Sir, is it now? Amazing what money can do.

So I make an arrangement with Gregory: I will call down to reception and summon him to do the filming.

'It'll just be on a phone,' I add, in the assumption that someone in there will have one. 'Probably not the standard of camera you're used to.'

He smiles indulgently at this pleasantry, now that we're friends.

'When you call down, just check with Fleur,' he tells me.

'Who's Fleur?'

Fleur, it turns out, is the woman I was flirting with at reception. Gregory is in no doubt that she will be 'cool' with our arrangement.

'Okay, but just make sure you get here quickly when I call for you. It could be any time,' I add mysteriously, 'depending on how things go.'

'I'll be there.'

When he's gone I press my ear to the door. There's a light murmur of conversation.

I breathe in strength. I breathe in courage. I push open the door. Every face turns towards me.

19

There are six of them sitting around a table, with me now standing in the doorway, a lucky seventh. This being The Drum, of course, it isn't your typical conference room – there's a restored refectory table surrounded by mismatched antique chairs and arrayed with mineral water and quirky drinking glasses.

Abaddon is sitting at the head of the table. He had been in the middle of saying something when I walked in. His face offers no clue to what he is thinking.

Alex is the first to speak. 'Will,' he says to me in the tone he reserves for tricky work situations, 'this is, erm … unexpected.'

'Be quiet, Alex. Hello everyone,' I announce to the rest of them, 'for those who don't know me, my name is Will.'

'Will, what on *earth* are you doing?' It's the boss woman, Stella.

'You too, please,' I say to her. 'Quiet.'

Still no one is moving, which I find a little surprising. I'd have thought at the very least Alex would have got up by now. I am aware that Abaddon is trying to catch my eye. I avoid looking at him, although I'm pleased to note that this is no longer through fear. I just don't want the distraction – I need to concentrate on my own performance. We all have our parts to play here.

The old guy, Nicholas, who took such a dislike to me last time we met, looks particularly unimpressed. The remaining two simply look dumbstruck at my appearance (both here in the room and, no doubt, my actual appearance). It's to them that I address my next remark.

'You must be the silent partners. I see now how you earned that title,' I quip.

I shut the door behind me, which changes the atmosphere somewhat. Stella looks at Alex, wanting him to do something. It is he who is responsible for my management, he is my keeper. But he makes a hang-on gesture to her with his hand.

'Okay,' I continue, trying to sound a little cheerier, 'since no one's going to introduce me, I'll just have to ask.' And here I do look at Abaddon, 'We know each other of course, as you have no doubt been explaining, in your own inimitable way. But you,' I point at the one nearest me, 'I have not met before. Name please.' He tells me his name. 'And you,' I accidentally bark at the next one, making them all jump a little.

He looks completely flummoxed. He looks at Stella imploringly. 'Stella ...?' is all he manages to say.

'Okay, let's stop this.' I look at the first guy. 'I've already forgotten your name anyway.'

Abaddon is trying to force words into my mind. My head is buzzing with the effort of keeping them out. I take a few deep, steadying breaths. *I am in control here*, I remind myself.

In this pause, Nicholas asks in an unconvincing bluster, 'Can we help you with something, Mr Pryce?'

I decide not to bother answering that, instead I walk a few paces closer so I'm right next to the table. I reach behind me. It's time to stop messing about.

One of them, the man whose name I can't remember, says, 'Okay now –'

Whereupon I produce the Glock and stand over them all, pointing it at the speaker's head.

The appearance of a weapon has had the predicted effect on Abaddon. Like any apex predator, he is unused to challenge, and in a situation like this it is especially problematic. I can tell that he is furious but to show it would be to break character at a vital moment, and shatter the thrall in which these people are held. His voice rattles into my head, *You dare to lift your heel against me? You dare to desolate His wishes?*

They all remain stock still, except for Nicholas, who starts to make a coughing noise. I take this to be a possible sign of a heart attack.

Still Abaddon's voice hisses through me. *Impudent pup. Extinguish your foolishness while you still have a chance. Turn that instrument on yourself.*

'Save your words,' I tell him. 'Did you really believe that this day would never come, when your lies would come crashing down about your ears?'

He feigns surprise at this, like he has no idea what I'm talking about, but I can tell that it unsettles him to see this change in me. His bullying has reached the hard flint of resistance.

'I will smite the shepherd,' I say, turning my attention back to all of them, because no one in this room is blameless. Each has been weighed and found to be wanting. 'And the sheep of the flock shall be scattered abroad.'

Nicholas's cough is worsening. 'Just try to find a comfortable position,' I tell him, 'on the floor if you have to. See if you can find a way to relax.'

He slides off his chair and crawls to the edge of the room. He sits there with his back against the wall.

'I'm okay,' he manages to say.

'I hope so,' I tell him. 'I wouldn't want you to miss this.'

This is the moment that Alex chooses. 'Will,' he begins, so softly that none of us are quite sure he has spoken. 'You're right,' he continues at a more normal volume, 'if you're thinking you've been treated unfairly.'

Stella isn't sure where he's going with this. He avoids her eyes, nor can he bring himself to look at me.

'And we need to talk about that.' He makes a monumental

effort and forces himself to glance up at my face. 'But that's a conversation to be had with cool heads, in slower time,' he says. 'Why don't we grab a coffee or lunch or ...' Even as he's saying it he can hear how useless it sounds.

'I think I'd rather talk now, Alex, if it's all the same to you. While I have my gun.'

The thing about these people – not these ones specifically but the schemers and doublespeakers of every generation – is that they always think they're the first to plumb the dark arts of persuasion. It's hilarious. People have been doing it from the get-go. Take my whole Resurrection gig as an example. The Great Defib, as I like to think of it. That was nothing, absolutely *nothing* to do with us. No divine involvement whatsoever. It was a one hundred per cent piece of human theatre. Some guys I'd seen hanging around Golgotha, no idea who they were, snaffled JC's body and subbed in a ringer to come stumbling out of his tomb. Honestly, if you could have seen it, you'd be in bits – he didn't even *look* like Jesus. But then, that's just the point: he didn't have to. They'd read the situation perfectly. Mass hysteria had kicked in by that point. Even his nearest and dearest (even, it pains me to say, my darling Maryam) bought into it. But that's grief for you – it'll make you see what you want to see, allow you to believe whatever it is you need to believe. Mark II (that's the name I give him in my head, partly because he actually looked more like Mark than Jesus – that same weak, sly mouth) saw the whole thing through with, I have to admit, considerable style. Even those who would have been starting to suspect something couldn't voice it at that stage, he was just too beguiling. He had them eating out of his hand.

'Anyone else want to have a go at handling me? No? Right then, let's get on with it, shall we? Could everyone please put their mobile phones on the table?'

Nothing. Not a single one of them moves. Abaddon is too

absorbed in my gun – he's watching it like there's nothing he's ever coveted more. The others, though, are simply in shock. I'm being too brisk. I need to slow it down, I need to soften my delivery and let them catch up. That's the trouble when you're having to act outside your comfort zone – it can all get a bit overzealous.

Luckily the Drum, louche bolthole that it is, has equipped its meeting room with a well-stocked honesty bar. I select a bottle of vodka from the tray.

'How about a little something to calm the nerves,' I suggest.

I do a quick tour of the table tipping everyone's water on the floor and replacing it with a few fingers of spirit. I don't want Nicholas dying on me, so I give him the option – vodka or water (a little nod to one of my more talked-about miracles). He points to the vodka, which makes me less concerned that he might be about to peg out on us.

'Why are you doing this?' Stella wants to know. She must be scared but she manages not to let it show. I have to hand it to her, she has class.

'You'll see.'

Alex is about to say something.

'No more talk.' I wave the gun at the drinks lined up in front of them. 'Down the hatch.'

Abaddon looks all tensed up, as if he's coiling his body back into the chair, preparing to spring. He would, after all, be the valiant hero if he wrestled me to the ground. I walk round to the end of the table opposite him and lean forward, letting the weight of the gun clonk down on the wood, reminding him how full of carefully engineered death it is. I glance at the drink in front of him – he alone has not touched his glass.

'It's only vodka,' I say to him, 'it won't kill you.' Then, straightening up, levelling the gun at his head, I add, 'But I will, if you don't do what I say.'

He hears the sincerity in my voice and downs the lot in one swig. All bullies are cowards at heart. Seeing him do this gives me an idea. I slide the bottle down the table to him, Western style.

'Fill it,' I say. 'Fill your glass to the brim.'

Again he complies, albeit with a little more reluctance this time. When it's full, he musters a voice I've not heard from him so far. It's injured, quietly outraged at what he is being made to endure. 'Surely you're not suggesting I drink that?'

'Not suggesting, no.' I cock back the hammer on the gun. It is a loud, crisp sound. 'Telling you.'

'Have some compassion.' Yet again it is Stella who has been brave enough to speak out.

A thin vein, watery blue beneath her skin, pulses at her temple. It is the only sign of emotion, that and the indignation in her voice. But what could she possibly know of my suffering? For it is in suffering, I would like to point out to her, that we find the real measure of compassion. *Com passio*. I suffer with.

Instead I ask, 'You think perhaps I am just a witness to human life?'

She looks away. To her, the question is unanswerable – a pointless non sequitur, further proof of my derangement. But to me, it is the vital distinction. With Jesus, witnessing was all that I did. There was only transient suffering then, the banging in of nails, the breaking of limbs, but nothing was really sacrificed. I let them continue in their lives believing that I would reappear. It prompted them to go surging out towards their own violent deaths. Even my Maryam set to wandering, eking out the last of her years in the conviction that she would once again be with me, in glory, in *lux aeterna*. All of them reduced to dust while I lasted on through the centuries. Where is the compassion in that? But this time it's different. This time I've made an investment of my own. I have skin in the game.

It takes Abaddon a while to finish his glass. Whether he's making a show of it for their sake or whether he genuinely struggles to force it down I neither know nor care. I wait patiently. Stella, who is sat beside him, touches him on the arm whenever he pauses. He smiles gratefully and continues. We'll see how long his charade of vulnerability lasts once the alcohol hits his bloodstream.

'Right then,' I clap my hands together, 'let's try it again: would everyone please slide their phones into the centre of the table?'

This time they do it. I notice the time on one of the screens – five to nine. Better call my cameraman.

I keep my gun on the group while I pick up the hotel phone and dial. It hasn't, of course, occurred to any of them that it might not be loaded. Its symbolic presence is too huge – the switch between life and death, immediate and irreversible change. Not something to be trifled with.

It is Fleur who answers the phone and I have to spend a minute or two chatting to her while she waits for Gregory to appear. At one point I hold the receiver against my chest to tell Abaddon to drink some water. He has started hiccuping. The taut readiness of just moments ago has already slackened into a look of crumpled nausea. His eyes are closed and his lips are moving, like he's trying hard to remember something.

The others murmur a bit, asking him if he's okay, until I jiggle the gun in their direction and they immediately fall silent again.

'Okay, thanks.' I'm back with Fleur. She has just sent Gregory on his way. 'And listen,' I add, 'maybe we could grab a coffee before I leave today.'

She agrees – maybe we could.

'I'll come and find you,' I tell her.

It's important to keep everything feeling natural. I wouldn't want any suspicions to be aroused, not when it's all going so well. I hang up the phone and am just starting to get Stella organised when there's a polite tap on the door and in pops Gregory. His face is a picture. He looks over at my subdued kennel of suits, then at me, then repeats the cycle. By the time he's done it a couple of times, he has managed to formulate a question.

'What have you been doing in here?' Then, obviously feeling that doesn't quite cover the extent of what he wants to know, he adds, 'What is this?'

'Just shut the door,' I tell him.

He reaches behind him and half closes it.

'All the way, please.'

Reluctantly, he clicks it shut.

Abaddon is talking to himself in a low grumble of Aramaic. His eyes are still closed. He's shaking his head and really hissing some of the words. It's upsetting the group. I tell him to be quiet, also in Aramaic so he knows I mean him. He opens his eyes. The word I've used, *dumah*, silence, is also a reference to a name he used for a while, in the distant past, for some of his bloodier work. He seems pleased to be reminded of it.

'You don't have the stomach for this.' He's using English again, but his voice has reverted to its old self, pointed and cruel. He seems to have forgotten all about the wronged and righteous act he was pulling just before.

'This is His world,' he adds, slurring slightly, 'not yours.' The phrase sounds familiar. No doubt he's parodying something I have said in the past. I don't waste a second trying to think what.

Gregory, who has been observing this exchange with increasing confusion, has had an idea. 'I get it,' he says, 'you're doing a role play. This is some kind of scenario, and I'm here to …' He runs out of steam at this point. In a less hopeful voice he asks, 'Why am I here?'

'I told you, you're here to do some filming. So I suggest,' I point at him with the gun, which I'm not sure he had noticed because I've been holding it down by my side for the past minute or two, 'that you take that phone,' I point to Alex's one in the pile, 'and get this woman here in the frame.'

It has a galvanising effect on the young director, who hurries over to take the phone. It has a less positive impact on Stella. She wants to know what I am planning to do with her. I hate to see the fear that, despite her best efforts, is now starting to get the better of her. I want more than anything to be able to tell her that this is just a short, unpleasant interlude for the betterment of mankind. *Grit your teeth and bear it*, I would like to say. *I will not hurt you. I could not.*

'It is not yet your moment to speak,' I tell her instead. I cannot afford to show weakness in front of Abaddon, who has emerged from the alcohol's temporary subdual into an embittered and dangerously confrontational state. He is breathing, more than breathing, growling at the end of the table, head down, eyes raised up.

'Little lamb,' he says, 'bleating, bleating.'

'For God's sake, man …' Nicholas's voice has faded to almost nothing. 'You'll get us all killed.'

Abaddon does not look at him. He keeps his eyes firmly on me. 'You are all but dead anyway,' he tells him. 'Return to your stupor.'

'Pay no attention to this creature,' I say, evenly, in control. 'It is too late for him to find a true path. But,' I look at each of them in turn, 'it is not too late for you.'

Only Stella meets my eyes, the others stay hidden within themselves, refusing to come out.

As gently as I can I coax Gregory into position across the table from Stella. 'If your hands are going to tremble like that,' I say to him, 'then perhaps you should rest your elbows on the table. I'm going to need a steady shot.'

Abaddon opens his mouth but before he has had a chance to speak I shout, 'Enough from you!' making everyone but him flinch in alarm.

He smiles and settles back into his chair. 'Carry on,' he says, sweeping out his arm in front of him.

Stella turns to him very slowly, one eye still on me. 'Mr Saint-Clair,' she says with all the dislike that three words can bear, 'this man has a gun and it is pointed at me. I would be grateful if you would please –'

'Harpy.' He closes his eyes and his voice drifts off with him, 'You know not of what you speak ...'

This is good, better than good. He is unable to disguise his contempt for them, just as I predicted. When people cannot be bent to his will, they are redundant husks to him. His vitriol is well-served to my purpose, it blackens his own cause. He cannot influence these people because he feels nothing for them.

Only from love can progress be formed.

I realise I have said these last words. It doesn't matter.

'Stella, it's time. I'm going to need you to answer some questions. But please don't look at me when you're speaking, look at Gregory here – look at the camera.' She seems unsure what to say. 'If you answer my questions with honesty in your heart, then you will be free to go. Okay?'

Still she says nothing.

'The truth,' I summarise for her, 'shall set you free. All of you,' I add for the benefit of the others. 'That's the only thing you need to think about.'

'Now Gregory, are you ready to do this?'

He valiantly says that he is.

'Good. Just make sure you get her squarely in the frame. Then, when we're done, I'm going to need you to save the recording in as small a file as possible. It has to be less than two gigs. So just bear that in mind.'

He nods.

'I'm assuming that phone is picking up the Wi-Fi here?'

He checks. Again he nods.

'I'm going to need some actual words from you, Gregory. Is it connected? Can you do what I ask?'

He looks a little tearful.

'Sorry, I didn't mean to snap at you.' This being an odd thing to say when you're pointing a gun at someone, I change that too. Lowering my hand to my side, I ask him, 'So how's it looking? Reception any good?'

'Reception's fine,' he mumbles. 'It's the high-speed connection Fleur was telling you about.' (*In a simpler, happier time* his expression seems to say – although my memory of him from earlier on is that he was singularly unhappy, in a complicated sort of way, so go figure.)

'Okay, that's good. Good lad.' It can't be easy, all this, when you're used to sulking about in a boutique hotel all day.

'Right then.' I place my non-gun hand on his shoulder. 'Count her in, Greg.'

And bless him, he does it like a proper media wannabe. The 'three' and the 'two' he says out loud but the 'one' he just mouths, and holds up a skinny finger, which he then points at her in a *And we're live* … sort of way.

'So then, Stella,' I say, being a little theatrical myself, 'would you like to tell the viewers at home exactly what you know about InviraCorp's offshore investments?' I smile at her. 'And please – don't spare any details.'

And to my surprise, she gets right into it. She answers all of my questions thoroughly and without a fuss. Inevitably, perhaps, we are forced to pause the recording a few times while I deal with Abaddon's interruptions and attempts to distract her. On the final occasion, I actually have to walk across the room so I am right next to him, with the gun touching his head.

I tell him, for the last time, to be quiet. His head shakes slowly from side to side, the short hairs at his temple scratch against the muzzle.

'Make me,' he says.

Even before the words have left his mouth I can feel myself starting to panic. Something in the set of his body tells me he has sniffed me out. He knows I couldn't use this gun, not on him, not on anyone. And for an awful moment I think perhaps he has realised it is empty, or worse, is about to snatch it from me. So I panic. Before I've realised what is happening, I've raised my hand above my head and cracked the butt of the gun down on his cheek. It sends him sprawling off the side of his chair.

I've never hit anyone before and I find myself paralysed in the moments after, the gun dangling loosely at my side. Adrenaline is emptying out of me like water down a plughole. But he is in no state to take advantage, he is kneeling on the floor with his face in his hands. A smear of blood at the side of his cupped palm turns my stomach and brings me sharply back to my senses.

When I return to my station opposite Stella, my outstretched arm is shaking so badly I have to hold it at the elbow. But no one else appears to mind what has happened. They almost seem relieved that Abaddon has been put to the ground and is now hunched there, at the foot of the table, like a dog. In a strange way, his presence was becoming more chaotic than my own. Order has been restored.

And when Stella resumes it is with an even greater clarity. Each phrase is turned to crisp perfection, no words are wasted. Previously, under the intensity of Abaddon's stare, she had taken to diluting her narrative with *it is possible that* or *it would appear that*, but now each revelation is couched directly – *we know, we have been aware for some time*. She uses a matter-of-fact, sometimes even rueful tone. She has a good instinct for knowing what people want to hear and she is now delivering it without impediment.

She explains how InviraCorp's assets are settled into the Jersey trust, how shares in unknown companies are used to keep people from seeing the Vatican's finances coiled deep inside there – the serpent in the woodpile. From time to time, I feed her extra information that I have acquired myself – names, account numbers, that sort of thing. She does not resist.

She even manages to bring an almost lightsome touch to her delivery, stripping it of the po-faced ambiguity that has become the hallmark of her trade. It feels real. So much so that I begin to wonder, as she rests her hands on the table in front of her, and says, simply, cleanly, *That's it, that's all I know*, whether in fact this darkness had not been festering inside her too. Perhaps there has been some measure of relief in having it extracted like this, brutally and suddenly. A non-elective procedure beyond her control.

'Good job,' I tell her. 'Now, I'm sorry to say, comes the painful part. You,' I say to Alex, 'are going to tell Gregory here how to access Abelwood's Twitter account.'

'I knew it,' says Stella, slumping forward in her seat.

'I need the bathroom,' says Alex, wriggling around in his.

'No one leaves the room,' I tell him.

'It can't wait.'

His lack of substance is particularly repellent in this moment, in the wake of Stella's bravura performance. For him I have no respect, no pity. I say some of this as I'm walking.

'Just do what I ask,' I conclude, more confidentially, as I arrive at his side.

Gregory is staring at us in the slow-witted way that some children stare at equations on blackboards.

'You do know how to upload video to Twitter, Gregory?' I ask, perhaps not as kindly as I could. It's Abaddon, he is unnerving me. He is back in his chair and has resumed his hostile staring. There is blood smeared on his face.

Gregory looks a bit flustered but he manages to nod, kind of.

'Of course you do,' I say to him, more gently. 'It's easy. Anyway, this one,' I give Alex a chummy shake of the shoulder, 'will help you. Right?' Alex groans and holds his stomach.

'None of you,' I say to the rest of them as an aside while Alex continues to groan, 'are here without reason. You have each, quite deliberately, rooted yourselves in a God-shaped hole,' I remind them (because, by the look of them, they need reminding). 'I shall now leave you to ponder that, without speaking or moving please – except for you,' I look charitably at Alex. 'You may use the bin over there for whatever it is you need to do.'

He doesn't wait to be told twice. He hurries over there, drops on all fours and retches over the wastepaper basket like a cat.

'Better?' I ask as he staggers back to his seat. 'Good. Now will you please get over there and help Gregory with what he needs to do.'

The next few steps need to be closely choreographed. First, Alex must be persuaded to let me change the administrator password for his company's Twitter account.

'Why?' he asks me even though he knows the answer.

'Because we wouldn't want the little scamps back at your office tearing down my messages the moment they appear.' I look at Stella, 'Would we?'

She smiles thinly. Abaddon contemplates her with weary malevolence. Like all the old school types, he is a committed misogynist. From Eve onwards, as far as they're concerned, the story can be told with weak, capitulating women at its centre. It is just one more reason to despise him.

'I can't,' Alex tells me.

Encouraged by this show of resistance, Abaddon finds his tongue again.

'You're right, Alex.' He is trying to show some solidarity, like they're all in this together, but as ever, he cannot quite manage to iron out the disdain from his voice. 'If you allow this to be published, which is what you would be doing, you would be committing a crime,' he tells him.

But in the end the wordless adjudication of my Glock wins the argument and Alex declares to Stella that he has no choice. He says nothing to Abaddon, who I am pleased to see is now almost on the verge of ranting. He is bandying around phrases like *corporate accountability.*

'It's okay,' Stella tells him, 'just let him do it. The first priority is that no one gets hurt.' She then turns to Abaddon and says, 'I am not quite sure what any of this has to do with you, Mr Saint-Clair. These are our clients and our responsibility.'

From the look on his face, Abaddon appears to be ruing the passing of an era, a Golden Age he would no doubt consider it, when he was able to simply murder people who had the temerity to question his jurisdiction.

Alex inputs a long sequence of letters and numbers into the password field and hands the phone back to Gregory.

'Now get on and upload this video,' I tell him. And because Abaddon is looking at the device with something approaching intent, I add, 'Come over here, behind me, and do it.'

I speak amiably to Stella while this is going on. I even see fit to lower my gun and take a seat. The other two, silent for all this time, also look as though they may emerge from their trauma, perhaps even say something. And from the rise and fall of his jacket, I would say that Nicholas, who is now lying on his side, is resting comfortably. A kind of peace has descended on us.

I explain to her why it was necessary to make her the reve-lator of this conspiracy. I share with her my observation that the whistleblowers, the corporate heretics of the digital age, have a single flaw in common: they make themselves the focus of the story. It eclipses the issue at hand, the very message they were trying to impart. In the end, we hear only about them, how mad they were, how bad, how demented.

'But,' I look at them all, 'what if the truth were to come from the culprits themselves? What if the perpetrators could be made to confess? That,' I say, 'was my vision of a modern miracle.'

I am about to say more. I am about to tell them that all of these photos and videos and tweets that are uploaded second by second to the internet are the substance of a history that is being written and documented in real time. This huge sprawling composite is a picture of life on earth, and emerging from this picture every so often are certain key moments, moments that can alter the course of history (I can't help but think of my own words spoken on the Mount, or my private grief, also caught in the amber of history). This, right now, I want to tell them, is just such a moment. But there's no time for ceremony. Gregory has finished the task at hand and is standing quietly at my side, waiting to be noticed.

'Okay, good,' I tell him when I've had a look. 'Now would you please send it out to everyone? I would do it myself but ...' I'm making reference to the fact that I have had to stand and move back across the room towards Abaddon, who was looking a moment ago like he might be thinking of putting a last-minute stop to all this.

'By the way,' I say, eyes glued to Abaddon, 'how many followers do you have?'

'Nearly ten thousand,' Alex tells me miserably.

'And how many of them are journalists?'

'Hundreds.'

I smile, thinking of Natalie. Stella sighs.

'Right then, Greg, type this, if you'd be so kind: He that hath ears to hear, comma, let him hear. Got that? Good, now attach the video and ...' I have arrived next to Abaddon '... send.'

247

It's just a moment's inattention, less than a moment, a second, as I wait for the sound of the phone, that magic tone to say the message has been sent. But it's enough. Abaddon springs from his chair and grabs my wrist. Prising the gun from my hand, he turns to Gregory and starts striding towards him, the Glock held out in front. *Click-crack, click-crack* goes the mechanism as Abaddon pumps the trigger and racks the slide, searching for rounds that are not there. I have no choice now but to run. I heard the message go, I'm certain of that, which means there's nothing left for me here. Abaddon will want to seal this in blood, and I have no appetite for violence, never have had. It was always said to be my great failing, after the last time – a recrimination that has rung in my ears for millennia. Too soft. Too weak to guide them.

As I move towards the door I see Abaddon's back, and Gregory and Alex recoiling before him. I see Stella, pushed back from the table, hands up at her face, shouting at him to stop. The other two, lunged forwards out of the line of fire, are silent. Their heads are bent down between their knees, like passengers braced for a crash.

Nobody hears me leave.

20

Fleur and the others look cowed and panicked as I pass by, suggesting that news of this morning's events has already broken loose. I'd like to think that Stella was the one brave and resourceful enough to have made the call. Goes to show, though, that you really do have to be going some to travel faster than bad news, and my progress has been faltering at best. The compression of that room has left me weaker than ever before. But this would be a bad time to rest. There is a security guard of some kind, or at least a well-built employee of the hotel, who for the time being has decided, or has perhaps been told, to keep his distance, which tells me that more serious people are already on their way.

Outside I keep to the smaller, less conspicuous streets but even they are teeming with people. Everyone is heading to work. Some seem to want to go, others look less happy at the prospect, but one thing they all have in common is the desire to be nowhere near me. And who can blame them? Every now and then I catch sight of Will, stooped and crazed in snippets of reflections, and even I am startled by it. I try to carry myself better, to measure out my steps but I am too exhausted to make it work. The state of neurotic alert into which I have forced this body has reached its end. This is not a decision, it is a fact. It comes from an ancient place, one of the few secrets that still remain balled up in that fist of reptilian brain.

It's amazing, in many ways, that I have lasted this long. My kind will always make short work of a body. We're too accelerated, too condensed to be housed in such flimsy form. In no time at all the frame begins to buckle and grumble just as this one has, like some jalopy that's been thrashed in a race, rattling up the final hills, grinding dangerously at every corner. It was the same way last time. Or at least I think it was… It's a funny thing, but my memories have kind of taken a step back in these past few days, into the dimmer light of something not quite my own. It's as if the pictures I once held in my mind, images of last time, of Jesus, have been stolen from someone else, or from books or paintings, lurid composites of things only glimpsed or imagined. They lack substance, I guess, is what I'm saying. Even my darling Maryam has become flat and unseeing, as dead as a board-painted icon. Why, I don't know. I assume it to be an effect of body-life, an inevitability of the downsizing I have suffered. It's stupid to be upset about it, and yet I can't help feeling as if I have lost more than I have gained. My own existence has now all but faded, leaving me to be troubled by the spikes and prickles of Will's past, a cuckoo in the thatch of another bird's home.

I have arrived in a smart little square with porticoed buildings whose shut, gloss-painted doors tell me that I have no business to be lingering here. But I can go no further. There is a tidy garden in the middle of the square, fenced off by black railings. I will take refuge there. I circle it once, slowly, pausing here and there to catch my breath and peer through the thick shrubbery that has been planted like a secondary perimeter just inside the railings – or perhaps it was there first, the vestige of a time when boundaries were softer, when people were better drilled on where they should and should not be. On completing my circuit, I have learned that there are only two entrances to this sanctuary, tall gates on opposite sides, and both are locked. Up and over is the only option.

I haul myself on to the roof of a parked car, to get a better view of entry points. It immediately starts to squawk and flash beneath me. I'd like to say that I feel like one of those characters the Greeks were so fond of, who always seemed to be leaping on to the backs of wildly complaining beasts. But it just seems a little sad to me now, all this. I'm struggling to see the point in any of it, to be honest. In fact, if I'm *really* honest, I'm wondering if I did actually hear that message get sent, and if I really did see Abaddon firing that gun, or if he wasn't simply snatching it away from me and hurrying over to join the rest of them. I don't know, I can't think, especially not with this car alarm screaming in my ears. I slide back down to the pavement. Just as I am about to start climbing, an indignant woman with a yapping dog approaches me and asks what in God's name I think I'm doing. It's a well-phrased question, given the circumstances, but it's not one I have time to answer.

Instead, I begin to hoist myself over the railings. She does not stay to watch. It's hard work. At first just one knee finds the right purchase, on an agonising little nub of bone-to-metal contact, but the pain soon spurs me on to hook my free foot on the sign that is bolted to the stanchions and I propel myself upwards. I then ease myself in a kind of tender slow motion over the spearing railing tops and roll down through the shrubbery into thick, bosky undergrowth. I lie face down for a while, breathing in the earth. It is as damp and cool as a well.

Eventually the car alarm stops and I am able to hear the sound of the birds and the rustle of my shoes in the grass as I walk. I have the garden to myself. That's not to say that those who are watching from upper-storey windows will not have called this in, of course they will, but for the moment at least, I am alone. *Like the panting hart*, I find myself saying, *spent from the chase*. Will's words, not my own, but this time I am glad of their comfort.

I settle myself at the foot of a large yew tree. The whorls and knots of its bark make smiling faces, encouraging me to rest. I allow my eyes to close. When I open them again a child is walking towards me, across the sunlit grass. As he gets closer, I see that in fact he is not a child at all but a fully grown man, just slight in his build and with an unusual lightness to his step. He is wearing something I can't quite describe except to say that it is familiar to me in some way. He stops just in front of me, his hands hanging at his side, smooth and fine-boned as a boy's.

'Why are you lying here?' he asks me.

I am looking up at him, up into the sun. His face is indistinct, curiously unmemorable.

'I am resting.'

'Are you tired?'

'I am very tired.'

He thinks about this.

'It has been a long time,' he says at last.

'Yes. Yes, it has.'

We are both silent for a while.

'I am sorry,' I tell him.

'Why are you saying that to me?'

'I feel like I know you.' I squint at him; he seems to be shifting around.

'You do not remember?'

'Not really.' I hang my head.

'I have failed them,' I say, when it is clear that he is not going to explain himself.

I feel his hand stroke my head, and yet when I look back up at him he does not seem to have moved. He is still standing a few steps away from me. I get the sense that he is looking beyond me, into the distance.

'It is nearly time,' he tells me.

I look around. I see no one else.

'You cannot fail them,' he adds softly, 'because they are not looking at you. You never did understand that. They see only themselves.'

'But last time ...'

He shushes me. 'Last time you just happened to be there. That is all.'

It is hard to focus on what he is saying. His voice is too like my own. His words seem to become lost in mine.

'They have forgotten the true meaning of our love,' one of us says.

'They will see it again. They always have.'

There is a loud noise behind me. I look round to see men in black uniforms flowing through the open gate.

'I'm tired of this,' I tell him.

But he has gone.

The men are yelling at me to put my hands in the air. I shuffle round on my knees to face them. They close in on me in a fast creep, the stocks of their guns tucked into their shoulders, looking at me down the sights, shouting, 'Armed police! Armed police! Armed police!'

'I want to rest,' I tell them but it is lost in their shouting.

I think about the future that awaits me now, jammed into the shell of Will's life. I think of his family, of the doctors who will stupefy me with pills. I start to move my left hand down towards my empty jacket pocket. It sets off a cacophony of voices. Some policemen are telling me not to move, to stop fucking moving. Other policemen are shouting to each other – *He's reaching! He's reaching!*

Still I continue, exhaling through the movement. *This breath I put back in the world.*

It's only as my hand is sliding into the silk of my pocket that I feel it happen. It hits me before the sound does. By the time I hear that brittle snap, I can already feel it spinning, tearing inside me. Then I feel a second one thud into my chest, right next to the first. Again that dry twig snap arriving just behind it. Some things move faster towards us, that's all it is. Just physics and numbers. Parts gentled into shape.

I am on my back, the sky far above me.

When I turn my head to the side, I see a pool of my blood running into the ground. My hand is flapping like a fish, my whole body shakes with it. Many feet are moving around me, many hands are on me.

But this time there is nothing else, nothing is tugging at me. He is not lifting me the way He lifted me from that hated cross, the way the tide bumps a boat off the sand. I am no longer His charge. Like all men, I must now lapse into darkness.

My heart is stopping. There's no mistaking it, the pressure just goes. I close my eyes. My moment. *Consummatum est*, for real this time.

One final beat. One last thing.

The hand of a child, Will's hand, enclosed in another's, the black of his sleeve, the band of gold on his finger, the path ahead of them both, and rising up there, at the end of it all, the mossy buttresses of his father's church set deep in the earth.

ACKNOWLEDGEMENTS

I owe a debt of gratitude to the following people, all of whom have helped in one way or another with the writing of this book. First and foremost, my extraordinary wife, without whose love and support I would be lost. My parents and my sister, for always being in my corner. The one they call Gerontion, ideas man par excellence, and Beloved Aunt, a fellow artist in disguise. My agent, Nelle, whose vision and encouragement made all the difference. And Andrew Lockett, for believing in this book.